THE
MISSING
BODY

BOOKS BY KERRY WILKINSON

THE
MISSING
BODY

KERRY WILKINSON

bookouture

Published by Bookouture in 2024

An imprint of Storyfire Ltd.
Carmelite House
50 Victoria Embankment
London EC4Y 0DZ

www.bookouture.com

ISBN: 978-1-83525-430-1
eBook ISBN: 978-1-83525-429-5

ONE

SUNDAY

'Heat rises', that's what people say. It's one of those certainties in life; like Popes being Catholic, bears doing their business in woods, and middle-aged men suddenly deciding they like salmon-coloured shirts.

Megan Lexington's current bedroom was the attic – and she had never been more aware of rising heat. The temperature was somewhere between sauna and centre of a microwaved apple pie. The skylight was open, not that there was any breeze to be, well, breezy. She sat on the edge of the bed, which was too soft, and plumped up a pillow, that was too hard.

The bed was directly under the skylight, blocked against the wall by an impossibly large chaise longue. A piece of furniture that answered the age-old question, 'What do you call a rubbish sofa?'

It had been a long few days, though beggars couldn't be choosers. Well, they could, but they'd only be showing a fundamental misunderstanding of what it was to be a beggar.

And Megan *had* come here begging.

Her suitcase was on the carpeted floor, unzipped yet unpacked. She knew she would be living out of it for the foreseeable future. That's how she was on holiday: no point in unfurling clothes into drawers and wardrobes, only to fold them back into a case a week or so later.

This was worse than a holiday. Not permanent and yet not exactly temporary.

The desk fan rotated on the nightstand, making a gentle *click* as it reached the end of its arc, before swinging back the other way. It was as effective as something could be when guffing hot air in an unsatisfying semicircle. Her phone lay charging at the side of the fan, the screen unwaveringly black.

Megan had nothing to do. *Nothing.*

The scream came from silence. There and gone so quickly that Megan wondered whether she'd heard it at all. Somebody downstairs probably had the television on too loud. It would be some detective show, with women – always women – getting bumped off every ten minutes. Or a true-crime Netflix thing with a drone hovering over some tiny town every five minutes.

Except nobody else was in. The house was empty.

Megan scooched across the bed until she was underneath the skylight. She knelt and twisted as she tried to angle a view towards the back of the house. The problem with windows slanting up was that it made it very difficult to look down. There was the blue of the sky and some green of tall trees a little past the property line. Beyond that, Megan couldn't see much of anything.

It was now so silent that Megan felt even more certain the scream was not imagined.

She shuffled away from the window and creaked her way across the attic floor. Her 'hello?' echoed along the landing and down the stairs, rebounding around the house that was definitely empty.

Megan edged down the first set of stairs and called another unanswered 'hello?', before continuing to the ground floor. Shoes littered the hallway near the front door and Megan grabbed hers from the pile as she headed towards the back of the house. There were a pair of mugs in the kitchen sink and more shoes by the door. A lined page had been torn from a notepad and stuck to the fridge, with 'DENTIST' written in scrappy block capitals.

It felt like somebody else's space because it was. Megan's own home didn't need written notes because she and her husband shared a Google Calendar, thank you very much.

Shame he didn't list *all* his scheduled events in there, of course.

Megan blinked away that thought and unlocked the back door with the key that apparently lived in the lock. Her husband had once told her things like that invalidated insurance policies, though he hadn't been quite so hot on things that invalidated marriage certificates.

She blinked away that thought, too.

Megan didn't have a key for the house, so she left the back door unlocked as she headed into the shaded garden. Mossy grass had grown over and around the paving slabs that Megan followed to the back gate, before she clicked it open and stepped through. She was so sure she'd heard a scream, a *woman's* scream, and yet the only noise was the gentle trickling of the nearby stream.

It was in the water that Megan and her sister would play when they were little. She couldn't remember specifics but they'd head out to the woods, with their friends, and somehow lose entire days jumping in and out of the stream. *In my day*, and all that.

'Hello...?'

Megan was in the trees now. The estate on which her sister lived had been built up against the woods, with barely a dusty trail to separate the two. Her voice ricocheted among the trunks, again unanswered by anything other than the dribble of the stream. Megan continued on, stepping across snapping twigs and skittering rocks. Another 'hello?' went unanswered, then another.

The water was loud, a rattling torrent pouring from the hills above. Megan stepped over a root and then stopped as the stream came into sight. It had rained the day before and the water was high on the bank.

A final 'hello?' rebounded around the trees, though there was still no reply. Megan moved to the edge of the water and looked up the slope, to where the stream was gushing over a plank of plasterboard. Someone had presumably put it down as a makeshift bridge, even though the flow was less than a metre wide and could be stepped over.

The scream must have been some animals fighting in the woods. Perhaps a deer had tripped, something like that? Megan paused a moment, considering the simplicity of those days with her sister, their friends, and a spot a lot like this. They would see deer then, too. Or tease each other with invented sightings of the various big cats that were rumoured to live in the woods. Someone would scream 'panther!' and they'd all run and hide.

That was a little further along the stream, closer to the pebble beach. Lots of things had changed in Hollicombe Bay, but not this.

Megan turned and had already taken a couple of steps back towards the house, when she spotted the flash of fuchsia a little down the slope. There were bushes and moss; leaves and grass – and among all that was a brighter colour. Megan moved slowly at first, tracing the line of the stream. She stepped around a trunk, half expecting the shape to disappear the moment it was out of view.

It didn't.

Something within her knew what it was, even as Megan told herself it couldn't be. As she got closer, the features became clearer.

The woman's long, dark hair was splayed across the ground;

her upper half contorted sideways, one arm above her head, the other underneath her body. Her top was pink, the lower part damper and darker as the water flowed across her hips and legs.

Megan crouched and rolled the woman onto her back, carefully pulling her away from the water. She was young, nineteen or twenty; her eyes closed, skin pale, chest still, and surely... *dead?*

TWO

Megan had never seen a dead body before. There would surely be blood, or bruises? The skin would be blue, or grey, or... what?

The girl, now on the edge of the stream, looked so peaceful, as if in the middle of a long sleep. Yet her chest wasn't moving; her nose wasn't widening and narrowing. Megan had dragged her from the water and she hadn't flinched or fought.

Megan stood and looked around, assuming there would be someone who knew what to do. A grown-up. She was an adult herself, of course, but a *proper* grown-up. Somebody who'd take charge and have the answers. She squinted through the trees and called a weak 'hello?', though there was only the distant chirp of a bird, the chattering flow of water, and the endless bed of twigs and dirt.

Why wasn't somebody around?! Trip over a kerb, or tuck your skirt into your knickers, and everyone you've ever met is somehow in the vicinity with a camera phone, ready to laugh about it. When something serious happens: nobody.

Megan could feel her heart thumping. There was something she should do. What was that advert? It had been on before the movie the last time Megan had been to the cinema. If someone wasn't breathing, you had to...

Megan was quickly on her knees, hunched across the woman. She angled in, pressing her ear close to the other woman's mouth and listening, *feeling*, for even the shallowest of breaths.

Nothing.

OK, the rest of the advert was the Bee Gees. Megan pressed one hand over the other and pushed hard into the centre of the woman's chest, before pumping up and down to the rhythm of *Stayin' Alive*.

Ah, ah, ah, ah.

One-two-three-four.

As she rocked backwards, Megan saw her own handprints in the centre of the woman's top. She must've got wet without realising. There was a crinkle of dirt, too, and Megan found herself having a future conversation with the woman in which she'd apologise and offer to wash her top.

No, back to the now. *Think!*

Megan leant in and listened for the sign of a breath that wasn't there – before trying again.

Ah, ah, ah, ah.

One-two-three-four.

She'd seen enough TV to know that, in this instance, the dead person would leap up with a huge gasp. It had to happen, because it always did. Whoosh, the person would be sitting, clutching their chest, coughing and wheezing. Everything would be all right.

Except it wasn't.

Megan tried one more set of chest compressions, humming the Bee Gees louder, while silently praying the volume would help. She listened for breaths again but there was nothing.

She was dead.

Really dead.

An actual person.

This poor young woman.

Megan stared at her, maybe for a few seconds but perhaps longer. She didn't know what to do. She said 'don't panic' out loud, quietly enough that only she could hear. She didn't know if this was actually panicking. Perhaps she should panic a bit more? If this didn't lead to a proper panic, what would?

No, she *did* know what to do. Megan patted her sides, trying to find the phone in her pocket. She'd call the police, an ambulance, or both.

Except she was wearing the shorts that didn't have pockets – and her phone was charging next to the fan back at the house.

Why did people keep making clothes without pockets?!

Megan stood and turned to take in the scene once more. It was all tree trunks, moss, small bushes, and the stream.

'Help?!'

It sounded more like a question as Megan called.

She shouted a second time, louder and firmer, but the only response was an echoing *coo* from a gull somewhere in the distance.

Megan knew she was going to have to leave the girl. There was no other choice. She'd get her phone, call for help, and then race back. She crouched one final time, touching the woman's forehead, hoping for some sort of miracle.

One second. Two.

When nothing happened, Megan was up and running. She followed the water upstream and then cut back through the trees. Roots and twigs clawed at her feet, desperate to send her flying; while something invisible pumped up and down on her own heaving chest. She couldn't remember the last time she'd run anywhere. Back when she'd worked behind a bar fifteen years before, there'd been some talk about putting together a team for the Whitecliff 10K. That had mercifully disappeared without Megan having to buy a pair of trainers.

Her heart thundered, as Megan's breathing got faster and narrower. By the time she surged through the back door of her sister's house, sweat was pouring from what felt like every part of her body. Her top clung to her as Megan bounded up the first set of stairs, slipping on the top one and catching herself on the railing. The second set leading up to the attic was at the end of the landing, and steeper than the first. The loft conversion was a few years old, back when her sister had been thinking about letting out a room. Then she'd watched a documentary about a serial killer who preyed on victims while staying in various Airbnbs, and that had been the end of that.

No, stop thinking about the loft conversion.

Megan's phone was where she'd left it, though she almost knocked the fan off the nightstand as she grabbed it.

The stupid face unlock didn't work, because it rarely did. What was wrong with the old fingerprint thing? Why did that have to change? Then it did unlock and Megan had already thumped in three nines before she realised she didn't have a signal. When she'd arrived with her suitcase, her sister had said that signal came and went in the house, as with the town itself. Something about there only being one phone mast. But weren't emergency calls supposed to connect anyway?

Megan tried to run back down the stairs but her body was having none of it. She limped down the first set and then held onto the rail for the second, like a granny in need of a stairlift. The front door was nearest, so Megan went through that, phone aloft. She was at the gate when a precious bar finally appeared and Megan pressed the green call button.

The handler was a woman and Megan tried to explain that she didn't know if she needed the police, or an ambulance. She was trying to say that she'd found a body, and then, before she knew it, she had been put through to someone actually from the police. There was a body, and a stream, and the woods, and...

What was her sister's address again?

It was such a blur.

There was a time when Megan would have claimed to be good in an emergency, except *that* was with something like a pan boiling over. Not a dead body in the woods.

Megan had forgotten the street name but then realised there was a sign diagonally across the road. Her sister's house number was on the front of the house, too, which felt obvious once Megan saw it.

She told them the body was in the woods at the back, and that, if officers followed the water upstream, they'd definitely find it.

Megan pictured the girl's face and those handprints on her pink top. The way it seemed as if she was sleeping. She knew the other woman was gone, yet she wanted to be with her when the police arrived. Wanted to say 'I tried', because she had. Wanted someone to be there to tell her that there was nothing else she could have done.

The handler asked if there was someone who could wait on the road and flag down the police car. And then Megan was at the end of the street, close to where the stream dipped into a tunnel and wound its way down to the rest of the town. She was waiting, listening for a siren, as the handler remained on the phone, saying something about the weather. Or perhaps Megan was imagining that? Or maybe she wasn't and the caller *was* trying to keep her calm by talking about the sunshine. And, if that was true, perhaps Megan *was* panicking – or at least sounded like she was.

Megan realised she was panting. Her face was damp and her top was stuck to her back. She wafted it back and forth, trying to cool herself in more ways than one. No, this wasn't a panic attack. Not like the ones from before.

Breathe...

That poor girl.

What had happened to her?

The siren started as a distant wail but, within seconds, it was a blasting beacon of noise. The town was so quiet that it came like an explosion. Faces immediately appeared in nearby windows, because that's what happened in places like Hollicombe Bay.

When the police car materialised over the brow, Megan began waving. The handler had hung up at some point, or perhaps it was Megan. She couldn't remember, though she was definitely flapping her arms, until the sound became too loud and she had to cover her ears.

The car pulled in, siren silenced, blue light still spinning. There was very little spoken between the two officers and Megan. One of them might have said something about a body but Megan was already a dozen steps into the trees, calling 'this way' over her shoulder.

She was running again but there was no trail. There were thorns and nettles, bushes and tightly packed trees. Megan fought her way through, dashing into the stream at one point as the officers' booming footsteps followed.

It wouldn't be far: a couple of minutes at most. The young woman would be on her back, hair still splayed, damp handprints on her top. Proper adults were here, real ones who'd know what to do.

It felt like a blink and then Megan was at the intersection with the trail that led across to her sister's house. She stopped, turned, and then saw the officers were far closer than she realised. They were a couple of paces back, neither particularly out of breath as they looked to her for guidance.

'Somewhere here?' one of them asked, except Megan was looking past him, back the way they'd come. They must have run past the woman without seeing her.

Megan stepped around them and took a couple more paces. She was in the same spot as when she'd first spotted the body. She'd seen the flash of pink from her top downstream, except...

She was walking now, slower. Still panting. Still sweating. Retracing the route they'd just been on, along the side of the stream.

And then Megan was there, standing in the spot where the young woman had been. The *dead* young woman.

Except she was gone.

THREE

Megan was sitting in her sister's living room as Nicola spoke to one of the officers in the hallway. They were whispering, Megan's ears tingling at the words she couldn't hear. They were definitely talking about her.

Ben was in the armchair across the room, gentle smile on his face as he pretended to scroll on his phone. Megan could feel her sister's partner eyeing her without moving his head, wondering what sort of nutter they'd let into their house.

A minute passed, longer, and then the officer was in the doorway. He was wearing his stab-proof vest, thumbs hooked into the underarm slots. He smiled, as if looking at a child who was struggling with the basics of standing up. *Poor love. You'll get there in the end.*

'Are you going to be OK?' he asked.

'All good,' Megan replied, forcing a cheeriness she didn't feel.

'We're going to head off in that case.'

Nicola had appeared at his side and was smiling in the same way as everyone else.

'If there's anything else, don't hesitate to call us,' he added.

'I've left your sister a card, or you can call nine-nine-nine if it's an emergency.'

'Got it,' Megan said. 'Thanks.'

There was another second of awkwardness – add it to all the others from the afternoon – and then he was on his way. Nicola followed him out and closed the door behind him, before reappearing in the living room doorway.

'Anyone want a tea?' she asked, cheerily.

'If you're offering,' Ben replied.

'Megs?'

'I'm fine.'

Nicola hovered for a second and exchanged a glance with Ben. They weren't married, even though they'd been together for ages. One of those couples who had gone so long without doing the deed that it was a point of principle. Also one of those couples who banged on about it all the time. *Oh, we're not married*, they'd laugh to anyone who'd listen. *It's just 'Miss', actually*, and all that.

Megan didn't know where to look, other than at her sister. Except... Oh, no. She was actually going to do it. Megan could see it in Nicola's face as her gaze flickered between Ben and her.

Nicola gulped, gave a little cough, and then a rehearsed: 'We know it's been a tough month or so...' she said gently.

That's what they'd been talking about in the hall. Nicola would have been telling the officer that her sister had gone through a few things and was now living in their attic. She was sure that no harm was meant and that nobody's time had been deliberately wasted.

'I know what I saw,' Megan replied, more defensively than she wanted. She'd already gone through this with two different police officers. They'd scribbled notes separately for some reason, while eyeing her over the top of their pads with what could only be described as suspicion. Or, worse, pity.

Nicola and Ben swapped another glance. They were having an entire conversation with a flicker of eyebrows.

'I know you did,' Nicola replied. 'I'm not denying that.'

'Sounds like it.'

There was a thunderous silence, though the smiles remained. The offer of tea was seemingly forgotten as Nicola leant on the door frame. She was a little over a year older and, to Megan, always had that way of looking down on her.

It was Ben who put down his phone and focused properly on Megan. 'How's the room?' he asked breezily. 'How was your first night? I was out so early, I didn't catch you this morning.'

It was a sledgehammered change of subject, though Megan didn't want to be rude. She'd arrived on the bus the day before, single suitcase in hand, texted offer from her sister to 'stay with us' as an insurance policy.

What was she supposed to say? That the attic was too hot? That the mattress had the consistency of a trifle? And the pillows were like bricks? Beggars, choosers, and all that.

'Good,' Megan replied instead. 'Thanks for having me. I'm hoping it won't be too long.'

'Stay as long as you like,' Nicola replied quickly. Too quickly, really. It was the sort of thing people said. 'Stay with us whenever you want' was British code for 'Don't come within half a mile of my house'. Everyone knew that.

Megan wanted her old house and her old life back before all the bad stuff. Not that she could say that to her sister. She had nowhere else to go.

The forced politeness was broken by the bang of the front door. It slammed into the wall, footsteps stomped on the hard floor, and then the door crashed back into place. Either an elephant had entered the house, or a teenager.

Feet were already clumping on stairs when Nicola called after her daughter.

'Jess!' she said, voice slightly raised, though not quite enough to be a full-on bellow.

'What?' came the sighed reply.

'Where have you been?'

'Out.'

'Who with?'

'Friends.'

Nicola sighed this time: like mother like daughter. There was more clumping upstairs and then, as if she'd momentarily forgotten, Nicola shouted: 'What have I told you about taking off your shoes?!'

The only answer was a slammed door.

'She's going to stomp right through the stairs one of these days,' Nicola said, talking to nobody in particular. She focused back on Megan. 'Sorry about that. She's—'

'Seventeen,' Megan replied. 'We were both seventeen, remember?'

They shared the merest hint of a smile and then it was gone because Megan was picturing the young woman and the stream. The handprints on her top. That poor girl hadn't been much older than seventeen. She was right there at the side of the stream and then... not. The police hadn't found any sign of her either.

Ben nodded towards the stairs. 'Did you ask her?' he said, talking to Nicola.

'She said she was fine,' came the reply.

The parents exchanged something of a shrug, maybe another raised eyebrow, and then Nicola began explaining for Megan's benefit. 'I thought I heard her being sick a couple of times this week. I know I told you about everything a couple of years ago. We were worried the bulimia was back.'

Megan didn't know how to reply. She wasn't sure she should even know this sort of thing. It felt like private family information and, even though she *was* family, the sisters didn't have the sort of relationship in which they shared everything. She also didn't think Nicola had ever told her that Jess had been struggling with an eating disorder.

Nicola was still talking, although the subject appeared to have changed. '...Have you seen the signs for Summer Fest?' she said. 'It's on Saturday?'

Megan was still thinking about Jess, though blinked back into the moment as she shook her head. Summer Fest happened every August and was vaguely connected to the day on which the town was apparently founded. According to the town's records some sort of festival had been going on for close to 1,500 years. Who knew what it was like back then but, from Megan's memories growing up, the streets were shut. There were stalls, markets, food, drink, ice cream, beer gardens, youths gathering in parks, and adults had competitions about who'd grown the best marrow, or whatever was in season. There were vintage cars, some tractors, face-painting. The usual. Or maybe it wasn't usual in other places? Every town appeared to have their own traditions, some stranger than others.

Nicola was saying something about 'Ben's dad's seventieth', to which Megan wasn't paying attention. She was wondering what she'd missed when she'd been daydreaming about the festival. Or, maybe, not thinking about the festival at all.

That young woman had been right there on the bank of the stream. Megan had left those damp handprints. She hadn't simply *seen* the girl, she'd *touched* her.

Megan blinked back into the room, realising Nicola and Ben were both looking to her. They were either deliberately trying to change the subject, or, perhaps, had already moved on themselves.

'Sorry...?' Megan said, looking to her sister.

'We're trying to get the whole family to go to the festival on Saturday. It's Ben's dad's birthday and he's in the baking competition.'

Megan stumbled over a word that might have been 'what?' There was a dead girl in the stream at the back of the house, her own life had imploded, and yet her sister was talking about baking competitions.

'I know it sounds weird,' Nicola added, 'but he keeps applying for *Bake Off* and not getting on. He reckons it's 'cos he's a straight white man and they're discriminating. Anyway, he's entered the Hollicombe Bay Bake Off on Saturday. It's on his birthday, too, so he's trying to get family support. Thing is, he and Jess haven't always got on. I've spoken to her but...'

Megan could feel everyone moving on. If she let it go, everything she'd seen would be as if it never happened. For Nicola and Ben – and seemingly the police – it *had* never happened. There was no young woman. They all thought Megan was mad, bad, stressed, or a combination of everything.

Megan sensed Nicola and Ben had had a different conversation about her when she wasn't there. Querying her state of mind and sanity. Wondering what state she was in.

'I suppose I can talk to her,' Megan found herself saying. She was living in their house, after all. Plus she and Jessie had always got on in the way aunts and nieces did, while mothers and daughters might not.

She was on her feet, taking a couple of steps towards the doorway and the stairs beyond. It felt inevitable. She also wanted out of the living room.

As Megan passed her sister, Nicola touched a gentle hand to her arm. 'We're there for you,' Nicola said earnestly. 'If you want to talk about anything. We know you're under a lot of stress.'

'Right, yeah, um...'

And then Ben was joining in: 'We know it's hard for you coming back to town after, well...'

There was that, too. The reason Megan had left Hollicombe

Bay in the first place. Another reason why they thought she was hallucinating.

Nicola was still rubbing her arm. 'Maybe get some rest after you've spoken to Jess, yeah?

Megan didn't doubt her sister was being kind, or trying to – but that condescending smile could absolutely do one. Megan wanted to shout, to say that she definitely *had* seen a young woman up by the stream. She'd tried to revive her, she'd felt the soft material of her top. It had all happened – and why wouldn't anyone listen to her?

She didn't say any of it. She nodded meekly, probably mumbled a 'thanks', and then headed for the stairs. She was barely at the top when the murmured whispers began once again.

FOUR

Megan tapped gently on Jessie's door. There was a vague hum of music from the other side and, when no reply came, she called a gentle: 'It's Megan.'

There was a muted 'oh' and the buzz dimmed, before the reply of: 'Come in.'

Jessie was lying on her bed but pushed herself into a sitting position as Megan entered. Her phone was in her hand, a laptop at her side. She croaked a 'hey' and reached for a can of some sort of energy drink on her side table. The sort of thing called 'CRANK!' or 'DRAGON FURY!'.

There was a redness around Jessie's eyes as she blinked rapidly while putting down the can. Megan closed the door and stood at the end of the bed.

'Have you been crying?' she asked.

That got a swift shake of the head. 'Just, uh... allergies. Hay fever and all that.'

It was a clear lie but Megan knew what it was like to be a seventeen-year-old. Secrets were important.

Jessie cleared her throat and had another sip of her drink.

'Mum said you're staying for a while. That you're gonna help in the café...?'

Megan nodded along, having forgotten she was starting work the next day. It didn't feel possible that things would continue as normal after she'd found the woman in the stream. Shouldn't that change things?

But then so much of her sisterly relationship with Nicola had been pretending things were normal when they weren't.

After Jessie was born, Nicola had slipped into what they now knew was postnatal depression. She had left Ben and moved along the coast to live with Megan and her husband for a couple of months. Ben would visit at weekends but there would be long periods of time in which Nicola wouldn't get out of bed, or would go out and disappear for hours. Megan was left to look after the infant Jessie. She would bottle-feed her and take her to the beach on nice days, or play with her indoors when it rained. Megan had put her life on hold until Nicola was eventually able to get appointments with a specialist. Perhaps that was what finally helped Nicola? Sometimes all it took was the passing of time.

Around six months later, Nicola had returned to Ben and Hollicombe Bay.

There had always remained a bond between Jessie and Megan, even though Megan doubted her niece remembered any of that. Even though, now, they only saw each other a handful of times per year.

It had been the start of summer, barely weeks before, that Jessie had caught the bus to Whitecliff to spend a day with Megan, doing touristy things. They'd played crazy golf, eaten vinegary chips, and then spent a couple of hours on the beach talking about everything and nothing. The sort of conversation that's gone in a blink, and from which not a single topic can be remembered, and yet the overall feeling is encompassing joy.

This was the first time they'd seen one another since then

and, as Megan looked down on her niece, she thought of her sister downstairs and 'the bulimia' potentially being back. It was impossible not to take in Jessie's frame. She didn't *look* that skinny, though that wasn't the point. Megan wondered if she should bring it up at all. It felt like an invasion of privacy.

Except she was there for an actual reason.

'Your mum sent me up,' Megan said. 'She wondered if I'd ask you about your granddad and—'

That got a roll of the eyes. 'I knew she wouldn't ask me again herself. She always does this. If I don't bow down to her, she'll send up Dad. Then it's someone else.'

Megan slotted onto the chair next to the dresser as she offered a weak apology. 'If it's any consolation, a Hollicombe Bay Bake Off does sound a bit rubbish.'

Jessie bit her lip as she crinkled a smile.

'Sometimes,' Megan added, 'with families, you end up doing things you don't want to, because it's better than hurting their feelings.'

It came out a little more piously than Megan intended, not that Jessie seemed to catch it. Most things adults said sounded overly self-important to younger people.

'Granddad wasn't so bothered about people's feelings when he called me fat,' Jessie replied. 'Straight up said it in front of everyone when I was twelve. I've not really spoken to him since.'

Megan took it in with an understated nod. She hadn't been there but she knew her sister would have defended it with some sort of 'different generation' justification. It was easier to say that granddad grew up in different times, as opposed to admitting he was a massive nob.

Suddenly, the bulimia talk from downstairs had taken a more sinister turn.

'I'm sorry he said that,' Megan replied. 'You shouldn't go if you don't want to. I probably wouldn't. I told your mum I'd pass on the message.'

She was now wishing she hadn't.

'I'll go to his stupid bake-off if *he* asks.' Jessie grinned, though it only lasted a second. The skin around her eyes was still red.

'Are you sure you're all right?' Megan asked.

Jessie shrugged it off and changed the subject not so subtly. 'Mum reckons you and Paul are getting divorced...?'

She probably hadn't meant it that way but the final word felt like a punch to Megan. 'Divorce' sounded so final. There wasn't much coming back from that.

'We're separated,' Megan replied, which was one of those stupid all-encompassing phrases adults used. Perhaps they *were* going to get divorced and the whole 'separated' thing was their way of pretending it wasn't happening? It felt like it.

Jessie glanced to her phone, likely sensing the clumsiness of it all. Megan tried to think of something else to say that a teenager might want to hear.

She stood, ready for a tactical retreat, but then realised what she wanted to talk about. 'I found a body in the stream at the back,' Megan found herself saying. It was too much to put onto a teenager, but nobody else believed her. She had to tell someone.

Jessie looked up from her phone: 'Huh?'

'A couple of hours ago. I was upstairs and heard a scream. I went out, into the woods, and there was a girl lying in the water. She was only a few years older than you. She wasn't breathing and I tried CPR.' Megan motioned as if pumping someone's chest and, for a flash, she was back on the bank of the water replaying the beat of the Bee Gees.

Jessie pushed herself sideways on the bed, until she was sitting with her legs over the side. 'Did she come round?'

Megan blinked and she was back in the room. She couldn't

quite manage the word, instead shaking her head. 'I didn't have my phone, so came back here to get it. I called the police and they had me wait on the street to flag down a car. By the time we got back into the woods, she was gone.'

Jessie's eyes narrowed with confusion. 'What do you mean?'

'I don't know. She was there and then, when I went back, she wasn't.'

The bewilderment deepened. 'You mean she wasn't dead? She got up?'

Megan was stumbling over her words. 'I don't know. I just...' A sigh. 'I don't know.'

Jessie was biting her lip again. 'Thing is... one of my friends went missing.'

FIVE

Jessie put down her phone for the first time since Megan had entered the room. She glanced towards the door, as if concerned someone else might be listening. Her voice was lower, not much more than a whisper.

'Maybe not "friend". Look.'

She picked up her phone again and began swiping with practised excellence, until twisting the screen for Megan to see. There was a video from the beach, where two topless boys were running a race against each other. People were laughing and talking across one another and, as the angle swung around, Jessie paused. She pointed to someone roughly her age sitting with her arms crossed.

'That's Helena,' Jessie said. 'She used to hang around with us sometimes.'

'From school?'

Jessie put down the phone. 'No, I don't know what school she went to – but she lived in town, for a while at least. We'd see her at the park, or the beach, wherever. She was always on her own, like she didn't have any friends, and I suppose we let her hang around with us.'

The phone was back in Jessie's hand, almost an extension of herself. She glanced at the still frame from the video and then continued.

'We talked once. Properly. I can't remember how it happened but we'd been at the arcade for some reason. I think the boys were on the punching machine.' She rolled her eyes and there was a moment in which Megan felt as if she *really* understood the younger woman. 'People started heading home and it was just me and her. We ended up walking up the hill. I asked about school and she kinda shrugged. I think she was Polish, something like that. She asked how long I'd lived in Hollicombe Bay – and I said forever. We were gonna meet the next day but she never showed. I've not seen her since.'

Megan asked to look at the phone again, momentarily certain that the girl she'd seen in the woods had to be the same person. She squinted and tilted the device, except, no matter what the angle, it definitely wasn't. The young woman on the bank of the stream had long, black hair. Helena's was short and a much lighter brown. It was hard to identify specifics, but there was something different about their noses – plus what looked like a light brown birthmark that curved around Helena's chin.

She handed back the phone. 'How long ago was that?'

'Easter-ish. Around the time town started filling up.'

Close to four months. Easter was usually the tipping point for when tourists returned.

Megan thought for a moment, chewed on it. 'Did you talk to any of your friends about Helena?'

'Not really. We didn't *know* her, know her – and it's not like she hung around with us very much. Just one of those people you see about.'

'Did you ask your mum?'

'She reckoned she was probably a traveller. Dad said "gypsy" and I had to tell him you can't say that anymore. They're such a state.'

Travellers in the summer had always been a part of Holli-combe Bay and the surrounding area. They'd park in a field, which would be followed by a local panic for a couple of weeks until the police moved them on to the next town. It sounded vaguely plausible that Helena was a traveller who'd shifted on with her family – although odd if she'd failed to mention it during the conversation with Jessie.

'What did she look like?' Jessie asked, and it took Megan a moment to realise she was talking about the girl from the stream.

'Sort of... normal,' Megan said, unsure how else to put it. 'Black hair, a bit pale, young...' She tailed off, because the woman really *had* seemed young. It was true that everyone did to her, nowadays. Megan had turned into one of those people who couldn't believe that what appeared to be literal children were apparently old enough to drive. To drink. To roam around town by themselves. Even Jessie was suddenly seventeen, having apparently been half that barely a blink before.

'You just described most of my friends,' Jessie said and there was a small smile.

Megan didn't know how to reply. It already felt as if her memory was fading of what the woman looked like. A murky fog of remembrance.

'What are you going to do about her?' Jessie asked.

'I don't know. The police think I'm wasting their time. Your mum keeps saying I'm stressed and seeing things.'

There was a roll of the eyes. 'Mum thinks a lot of things.'

They shared a momentary glance of acknowledgement. Megan didn't want to take sides in whatever mother-daughter tension was going on.

'I believe you,' Jessie said.

She was reaching for her phone, moving on. It was the simplest reply but, even though she was only seventeen, for

Megan, it was someone – *finally* – who'd said what she needed to hear.

But what now? Who was the girl in the stream, and where had she gone?

SIX

MONDAY

Nicola tapped the polished chrome of the large coffee machine, then wiped away the smudged fingerprint with her sleeve. 'This works pretty much like the one at the house,' she told Megan, while pointing to various parts. 'The coffee goes in there and the water there. You have to wait for the light to come on and then you're away.'

Megan was listening in a not listening sort of way. In the best way she could when she'd found a body the day before and was now being told how coffee worked. By her older sister, of all people.

'You warm pastries in there,' Nicola said, moving on and pointing to a small toaster oven on the back counter of the café she and Ben owned. 'That's a microwave,' she added, pointing – somewhat unhelpfully – to a microwave, as if Megan had never seen or used one before. 'The rest of the food is made in the kitchen,' Nicola continued. 'You can just use the hatch.' She pointed towards something that looked more like a large letterbox and then finally relaxed by leaning on the spotless counter. 'It'll be good for you to get back into a routine.'

The girl from the stream hadn't been mentioned since the

day before, with the implication that this new 'routine' might stop Megan from imagining things.

Megan found herself agreeing that, yes, a routine *would* be good. Waking up at six every morning and heading into town to work in her sister's coffee shop for cash in hand *was* the ideal way to spend a summer.

The café hadn't yet opened for the day, though it wouldn't be long. It was a traditional seaside tea shop, with tables that were a little too close to one another. The sort of spot in which patrons had to apologise their way around each other whenever they moved. It sold fry-ups and cheap teas, alongside espressos and muffins. Starbucks with a sticky laminated menu that hadn't been changed in twenty-five years. Costa plus chips with everything.

A pile of menus was on a shelf near the door, the sticky-backed plastic warped brown with age and too much sun. The menu was repeated on a giant blackboard behind the counter, above the coffee machine. Megan knew people would still get to the front of the line without knowing what they wanted. It was the same everywhere. They would queue for ten minutes and then somehow ask with a straight face if there was egg in an egg sandwich. That, or spend five more minutes looking for a bank card. Or telling Little Noah to stop touching everything with his grubby fingers, else Mummy would get very angry. Spoiler alert: She wouldn't.

They'd moved across to one of the tables and Nicola was scratching at an invisible something on the surface. 'Pam will be in soon,' she said. 'She knows everything better than me now.'

'How long has she been manager?'

'Almost a year.'

Megan nearly said that she didn't realise her sister had handed over day-to-day duties to someone else. She was ninety per cent sure it had never come up in their semi-regular text conversations. Except that other ten per cent niggled in that she *might* have been told and simply forgot. It was easy to get caught up in your own world when only seeing family a few times a year.

'When was the last time you worked in place like this?' Nicola asked.

Megan had to think. She'd left Hollicombe Bay to move to Whitecliff when she was nineteen – and then there was bar work, office work, more bar work, a week at the service station, back to bar work and then...

'Eight or nine years ago,' Megan replied.

Trying to figure out what life things happened in which year after hitting forty was like dropping a jelly and trying to put it back together. Memories of everything were there somewhere: but it was a gelatinous mess, covered in dust, and looked genuinely distressing.

'It'll be like riding a bike,' Nicola said. 'You never forget.'

That was part of the problem. Megan *wanted* to forget her experience in the service industry. If it wasn't for all the customers, it would be a pleasant job. But, oh no, in they'd come with their 'double froth, half almond, half cashew milk, three stevias and whip on top' nonsense. Or they'd order an almond croissant, before saying they were allergic to almonds and 'can you do something about that?'

Why was she going to work with the general public again?

When Megan had texted her sister to ask if she could stay for a week or two, the reply of 'sure!' had come back quickly enough. What had also followed was 'you can do some shifts at the café if you fancy some cash in hand?' kiss, kiss, smiley face, thumbs up, laughing emoji.

Somehow, Megan had said 'yes', figuring it would take her mind off things in Whitecliff – and that the extra money would certainly help when it came to sorting out the mess at home.

That was the theory; the reality was here and now.

The door rattled as a woman fiddled with a key and barged

it with her shoulder. Nicola called 'already open' as the pair waved at each other through the glass. Pam blustered into the café with the grace of a brick through a window. She dumped her dumbbell-like bag on the nearest table and then immediately asked if Nicola had heard the sirens the day before. 'Nearly gave my Jimmy a heart attack,' she said. 'He was scratching at the door. Jackie on Facebook reckoned it was someone playing silly buggers, do you get me?'

Megan shrank into her seat. She'd somehow missed the fact that nothing remained private in Hollicombe Bay. It wouldn't be long before everyone knew someone had hoaxed the police by reporting a fake body in the woods. Then they'd know it was her.

This was part of why she'd left town in the first place.

Nicola sidestepped the conversation. 'Jimmy is Pam's dog,' she said, talking to Megan – as if she might have somehow thought Jimmy was a downtrodden husband scraping at a door. Nicola introduced the pair, without saying Megan was responsible for the blazing sirens the day before.

Pam looked Megan up and down in the way a plumber might eye the work of any other plumber. *You've got a right cowboy on your hands, here.*

'Megan, is it?' she asked, even though they'd only swapped names seconds before. They shook hands and then Pam nodded to the counter. 'Heard you've done this before...?'

Before Megan could reply, Nicola was on her feet, bag on her shoulder, saying she had to get off. She said she'd see Megan later and then let herself out, heading over the road to where she'd parked her maroon Mini. Nicola had wanted a Mini since they'd been young and, though the newer ones were nowhere near as small as the ones she'd craved, Nicola had finally bought herself one a year or two before.

Megan watched her sister for a moment and then realised Pam was tapping her toe gently, still waiting for the answer.

'A bit,' Megan replied, avoiding eye contact. Pam had the sort of stare that could make a stinging nettle wilt. 'I've worked in a few pubs and did nine months in a café in Whitecliff.'

It wasn't on purpose but she'd made it sound like a prison sentence, though that wasn't too far off. She didn't say that her most recent job had been working on reception in a gym.

'It's busy season,' Pam said. 'Lakshmi will be along in a bit – but she's young and a bit, well...' she lowered her voice, 'she's a bit dim. Tries her best, poor thing, but she's not the sharpest match in the box, do you get me?'

It felt as if Pam wanted a mutual moan about young people, which Megan ignored. 'I grew up here,' she replied instead. 'I know it's mad in the summer.'

'Not as mad as it used to be. Did Nic show you the coffee machine?'

'Yeah, she—'

Without being given much of a choice, they were off again. Pam giving instructions for everything Megan had already been shown. She had an annoying habit of ending at least half her sentences with 'do you get me?' *This is where you put the coffee, do you get me? This is the fridge, do you get me? You put money in the till, do you get me?*

Megan nodded her way through the lot of it, though her mind was still at the stream. She hadn't been back since that moment with the police. They had made their way back to the police car and then along the street to her sister's house. Then she'd given statements, while waiting for Nicola to get home.

And now, here she was listening to someone a few years older than her asking if Megan knew how 'they' get milk from oats. 'It's beyond me,' Pam added.

Megan smiled politely, saying she didn't know either, while thinking it probably involved water and a bunch of squeezing.

They were at the end of the second tour of the day when they reached the letterbox posing as a hatch. 'Put the food orders through there,' Pam said. 'You don't need to bother the cooks. They keep themselves to themselves, do you get me?'

From Megan's memories of front-facing customer service, the cooks had the right idea.

A minute or so later and Lakshmi appeared. Far from being 'a bit dim', as Pam had called her, she was on summer break from university and back in town, living with her parents. She was breezy and enthusiastic, something Megan didn't feel herself.

And so the morning continued. There was a steady stream of making hot drinks and iced drinks, putting pastries on plates, telling every customer that the card machine 'does that sometimes' when it was being a pain in the arse. Pam's managerial style appeared to be chatting to her friends whenever they came in, while Lakshmi enthusiastically did everything asked, and unasked, of her. It was a relief she knew what was going on, because Megan had instantly forgotten everything she'd been told twice. She shuttled food from the kitchen hatch to customers, and then dirty dishes back the other way. It felt as if the morning had passed but, when she checked her phone, it had been an hour and a quarter.

She had forgotten what it was like to be on her feet all day and was struggling to remember why she said she'd do the job. After Nicola had said she could move in, she would have probably said 'yes' to anything.

As well as the tapped cards, phones, and notes, customers were paying with what Megan first thought was monopoly money. Lakshmi laughed to say they were 'Bay Bucks' and that it was a currency only accepted in local shops. It occurred to Megan an hour or so later that she should probably check with her sister that she was being paid with real money. Someone should've probably mentioned it earlier.

None of those thoughts lasted longer than a moment or two. Every time Megan found herself thinking of something else, she'd drift back to the day before and the girl in the stream. Did the chest compressions work, but only after Megan had left? Had she been alive all along but stoned, or something like that? She'd woken up in the minutes Megan was gone and headed home? Who was she?

Every time a young woman entered the café, Megan would spend a millisecond thinking it was the person she'd seen in the woods. It never was.

It was a little after twelve when Pam told Megan she could take a break. 'We take it in turns,' she added.

'How long?' Megan asked.

'Forty minutes, then you can cover for me.'

The sun tickled Megan's arms as she stepped into the afternoon. She was still wearing her apron but couldn't be bothered heading back inside to drop it off.

Gulls circled the bay as salt and vinegar coated the breeze. There was a line for the ice cream van across the street, while the tat shop had piles of fluorescent buckets and spades on the street going unsold. It was a lot of what Megan remembered from growing up. Sure, iPads were great, but had you ever dug a really big hole in the sand? Not just big, *really* big?

Thirty-seven minutes. Megan had somehow wasted three.

She set off at a pace, weaving around the queue for ice cream, plus the sunburned bloke with his top off who had 'PRIDE' unironically tattooed across his belly. Posters seemed to be on every telegraph pole and lamp post advertising that weekend's Summer Fest. Megan even saw a few for the Bake Off, which offered the chance for anyone who showed up to taste the cakes and bakes after judging.

Perhaps it didn't sound so bad?

Megan was through the centre in a few minutes, and then off and up the hill on which Hollicombe Bay sat. It was hard to know why, with all the flat land elsewhere from which to choose, some maniac had looked at the ten per cent gradient and figured it was as good a place as any to start building. Instead of using the summer fete to celebrate 1,500 years of the town, someone should be asking some serious questions.

For the second time in as many days, Megan was sweating through her clothes. This time it was from struggling up the lower part of the hill, past the shops, restaurants and the B&Bs of the seafront, and onto the outskirts of the houses. She was at the next corner when she stopped, realising where she was.

The low wall had once seemed tall, the railings so imposing. The harsh tarmac of the playground had been replaced by some sort of springy rubbery surface, on which children would have to try really hard to scuff their knees.

Hollicombe Bay only had one secondary school: there simply weren't enough children to justify more than that. It meant everyone of the same age ended up in the same place. Lifetime friends and enemies were made; relationships that might last decades, or hours. Even babies were sometimes created.

It was nothing special, not really: one big building, three storeys tall. There'd be similar schools all across the country and probably offices that looked similar.

Except...

Megan found it hard to believe it was still in place after everything that had happened inside. That it wasn't a pile of rubble. That's what happened to sites where something awful had taken place. They knocked them down and built a memorial.

Not here. They put it back together and carried on as if nothing had happened.

Twenty-eight minutes.

After hauling herself away from the school, Megan continued up the hill. She skipped across a couple of streets, winding her way diagonally across the town as gulls continued to chirp above. A group of lads passed on the other side of the road, all trying to be the loudest as they elbowed and shouldered each other on the journey down to town. Past them, Hilltop Park, which wasn't at the top of the hill, was crammed with young children charging around the play area as parents watched from the benches. A tanned mum was fanning herself with a magazine while a boy, presumably her son, rolled in the dirt close to the fence.

Megan kept walking, trying to move faster, even as her calves burned. Every time she returned to her hometown, it was as if she'd somehow forgotten how steep everything was.

Up another street, and Megan reached the spot where the stream dipped into the tunnel. The water lapped gently over the rim of the pipe as Megan wondered how long it would be before it dried up. Weeks, rather than months. Perhaps days.

There was a person-shaped hole at the side of the bush and Megan shoved through as she had with the police the previous day. She followed the stream up the slope, sliding around the trees and other shrubs, before the growth started to clear.

A couple of days before and it would have all looked the same. Seen one tree, seen 'em all... except Megan now knew this patch of ground as if she had spent a lifetime visiting. That's what happened when a person closed their eyes and saw the same thing over and over.

Most of the ground had a thin carpet of moss, grass, and roots – but a shallow, naturally carved dimple sat at the side of the stream. It was a couple of metres wide and clear of anything except dust and dirt.

It was the place Megan had laid the young woman after pulling her clear of the water. Where she had pumped her chest and hummed 'Stayin' Alive', praying that's what would happen.

She stood at the edge of the clearing, listening to the crinkled drizzle of water creeping downstream.

Megan hadn't noticed the day before but there were scuffed footprints in the dirt. She realised she was holding her breath.

There were scrapes from a person with huge canoe shoes, plus someone else with much daintier feet.

The girl *was* alive!

These were her prints. She'd stood and walked upstream.

How had they all missed it? What kind of police officers failed to spot something so obvious?

Was there some sort of medical thing, where a person could receive CPR and then come around a few minutes later? There had to be, except...

Megan crept into the clearing, softly at first, not wanting to disturb anything. It was only as she gently pressed her heel into one of the prints that she realised – slowly, devastatingly – that she had been looking at the marks from her *own* shoes.

There was a couple of seconds in which it felt as if she was sinking. The more she stared at the scuffs, the more Megan couldn't understand how she'd been so wrong – even if for only a moment. The larger prints clearly belonged to one, or both, of the officers from the day before. That's why they hadn't spotted such obvious indents: their small group had been the ones to make them.

Nineteen minutes.

Megan was not going to get back to the café in time. She'd be late on her first day. It was hard to remember why she'd returned to the spot in the woods, other than that she'd felt drawn there. The missing woman was a ghost in a town where Megan had more than enough of her own.

Eighteen minutes. She'd been staring at the footprints and the stream for a full minute.

Seventeen minutes. Two full minutes of looking at the floor.

Megan had rushed through town to get to the stream, only to have to turn around and head straight back. She'd achieved nothing, even failing to make herself feel better. If anything, after the momentary confusion over the footprints, she felt worse. Megan couldn't think of an explanation for what had happened the day before. The young woman had been there – and then she wasn't. She was dead and then... what? Alive?

She turned to leave, deliberately scuffing away the prints she'd made the day before. Perhaps it was that extra second; or maybe it was the delicate, imperceptible shift in the position of the sun, but that's when Megan spotted it sitting on the other side of the stream on a dry mossy bed.

Megan crouched and picked it up, squeezing it hard between her fingers until she winced. She needed to know it was real.

And it was.

A single, stubby, yellow-white tooth.

SEVEN

Staff shared a toilet with customers at Nic's café. It was a single cubicle next to the door that led into the kitchen. There was a list on the wall, where staff ticked off each hourly clean. Megan sat on the closed toilet seat and stared at the tooth in her palm. It was a fraction narrower than her little fingernail, and not much longer; almost a rough, rounded square. She didn't know much about dentistry but, if Megan had to guess, she'd have said it was a *front* tooth. It had looked whiter under the dappled sun from the woods but, now, in the bright of the humming strip lamp, it was a mucky yellow.

Megan rolled the tooth around in her palm, wondering if there was a way to know whether it came from a man or a woman. There probably was, but it would involve testing. To her untrained eye, it looked bigger than her own front teeth, plus there was something about the grimy colour that made her think it didn't come from the woman in the stream. She had been young, probably in her early twenties. It felt as if a person would have to do a lot of coffee drinking, with not much brushing, to end up with incisors that colour.

The thump of fist on door made Megan jump with what she

hoped was a *silent* squeal. A woman's voice called, 'Someone in there?' Megan flushed the unused toilet and set the taps running as she slipped the tooth into the otherwise useless micro-pocket at the back of her trousers. Whoever had designed them must've been into teeth smuggling, because they weren't going to fit much else. There was barely space for a key.

The gushing water left Megan momentarily thinking of the stream, before a second, gentler bang on the door.

'One minute,' Megan called.

She considered calling the police for the second time in two days – except they already thought she was a weirdo and possible troublemaker. What would she say? It was true that she'd returned to the stream and found a tooth, but it sounded like a lie. Why go back? Whose tooth was it? They'd probably think she'd planted it. They would have more questions and she'd have fewer answers than her embarrassing attempts the day before.

Megan opened the door to find a mum holding a red-eyed toddler by his wrist. He was covered in what Megan hoped was chocolate and the woman shrugged an apology as they passed. 'I can't take him anywhere,' she said, before dragging her son into the toilet and locking the door.

Megan wondered if cleaning the toilet was her job for later? Neither Nicola nor Pam had told her to put her initials on the check sheet in the cubicle, so, with a bit of luck, it was someone else's.

The rest of the afternoon dragged. It was warm and anyone sane was looking for ice cream and soft drinks, as opposed to coffee. Fewer customers meant less to do, and not as many people for Pam to chat with. Lakshmi was a cheery machine, hustling from task to task without needing to be told. She was so efficient that Megan felt in the way as she tried to learn on the spot.

Across the day, Megan saw a host of semi-familiar faces.

Either people with whom she went to school, or their siblings, or children. A few blinked, or widened their eyes when they saw her. She heard a couple of 'Oh, you're back?', and 'I've not seen you in ages'. The small-talk was polite and predictable. 'Where've you been?', '*How* have you been?', 'Are you back for long?' Megan knew her replies were largely irrelevant, as were theirs. The vague familiarity was what mattered. If they saw each other in future days, they'd nod awkwardly, and carry on as before.

The café slowly emptied until they were down to one straggler with a laptop. He said things like 'ciao for now' and 'shoot me an email' into his phone.

Ben appeared late in the afternoon, not long before they were due to close. Megan's brother-in-law was some sort of marketer, although details were vague about what that actually meant. Either that, or, more likely, Megan had never really listened. It was one of those jobs where the description guaranteed an instant switch-off. Sure, people like accountants, marketers, and consultants probably did *something* – but the specifics were lost among mists of deathly boredom.

Megan's brother-in-law sat at a table with his laptop until Pam joined him shortly afterwards with a cappuccino. It felt like this happened semi-regularly as Ben sipped his drink, didn't bother opening the laptop, and instead listened as Pam told him it had been quiet after lunch. Megan did a general bit of table wiping, partially in an attempt to overhear whether Pam brought up that she'd been late back from lunch. It hadn't been mentioned earlier, though Megan wondered if the other woman had been saving it up.

Instead, Ben waved her across to their table. 'How's it gone?' he asked.

Megan struggled not to picture him the day before, having entire conversations with Nicola with barely a shift of the eyes. Neither of them believed her about the woman in the stream.

'Good,' Megan said, unsure how else to reply.

'Are you over everything from yesterday?'

Megan stared for a second, feeling the metaphorical weight of the tooth in her back pocket. He spoke so casually, as if asking if she was getting over a sore shoulder. Megan stumbled a reply, managing something about it being good to be busy. It didn't answer the question, though he wasn't listening. Instead he'd turned to Pam.

'This one gave us quite the worry yesterday,' he said. 'Reckoned she saw a body in the stream at the back of ours. We had the police over and everything.'

Megan refused to catch Pam's eye, as she felt the puzzle pieces around the sirens falling into place.

'What sort of body?' Pam asked, as if there were multiple types that people found.

Megan felt both of them looking to her now, so she focused past them on the lone bloke who was single-finger typing on his laptop.

'How was your day?' she asked, talking to Ben and pretending she hadn't heard Pam's question.

There was an awkward pause until Ben replied: 'Busy. I was doing a cash-and-carry run. The local business association pools together because it's such a long journey. We take it in turns to drive out and pick up everyone's orders. It was supposed to be Trev's turn today.'

'Trev from the sweet shop?' Pam asked.

'Right. He pulled out at half-eight this morning. Asked if someone could swap. Something about needing emergency dental work.'

EIGHT

Ben had already moved on when Megan halted him mid-sentence. 'Emergency dental work?' she asked.

Her brother-in-law had been saying something about road-works but stopped and turned from Pam to Megan. 'I don't know the details. Something about losing a front tooth.' Another pause. 'Do you know him?'

'I don't think so,' she replied.

Even with the denial, Megan wondered if she did. The name 'Trevor' didn't seem familiar, though she might know his face if she saw him. Either that, or he'd turn out to be the dad of someone she used to know. She tried to remember who used to run the sweet shop when she last lived in town, though a name didn't come. Hollicombe Bay had a locally owned one or two of everything. There was a sweet shop, ice cream parlour, tat shop, toy shop, chip shop, bookshop, antiques shop, bike rental place, pub. There was no Greggs, but there was a Betty's Bakery, even though Betty had died during the Major government. No Starbucks or Costa, but there was Nic's. The closest the town came to embracing modern capitalism was the Tesco Express at the end of the high street.

The tooth felt as if it was burning through Megan's back pocket. Whoever this Trevor happened to be, did Megan have his tooth? She'd found it steps away from where she had seen the dead girl the previous day. It had to be connected.

'...Anyway,' Ben continued. 'I dropped everything and took the van out to the cash and carry. Only just got done delivering everything. Trev said he'll cover my turn next time. Always worth having him owe you one.'

He sounded pleased with himself, even though it got no reaction from either of the women. Pam was still giving Megan a sideways glance, presumably about the body and the siren thing.

Ben didn't appear to notice any of this. He really was a talker, not a listener. 'Did, uh, Nic talk to you about the, uh...' Megan realised he was talking to her as he lowered his voice. '...cash thing?'

Lakshmi was behind the counter, clearing up; while the laptop lingerer was typing at about six words a minute.

'She asked if I wanted to work cash-in-hand...?' Megan replied.

Ben tensed, even though nobody other than Pam had overheard. She presumably knew, and seemed unfazed. 'We'll sort you out from the till at the end of the week,' he said quietly. 'I just wanted to make sure you weren't short between now and then. If so, we might be able to...'

He didn't finish the sentence and probably hadn't planned to. Megan's return to Hollicombe Bay, or, more to the point, her escape from Whitecliff, was nothing to do with money. When Nicola had asked if she fancied a few shifts, she'd said 'yes' almost by default. What was the worst that could happen? The best was that it would take her mind off everything else.

'I can wait,' Megan replied.

Ben started talking to Pam about the 'float' and leaving it to him but Megan had heard enough. She drifted off to help

Lakshmi finish the real work and, when that was done, said her goodbyes. Without looking up, Ben said he'd see her later. Pam reminded Megan that her dog didn't like sirens, while Lakshmi said she was off to meet her boyfriend on the beach.

Megan knew where she was going. The sweet shop was near the end of the high street, just before the start of the steep slope.

There was a late-afternoon buzz to the town as Megan hurried along the high street. The tables outside the ice cream parlour were full, with the inside seemingly packed as well. A line stretched out the shop and along the pavement. The sandwich board advertised twenty-three flavours, which seemed oddly specific.

Past there, Betty's Bakery had closed for the day, though the sign in the window said they were doing three doughnuts for a pound. Megan vaguely remembered when ten were sold for the same price. She and her friends would save some of their lunch money and then pass through town on the long way home from school to share a bag that was eighty per cent sugar.

The bookshop had a bunch of faded, crusty paperbacks in the window that had likely been there since before mobiles were a thing. The pub was as rammed as would be expected, while the toy shop sounded busy. The pet store had a bright yellow bird in a cage near the door, with the creature chirping noisily as it sat on its perch.

On the other side of the street, people were making their way back from the beach, some barefooted, others in sandals. There was a steady dusting of sand across the pavement.

Hollicombe Bay Sweets had a sandwich board at the front, saying it was open until seven. The note underneath told customers to 'ask about our custom rock', which would have excited Megan as a child.

The outside smelled of sugar and sweetness, which sent Megan tumbling through time. She and Nicola would come as seven- and eight-year-olds to spend the pocket money that they got for washing- and drying-up. She couldn't remember the point at which she'd stopped eating such stuff.

The window display was full of bright logos, advertising what was inside. A pair of young girls exited as Megan waited, each with some sort of pink stringy spiral thing on which they were sucking.

As Megan entered and the door closed behind her, the cloying sweetness was almost too much. The walls were lined with large tubs and jars, plus there were two racks of chocolate bars. Comics and children's magazines were on a separate rail towards the back of the shop, next to a door with a 'staff only' sign.

A bored-looking young woman sat behind the counter, phone on her lap. She glanced up, taking in Megan momentarily, and then returning to her phone. Unless naming conventions had changed dramatically, she was not Trevor.

Megan browsed aimlessly, picking up a comic and returning it to the rack, then eyeing the 'American candy' corner. There were boxes of breakfast cereals above that, most of which appeared to involve entire bowls of cookies.

'This is all the fresh stuff,' the girl said.

When Megan turned, she realised she was being watched.

The young woman motioned towards the counters in front of her. 'It's made in the kitchen every day,' she added, nodding towards the staff only door.

Megan crossed towards her and took in the rows of various sweet things. There were lots of flavours of hard sweets, something called a 'sour bomb'; plus various fudgey and chocolatey concoctions. Megan asked for a fiver's worth of something called an almond crunch and then watched as the girl measured it out.

Even with a summer of tourists, it was hard to know how such a place could keep going. It wouldn't make much in the winter and yet there were no signs advertising an online shop, or anything similar.

Once the transaction was complete, the young woman passed across the bag. When Megan didn't move, she frowned a fraction. 'Can I help with anything else, or...?'

'Is Trevor around?' Megan asked.

That got a shake of the head. 'He's been off all day. Had to go to the dentist.'

'What happened?'

'Dunno. He texted to say he lost a front tooth. Asked if I'd open up.' She paused, suddenly hesitant. 'Do you know him...?'

Megan avoided the question: 'I used to live here a while ago. I've not been back in town for long.'

The young woman nodded along, apparently accepting that as an answer. 'So... can I get you anything else?' Her hand slipped towards the phone that was sitting next to the cash register.

Megan was about to leave when she realised the girl's age. She'd be late teens, perhaps early twenties.

'This might sound like a weird question,' Megan said, 'but do you know of anyone who's missing?'

That woman by the stream had rarely left Megan's thoughts since she'd found her. She was close to the same age as *this* girl. Probably around the same age as Jessie's friend, Helena, too.

Not that there was any sort of recognition. 'Missing... how?' came the reply.

Megan wasn't sure how to respond. 'I suppose if any of your friends, anyone you know, just sort of... disappeared recently?'

The shop worker's eyes crinkled with understandable bemusement. Young people already thought anyone older than them was an embarrassment and borderline weirdo. This was hardly helping.

'I, uh, don't know what you mean,' she said. 'Are you missing someone, or...?'

'No, it's not that. I, er...'

Megan tailed off as the girl picked up her phone, angling it up in a way that made Megan think the other woman might start filming. She took a step backwards, gave a needless wave that came out almost involuntarily, and then disappeared out of the shop.

It was an embarrassing retreat up the hill, away from the centre. Megan wasn't quite sure why she'd asked such an odd question, other than that a part of her genuinely expected the girl to say 'yes'. She would have revealed her friend was missing, Megan would describe the person she'd seen in the stream, and then it would all be real.

Except there was now one more person who thought Megan wasn't quite all there.

Megan walked slowly up the hill. It was the hottest part of the day and she could feel her skin tingling. That was the thing when leaving home in a hurry: basics like sun cream got left behind. Her decision to go had happened in a rush. She'd asked Nicola about coming to stay on Friday, caught the bus on Saturday, saw the girl in the stream on Sunday, and had somehow started work on Monday. She hadn't carefully planned what to pack, or thought about what she'd need. Megan had hoped moving would help give her some degree of clarity about the issues in her life. Instead, she'd found the girl in the stream and given herself something much more serious about which to be concerned.

With the spare key Nicola had given her that morning, Megan let herself into her sister's house. She patted her back pocket as she entered, ensuring the gentle dimple of what she presumed to be Trevor's front tooth was still there.

It was.

Megan was planning to head up to her attic room to have a good look at the tooth in a new light, in case there was an unlikely clue she'd missed. Instead, as she passed the door to the front room, Jessie's voice called through.

'Mum and Dad are out,' she said. 'Dunno where.'

Megan paused in the doorway, much in the way her sister had the previous day. 'Your dad was at the café not long ago,' she replied.

That got a curious look: 'Doing shifts?'

'Something about a cash-and-carry run.'

Jessie started nodding slowly. 'I think they're still annoyed I don't want to work there this summer.'

'Not your thing?'

'Is it anyone's? I mean, have you *met* people?'

She had a point. Megan had met many of them through the day. There was the woman who ordered an espresso for her nine-year-old, another who let her kid run around the café screaming, someone else who gave her son an iPad and refused to turn down the volume and/or give him accompanying head-phones. Many more who wouldn't clear their snotty tissues from the table, or who'd wheel their massive pushchair inside and refuse to move it. That was all barely scratching the surface.

'What are you doing with the summer instead?' Megan asked.

'Now you sound like Mum.' Jessie replied with a gentle smile but there was an edge. 'She won't stop going on about it but I've still got savings from helping out last summer,' she added. 'I didn't want to lose another one. One of my friends is working in the ice cream shop all summer because her dad owns it. I've hardly seen her. I know a couple of others working at the camp, just out of town. But it's like...' she tailed off, searching for the words and then added: 'You have a whole life to work summers, don't you?'

'You definitely do,' Megan agreed.

She hadn't had a job as a seventeen-year-old, other than

delivering the free papers once a week. Maybe she and Nicola had been the exceptions? It felt like everything was a hustle now. That every free moment not spent trying to earn was wasted and lazy. Nobody could ever just live.

Jessie reached for her phone, and the conversation felt over, except she never picked it up. 'Can I ask you something?' she said. 'I kinda wanted to do it last night but then you talked about the body and...' She tailed off and Megan knew what was coming. Probably because of that, Jessie didn't wait for a reply. 'Mum never talks about what happened at the school. I have asked but she always says it's not the time. But it's *never* the time. I know you were there, too, so I suppose...'

Megan was staring at the television, which was switched off. She'd somehow crept a few paces into the room without realising and there was no easy way to escape. In a blink, it felt as if the walls were slightly closer, the ceiling a little lower.

'I know there was a fire,' Jessie added. 'I know people died... but I guess I've always wanted to know what actually happened.'

NINE

'*Children* died...' Megan whispered. The walls were even closer, ceiling lower. Her arms were prickling with the heat once more, though it wasn't the sun from outside. It was the same whenever she was near a hot oven, or sizzling pan. A tingle would begin and she was back in the classroom with her sister and all the others.

A moment had passed, hard to know how long, but then Jessie was speaking again: 'I shouldn't have asked,' she said.

There was another moment of silence as Megan wondered how to reply. She wanted to say something, but where to begin?

Jessie's phone buzzed, short and sharp, and the teenager snatched for it, glancing to the screen. Her features sank as she returned the device to the arm of the sofa. When she looked back up, Megan still felt frozen.

'There's a plaque at the school,' Jessie said. 'We walk past it every day in reception, right by the scanners.'

'You have scanners?' Megan asked. It felt a world away: London with all the knives and the United States with all their guns. No need for such a thing in Hollicombe Bay. Except it was here that she'd been trapped in that classroom.

'We have a minute's silence every year on the anniversary,' Jessie added. 'They say it's to remember what happened – but they never really tell us what happened. Not properly. Just that there was a fire.'

Megan was nodding along. That was how things went with modern history. Children were taught what it was like to live in Victorian times but not what it was like to be shopping in the middle of Manchester or Warrington when a bomb went off. They would know every facet of Henry VIII's reign, which had no bearing on their lives, while not being told why they had to take their shoes off at the airport.

And they'd walk past a plaque every day without really knowing why it was there.

Before Megan could say anything, a key began scratching at the front door. It scraped the metal and then there was a bluster as the door was shouldered inwards.

Nicola appeared in the hall, a bag for life over her shoulder, massive sunglasses covering a third of her face. She closed the door and took off her glasses, blinking into the dimmer light as she noticed Megan.

'Oh, hello. How was your day?'

'OK,' Megan said. The standard response to cover everything from 'I was on a bus that slipped over a cliff into the sea', to 'All my wildest dreams came true, and then I won the lottery'.

Jessie picked up her phone, which was a statement of sorts.

'Did your granddad talk to you?' Nicola asked.

'No.'

Nicola hmmed to herself. 'He did say he was going to come over to ask you about Saturday. You know what he's like.'

'Rude?'

Nicola didn't answer that, not that Jessie was bothered. She was on her feet and part-way upstairs before her mum moved into the living room. When she had gone, Nicola plopped onto the sofa in the same spot her daughter had been. Megan took the armchair opposite.

'She doesn't know how good she's got it,' Nicola said. 'Dad made us work when we were her age. Remember when I spent a summer selling tickets at the old cinema?'

Megan had forgotten that cinema existed. In the days before giant multiplexes and ten screens showing the same thing, there was a small cinema in town that had a single screen in a spot not much bigger than a living room.

'You hated it,' Megan said. 'Used to come home stinking of smoke because they had a smoking section on one side and none on the other.'

Nicola let out a low whistle. 'I'd forgotten that. There was an aisle down the middle but it made no difference because smoke is, well... smoke.'

'Imagine trying to explain to Jessie that people her age used to have to work in a place that would give them lung cancer – but adults thought it was all right, because there was an aisle.'

Nicola was silent at that. It felt like a different age, yet it was their youths. 'I'm not asking her to get lung cancer,' she said, a bit quieter.

'We hated working through our summers – and now you want her to do the same.'

Nicola opened her mouth, then closed it. *You don't know what it's like, you're not a mother* had almost come out, and Megan knew it.

'Dad did a lot of things,' Megan added, and then: 'When was the last time you saw him?'

Nicola chewed the inside of her cheeks for a moment. 'About a month ago in town. I was on the other side of the road and I don't think he saw me. It's not like I was going to chase after him.'

'When did you last talk to him?'

'Maybe Christmas? He came to the café and I was on shift.

He wanted to talk but I told him he'd have to come back after we closed. He went off and that was that.' A pause. 'You?'

Megan needed a moment to think. The last few weeks had crashed into one another and time before that felt difficult to judge. 'Three years ago,' she replied. 'Something like that. He called my mobile from the old landline number. I didn't even know he still had it. I don't know how he got my number.'

'I didn't give it to him.'

There was a snippiness that Megan ignored.

'I never thought you did. Anyway, he said "happy birthday", even though it was about six weeks *after* my birthday. When I told him, he mumbled something and hung up.'

Nicola didn't seem remotely surprised. She didn't ask if Megan had called back, because of course she hadn't.

'When did you last see the house?' Megan asked.

'I drive past it now and then. Maybe a month ago? A bit longer? I was picking Jessie up from somewhere and went the long way around. The garden was overgrown and the gutter was hanging off the wall. It looked like there was a crack in the window of your old room.'

Megan found herself sighing at that. It had been twenty and a bit years since she had last slept in that room and yet, in truth, she probably did still think of it as hers. She wondered if any of her old schoolbooks remained under the bed, or posters on the wall. She used to collect magazines and they could even be in there somewhere.

'Sometimes I think about Jess and her granddads,' Nicola said, along with a half sigh of her own. 'They both live around here but she doesn't see either of them. Ben's dad called her fat, and she's not forgotten it, and ours...' Nicola tailed off momentarily and then picked up the thought. 'Did I ever tell you Dad grabbed one of her friends in town?'

Megan said 'no', even though she had been told. Sometimes

she thought she needed to be reminded of the reasons why she didn't visit her father.

'Jess was in town with her friends about a year ago. They were hanging around near the arcade, like you do. One of her friends said there was an old man staring at them, and Jess realised it was Dad. She said he sort of charged at them and grabbed one of her friends. I don't know what happened, or why, but he shook her a bit – and then ran off. Jess was really upset, as you would be. I tried to talk to Dad about it but he said he didn't remember.'

It wasn't entirely a surprise and certainly seemed like the sort of thing their father might do in a moment of madness.

'Did anyone call the police?' Megan asked.

'Jess told her friend not to, because it was her granddad. But she's not talked about him since.'

It was hard to blame her.

The sisters sat quietly for a while and Megan suspected Nicola was thinking the same things as her. They had each reached a point where trying to have any sort of relationship with their father wasn't worth it.

'How was the café? Nicola asked. 'Lakshmi's great, isn't she?'

It sounded like a polite way of admitting that the youngest member of staff, likely paid the least, did the most.

'You'll miss her when she goes back to university,' Megan replied.

Nicola nodded in agreement. At least she had some idea of what she had with Lakshmi.

'I was at the second site today,' Nicola said. 'I've told you about that, haven't I?'

This was something Megan definitely hadn't heard.

'We're trying to open a second café in Steeple's End,' Nicola added. 'There's a site close to the market we're renovating.'

'So you're becoming a chain?' Megan replied.

Her sister frowned, as if it had been an insult. 'Maybe,' came the reply. 'It needs a lot of supervising out there, so I promoted Pam to manager to cover me while I'm away. She's harmless enough.' Nicola made eye contact and then added: 'Do you get me?'

Megan sniggered at that – and, for the briefest of seconds, they were giggly teenagers again. Some girl had turned up to school with a dodgy haircut and it was the funniest thing in the world.

'How were the regulars?' Nicola asked.

'I don't know who's a regular, and who isn't.'

'What about Chrissy, with her giant pushchair and the whybrows?'

Megan had certainly seen the woman with the oversized buggy. 'Whybrows?' she asked.

'Y'know. She's done something mental to her eyebrows, and you think "Why?" Whybrows.'

Megan laughed at that – and there were a few more seconds to forget about everything else. This was how life had been when they were sisters growing up, one only a year older than the other. They had been close to inseparable for a while.

And then she remembered why she was now living in her sister's attic. Why she'd left Hollicombe Bay in the first place. And the young woman in the stream. It was weight after weight.

'I meant to ask,' Nicola said, moving on, 'are your documents safe? I know you left your place in a rush but do you have your passport and that sort of thing? Just in case.'

Megan hadn't thought about such items and it took her a second or two to consider the change of subject. She didn't think she'd need a passport any time soon. 'Everything's still at the house,' Megan replied.

'If you do go back to get them at some point, we can put

them in the safe. Our passports and birth certificates are all in there.'

Megan wasn't entirely listening. Now the woman from the stream had popped back into her mind, she was trying to figure out how to shoehorn Trevor into the conversation. She knew he worked in the sweet shop, maybe owned it, and that he'd recently lost a front tooth.

'Sounds like Ben had a busy day,' Megan said. 'He was in the café, saying he'd had to cover a cash-and-carry run...'

'Yeah, Trevor somehow had his front tooth knocked out. Had to have emergency surgery.'

'Do I know Trevor?' Megan asked. 'Is he one of the old-timers?' Some of the business owners in Hollicombe Bay had seemingly been around since Edwardian times.

Nicola sniggered. 'Sort of,' she said. 'Trevor's dad was Harry. He used to be on the council and ran the football club.'

It wasn't as if teenage Megan followed either council meetings, or football, but people like the mayor and councillors were known almost through osmosis. They'd be the only people in suits when it came time to open Summer Fest, or anything else around town. They'd sometimes end up giving a talk for a school assembly, or would be on the front page of the local newspaper. The sort of people everyone's dad would stop to speak to on the high street for a needless half-hour.

'He lives in that farmhouse up by the old church,' Nicola continued.

'The *white* church?' Megan asked.

'The one where Dad used to take us for Christmas Eve. It's a wreck now. Nobody's gone there in years.'

Megan knew the place. It was further up the hill, on the way out of, or into, town. She was fairly sure she'd been christened there, which meant Nicola probably had as well. Those were simpler times, when they and most of the rest of the town would pack into a hall for Easter Sunday, or to listen to carols late on Christmas Eve. Megan used to enjoy those times, with the singing and the stories – even though her dad told her not to believe any of it. 'Fairy tales,' he'd call them.

'It's not a farm anymore,' Nicola said, still talking about Trevor. 'It's been in his family for years but the whole place is run-down. He owns the sweet shop and the chip shop in town.'

Megan thought on that for a moment. It was more information than she'd hoped for. There was a decent chance she'd know Trevor if she saw him. He was from one of those Hollicombe Bay legacy families. The ones who'd lived there forever, who owned everything, and who ended up on the council, making decisions. Every small town had a family or three who were the same.

Nicola was still talking. '...Anyway, are you feeling better? No more walks in the woods?'

Megan was back in the room, though had no idea how to reply. She *had* been back in the woods.

'Not today,' Megan managed.

'Good. You'll have the whole town talking about you.'

It might have been the way she said it, or perhaps the gentle accompanying laugh. Either way, Megan knew without question that her sister had spent at least part of the day talking about her.

TEN

TUESDAY

Megan's phone read o1:28 when she heard another scream.

She sat up sharply in bed, sensing the sloped ceiling a fraction above her head. The window was cracked an inch or so: an attempt to cool down the attic, while hoping a bird didn't fly in during the night. Megan breathed, listened. The sky was dark, though there was a gentle swish of tree branches somewhere towards the back of the garden.

Had there been a scream? She'd heard *something* and yet it was so quiet now. Had she dreamed it?

Megan pressed the thin sheet aside and stretched to open the window wider. She knelt on the bed and craned outside, welcoming the cool air that whispered across her face.

It was quiet. There probably hadn't been a scream. Even if there had, what was she supposed to do? Follow the trail into the woods once again? It hadn't gone so well the last time, and that was when she could see where she was going.

Megan lay back on the bed, on top of the covers, window still wide, as she listened to the whispering trees. From what had been the depths of slumber, she was wide awake with the sort of late-night clarity that meant she wouldn't be getting back to sleep any time soon.

What to do?

She hadn't brought any books with her, not that she'd read much recently. There would be some argument raging on social media, because there always was, and she didn't fancy that either. Even though young people seemed to manage fine, Megan had never quite got her head around watching anything that lasted longer than a few seconds on her phone.

Aside from the bed, chaise longue, nightstand, and an uncomfortable-looking wooden chair, the only things in the attic had come from her suitcase. Megan was blocked in by the wall on one side and the chaise longue on the other. She shuffled herself down to the bottom of the bed, the image of the sweet shop suddenly in her mind. There was some sort of connection from that to Trevor, to the girl she'd seen in the stream. Megan knew she wasn't going to get back to sleep until she'd at least made some attempt to see if there was something obvious she had missed.

She grabbed some clothes from her case, took her phone and her sister's spare key from the nightstand, and then descended into the house as softly as she could. There were creaks and squeaks, though nothing that should wake a person.

Megan slipped on her shoes in the hall and then quietly left the house with a barely perceptible click of the door.

For the first time since she'd arrived in Hollicombe Bay, there was the mildest of chills to the air. A high, bright moon cast a bleached glow across the street. There were barely any lights in the windows along the street, and the town was so quiet that the simmering ripple of the ocean flittered on the air.

Megan started to make her way down the slope towards the centre of town, more following the noise than anything planned. Whitecliff had a row of pubs along the seafront that would be open late through the summer, making the early hours prime time for a steady trickle of tourists to be walking, stumbling or crawling their way back to the hotels and caravan parks. The smaller town of Hollicombe Bay had none of that. By the time it was midnight, everything was shut and more or less everyone was home. It was seemingly the way it had always been, and just the way people liked it.

On down the hill, and Nicola's 'you'll have the whole town talking about you' still felt crisp in Megan's ears. Ben had told Pam about what Megan had seen in the woods – and Pam seemed the type who would share it with everyone for the rest of the week. It also sounded a lot like Nicola had been talking. Perhaps those moments of recognition from customers across the day had been more than Megan had realised? She thought it was people she used to know saying hello but, in reality, it was people coming to have a stare at the person who saw ghosts in streams.

The street lights were gloomy in the town centre. Not those bright white LED bulbs that turned night into day, more those dark orange things that couldn't light a cupboard under the stairs.

Megan passed a phone box and wondered if it still worked, then a postbox. Next to that, the back of a bus stop had been kicked through. A poster was taped to the nearest lamp post, with the word 'handyman!', plus a phone number underneath. It was simple yet effective – presumably not the sort of marketing with which Ben was involved.

Paul was a handyman. Megan's husband. He'd started his own business close to fifteen years before, and was still going strong. People used to tell Megan she was so lucky to be married to a person so good with their hands. Someone who could fix more or less anything. And they were right... except, once separated, it quickly became apparent that if one person in a relationship knew how to do everything, the other ended up knowing very little.

Megan was halfway along the high street, swallowed by the shadows of the awning outside the pub. She was thinking about her husband, wondering if he was sleeping in their house at that moment, when there was a flicker of movement from the alley ahead. There was the sound of a car door opening and then a man saying something lost to the night. Megan edged forward, keeping to the shade as she reached the end of the cut-through. An SUV was parked a little way along, lights off, with one of the back doors open and a big dent in the back bumper. The side door of the sweet shop was also open and there was a flash of movement from vehicle to building.

A man was leaning on the back corner of the car, and he hissed a 'Get on with it', as one more person hurried into the back of the shop. With that, he slammed the SUV door and then moved into the building himself, closing that door behind him. Megan was at the front of the sweet shop, though the bright displays had been replaced by stifling metal shutters. A graffiti tag was sprayed across the front, with some sort of spiral and devil horns.

The town was still again, and Megan found herself continuing along the alley, around the vehicle, and to the back of the shop. A large metal wheelie bin was underneath a window, with a series of empty boxes to the side. It was dark at the back of the shop, the shadows stealing the moonlight, leaving only a muddy murk. Megan wasn't sure what she was doing, other than being nosey. She'd felt drawn to the place by her restless sleep.

She waited in the gloom, listening as the relative silence of the ocean was replaced by a gentle hum of machinery. The woman behind the counter of the sweet shop had said that new confectionary was made in the kitchen every day, though Megan would not have guessed that meant two in the morning.

As the hum of the equipment was joined by a steady *thunk* of something being mixed, Megan figured she would head back to the front. Perhaps complete a lap of town and then return to Nicola's to see if she could fall asleep again?

She'd moved to the corner of the building, close to the parked car, when the side door of the shop opened with a creak.

If he had turned to the side, the man who'd emerged would have seen Megan standing a couple of paces away. Instead, he angled the other way, humming tunelessly under his breath, as he closed the door. He was a silhouette under the merest of light: stocky, to be polite, with a beefy chest.

He stopped whistling almost as quickly as he'd started, swearing under his breath and muttering something about a tooth. At the mention of that, Megan crept backwards, into the darker shadows, watching as he rounded the car, to the driver's door. He pressed on the side, holding up his phone, and stabbing at the screen as white light slinked across the lower half of his face.

The swollen top lip and gums were unmistakeable. He'd either had a filler injection that had gone *badly* wrong, or he'd been smacked in the face.

The man put the phone to his ear, waiting for someone to pick up the call. He tapped his foot and grumbled under his breath, then swore again when it went unanswered. With a sigh, he clambered into the SUV, before quietly easing out from the alley, onto the road, and out of sight.

It had to be Trevor.

Either that, or two people in the small town had gone through emergency dental surgery that day.

Megan hovered in the alley, wondering what to do – if anything.

Trevor's original tooth was wrapped in a sock, in her suitcase, back at Nicola's house. She was certain he'd been somewhere around the stream when she'd found that young woman. It was probably a bit late to tell that to the police now, and she still wasn't sure she'd be believed. Plus, with Trevor being one of the legacy families in town, she had a nagging sense that any local officer might be a little *too* friendly with him.

With that, Megan returned to the back of the shop. The window was too high but she hauled herself up onto the bin, feeling the crunch of her knees on the metal, before managing to stand. The hum of machinery had become part of the night's patchwork, as if it had always been there. Every few seconds the solid, juddering *whump* of something metal would cause a minute earthquake that was more of a feeling than a noise.

Megan pushed herself onto tiptoes, giving her a stunted view of what turned out to be a kitchen. A large mixer was in the back corner, its arm metronoming in an arc, as somebody stood over the bowl, watching the action. There were a couple of others in the kitchen: someone standing at a counter chopping; another stacking plastic trays in the other corner.

The kitchen was bright and clean, and the trio of cooks were all in aprons and hairnets. Aside from the hour, it felt perfectly normal. Megan wondered who they were, and whether they were getting overtime. Was this a nightly thing, or a one-off because Trevor had spent the day with a dentist, instead of at the shop?

None of it seemed to matter – and Megan was about to climb down – when the person at the mixer turned around. It was a woman, a *teenager*, probably, although it was difficult to tell from the hairnet. The man stacking trays said something and she looked across to him, half smiling, before replying.

Megan had seen her before, and even with the late-night memory fuzz, she knew where.

It was Jessie's missing friend, Helena.

ELEVEN

More because of surprise than anything else, Megan was a moment away from tapping on the glass. Then she realised it would lead to three people staring up to the high window, wondering why some nutjob was watching them in the early hours of the morning. Wondering why that same nutjob was trying to get their attention.

Megan ducked out of sight and then climbed down from the bin. She wasn't sure why it felt like such a surprise. Jessie's friend hadn't gone missing, she'd got a job that likely meant she slept a lot during the day. Not only that, Jessie had been the first to say they weren't close friends. Megan had told her niece about the woman in the stream and, naturally, Jessie had tried to make a connection. It had been her polite way of saying that Megan *wasn't* a maniac – and Megan had seized it.

Except nothing strange had happened with Helena.

As Megan reached the high street once more, the hum of the machines was gone, replaced by the wash of the sea. It felt colder than moments before, and she'd left the house without a jacket. The late-night walk felt even sillier. It had woken her up

– and all she had achieved was making herself feel like a conspiracy theorist.

Megan turned in the direction of the house and started walking. She was near the blackened windows of the chip shop when a man's voice sliced through the night.

'Megan...?'

She turned to see a man on the other side of the road, standing under a street light. Her first instinct was to touch her pocket, to make sure the key was still there. She might need it in her hand if he came at her. Either that, or she'd have to run. Or shout. Or a combination of all three. She was on her own in the middle of the night.

As if reading her mind, the man held up both hands, arms out, fingers wide, showing her he wasn't holding anything. 'It's Daniel,' he said.

Megan had known a couple of Dans in her time, probably a Daniel here or there – but there would only ever be one *proper* Daniel.

He'd been in her class through primary and secondary school. Once Megan had hit that certain age, he'd become the sort of boy or girl that everyone had in their lives. The type where theoretical fantasy wedding plans would be made, even though they were fourteen and barely spoke. She had written 'Dan', 'Daniel' and 'Danny' in the back of her exercise book to see which she preferred, even though it wasn't up to her, and they had never been boyfriend-girlfriend. They weren't even friends, more just people in the same year.

She had once got a red bag because one of his friends had told a different friend, whom Megan had overheard telling someone else, that Daniel supported Liverpool. They apparently played in red, and she wondered if he'd be impressed. If he was, he never mentioned it. As far as she could tell herself, he wasn't even into football.

Megan assumed everyone had a Daniel in their life... and

then, at some point, those feelings slipped into nothing but memories.

As she looked to him across the road, Megan saw the rippled, damaged skin on Daniel's palms. Everyone who'd been in the fire at the school had their scars, but, for some, they were physical.

'What are you doing out so late?' Daniel called.

'I could ask you the same.'

He looked both ways and started crossing the empty road towards her, hands now in his pockets. 'Someone said you were back home.'

Megan didn't quite know how to reply – partly because she wasn't sure if Hollicombe Bay *was* home; partly because Daniel Clarkson, the *actual* Daniel Clarkson, was talking to her.

When no response came, he stopped a couple of paces away. 'You look a bit lost,' he added. And he was right, though not for the reasons he might have thought.

'Couldn't sleep,' Megan replied. 'I thought a walk might help.'

'I guess that means we're both night owls,' he laughed. 'Is that the saying? Night bird? Night hawk?' He didn't wait for clarification. 'Do you want company for your walk?'

'I was about to head back to Nic's house. That's where I'm staying.'

He nodded along. 'It's OK. I was heading home myself. I can let you go—'

'No,' Megan spoke a little too eagerly. 'Company would be good. Maybe a slow walk back?'

Daniel stepped onto the pavement, so he was at her side. 'I only really do slow walks nowadays. Messed up my knee playing hockey a few years back.' He paused and then added: 'Which way?'

Megan pointed in the direction of her sister's and they slotted in at each other's side. Megan had to stop herself from laughing at the absurdity of it all. Her teenage self would have dreamed of this, although perhaps not at such an early hour.

The moon coated the dark ocean waves a frosty white as they rippled in to shore. There was a sharp, harried intake of air – and then a gushing rush of water across the barren sand.

'How have you been?' Daniel asked.

Megan laughed, a real one that sprang from the emptiness of what her life had become. 'It's quite hard to sum up twenty years in a sentence,' she said.

Daniel sniggered as well. 'Good point.' She felt him smiling, even though Megan didn't turn to look. They were matching each other's pace. 'When was the last time I saw you?' he added.

'Francine's wedding?'

'Did you hear they're already divorced? Only lasted eighteen months. Someone told me her parents spent twenty grand on the venue.'

Megan didn't know any of that. Francine was a person from school who was more Nicola's friend than Megan's. She wasn't sure how or why she'd been invited to the wedding, other than that *everyone* from back then seemed to be on the list. Her only reason for returning to her hometown in the past decade or so had been for weddings, funerals, and the like. Her teenage obsession with Daniel had gone unrequited through school – and the first time she'd ever spoken to him in a real way had been at someone's wedding a few years back. They'd reached for the same sausage roll, both insisted the other take it, and then gone halves.

'How is Nicola?' Daniel asked. 'I see her in the café now and then. I know Ben from the business association.'

'She's fine,' Megan replied. 'Talking about opening a second café.'

'What about you? I forget your husband's name...?'

Perhaps it was an innocent question, or maybe he'd heard

something about why she was back. Megan let it sit for a moment. The words didn't sound right from her lips. 'We're separated,' she said, and there was an edge to it. No more questions, your honour. To ensure he couldn't follow up, she continued talking: 'What about *your* wife?'

'Divorced,' he said, less firmly. 'Papers came through six or seven weeks back.'

Megan almost asked what had gone on, though it was hard to be nosey about the breakdown of *his* relationship without expecting questions around her own. She'd seen some Facebook posts from mutual friends a while back about the actual wedding, though she and Daniel weren't connected on the website. She'd not seen much since.

They were off the high street, at the bottom of the steep slope up towards the housing estates. A sandwich board for the tapas restaurant had been chained to a cycle rack and Daniel had to sidestep closer to Megan to get around it. She felt a second of his warmth, and then he was back on the other side of the pavement.

'How long has there been a tapas place?' Megan asked.

'Opened just before Easter.'

'Only took twenty-odd years to reach the twenty-first century.'

Daniel laughed at that and Megan allowed herself to join in. That teenage part of her still existed, telling her to be cool. Don't laugh too hard. Don't snort, for God's sake, don't snort.

'It's not bad,' Daniel said, which was British for 'It's incredible'. 'Makes a change to burgers at the pub, fish and chips, or fry-ups.'

They were safely away from the subject of their respective break-ups, which was fine by Megan.

There were a few seconds of silence as they began the incline and then: 'What are you up to in town?' Daniel asked.

'I'm doing a few shifts for Nic in the café,' Megan replied. 'Do you still run the arcade?'

'I own it outright now. There was a bit of money in Dad's will that I used to pay off the bank.'

'Oh... wow.' A pause. 'I reckon I partly paid that off with all the two-pence pieces I used to feed into your coin machine.'

He laughed at that, so she continued.

'You can tell me now. It's all a scam, isn't it? Nobody ever wins on those things.'

Daniel held up his crossed fingers. 'It's all legit. Scout's honour.'

'I don't remember you being a scout.'

'Either way, it's too late now. Your two-pence pieces are all mine.'

Megan snorted at that and then wished there was a little more elegance about the laugh. When she'd been younger, she'd spent plenty of time in the arcade, in part because she knew Daniel's family owned it, and she was hoping she might get a glimpse of him somewhere among the machines. A cheap way of wasting time was slowly feeding 2ps into the ramp machines and hoping some of it paid out.

'Do you still have those machines?' Megan asked.

'Only for ten-pence pieces.'

'I know inflation's bad but that's ridiculous!'

'Everyone having PlayStations and Xboxes at home has changed the business. We have to buy in dance machines, or driving cockpits to try to offer something different.' He sighed and added: 'Covid hit us hard and not everyone's come back.'

He was no longer laughing and it felt like the first moment of seriousness. Megan wasn't sure how to reply, but he was still talking.

'The whole building's a mess. There are so many store-rooms at the back. They used to be filled with old machines but I got rid because they were a fire hazard. Dad had all sorts of stuff back there. There's a big open space. I'd like to redesign the whole layout, but it's expensive.'

He tailed off and it felt as if he was sharing something with her in the way she'd shared with Jessie. Big things on a person's mind, with nobody obvious to tell. They didn't really know each other and had been walking for less than ten minutes. Perhaps that's why it was so easy to talk about true feelings?

'Everyone in town is struggling,' he continued. 'Heating bills are ridiculous in the winter – and nobody's here in the off-season. We're all desperate to get the money back in summer. That's why I'm out so late. I was finishing off some bits at the arcade.' He sighed and then added: 'Sorry, I don't know why I'm telling you all this.'

Megan was huffing from the effort of the hill and, without needing to discuss it, they stopped to sit on a wall. They were facing back towards the town, watching the tide ripple towards the shore. In the distance, out past the rocks, the lighthouse bled white across the waves.

There wasn't a lot Megan could say as a direct response, and it felt like Daniel didn't want one anyway. Having some-body actively listen was enough. She thought about telling him of the young woman in the stream. How she'd been there and then she was gone. Perhaps even about the tooth that probably belonged to Trevor – except she didn't want one more person to think she was a fantasist.

They sat quietly for a minute. Longer. It was good to be with another person and not feel that need to talk for the sake of talking. When she glanced down, Daniel's hands were resting on his knees, and it was impossible to miss the scaly scars that snaked up to his wrists. She had scars, too – though hers weren't as visible.

'We have a book club,' Daniel said after a while. 'We meet in the back room of the Labour Club. Our next meet is tomorrow, if you fancy it?' He stopped and checked his watch. 'Well, technically, I suppose it's later today.'

Megan thought on it for a moment. She'd never been to such an event. 'I wouldn't have read the book,' she replied.

That got a gentle snigger. 'Half the people haven't. We always pick something where there's a movie as well. It's an excuse to hang out, drink wine, and eat cheese. You should come.'

Megan almost said 'no' by default, except there was something about the normality that she craved. 'What's the book?' she asked.

'*Tinker Tailor Soldier Spy.*'

'Have you read it?'

'Years ago. I can tell you that Gary Oldman's very good.'

Megan giggled at that. There was something charming about a movie club posing as a book club because it sounded more respectable. 'I'll see if I'm free,' she said, knowing she was, and getting to her feet, without committing. She was still married, after all.

They continued walking together up the hill as Daniel told her how they took it in turns to bring the wine, and that there was far more competition over that than anything to do with the books. She listened and she laughed, and it was only as they reached the crossroads near Nicola's house that Megan stopped and pointed.

'I'm that way,' she said.

'I'm *that* way,' he replied, pointing back in the direction they'd come.

They hovered awkwardly for a few moments, neither apparently sure how to say goodbye. It was Daniel who finally took the moment. He reached and touched her upper arm gently, momentarily. Perhaps odd without the context, yet right for what it was. Enough.

'It's been good chatting,' he said.

'It really has.'

'If you're not at book club, maybe see you around for another late-night walk?'

Megan wasn't sure whether he was joking. She took a step away and glanced sideways towards the stream and where the water disappeared into the tunnel. She *so* wanted to tell him about the young woman.

'Maybe,' Megan replied.

They stood there for a moment longer and then Daniel turned to head back down the hill. 'Night, night,' he called.

TWELVE

Megan's alarm was going off what felt like moments after she'd put her head on the pillow. She had time-travelled to 6.40 a.m. and groaned herself out of bed with a series of yawns and stretches. Considering how late she'd been out, Megan felt surprisingly fresh. That short period with Daniel had somehow helped make everything feel a little better. She even managed a few seconds in which the drama of the last few weeks didn't invade her thoughts.

Then she remembered everything that had happened in Whitecliff with her husband. Plus the young woman from the stream. The crushing weight was back.

Downstairs, and Nicola was already up, though still in a slouchy set of pyjamas. The laptop was open on the kitchen table and she was sipping from a mug of coffee. She took off a pair of reading glasses that Megan didn't know she needed and peered over the screen. 'I can drop you at the café, if you want a lift in?' she said.

That meant Megan would get at least fifteen more minutes of sitting around.

Nicola nudged the coffee pot across the table and nodded

towards the mugs hanging from the underside of a cabinet. 'No one will be around to pick you up,' she added, nodding towards the back of the house. 'If you don't fancy walking, you can borrow my bike. It's in the shed.'

'I've not been on a bike in years. Probably since we were kids.'

From nowhere, Megan had a clear memory of waiting at the top of one of the hills for traffic to clear. Once they were sure no cars were on the way up, they'd pushed off on their little bikes and freewheeled to the bottom. There was the rush of the wind and that stabbing midge of fright at the uncontrolled speed.

'Ben picked it out when he was trying to get me into cycling,' Nicola explained. 'I've only used it about ten times – but it's pretty new. Even *I* managed to get up the hills with it.' She paused and then added, 'Are you still learning to drive?'

It was an innocent question, although one that was hard not to take personally. One of Megan's great disasters was that she'd failed her driving test five times. Nothing had ever seriously gone wrong. It's not like she'd run over a cat, or clipped a lollipop lady – but there was a series of little things. She'd got in the wrong lane after confusing the examiner's directions, then panicked, and returned to the correct lane without indicating. She'd accidentally cut off a mail van when she was supposed to give way at a junction. She had somehow mistaken a 30 sign for a 20. Each failure had felt more devastating than the last, to the point that getting into a driver's seat brought with it rivets of anxiety.

'It's on hold at the moment,' Megan answered, which was her way of saying that she'd stopped getting lessons a little over a year before. In case any follow-ups came, she quickly added: 'I ran into Daniel yesterday.'

Nicola had picked up her glasses but immediately put them down as she closed the laptop lid with a snap. They were teenagers again. 'Daniel from the arcade? Daniel Clarkson? Clarky?'

Megan pushed away the grin that had snuck onto her face. She didn't mention she had run into him at two in the morning.

'How is he?' Nicola asked. 'I heard he owns the arcade outright now.'

'He mentioned that.'

Nicola smirked. 'Did you tell him how you used to write his name in the back of your exercise books?'

'I didn't.'

They both smiled at that and, for a few seconds more, Megan forgot the chaos of her life.

'He invited me to his book club later.'

'A date!'

'Not a date. Just some wine and cheese.'

'Megan and Daniel sitting in a tree...'

Nicola was teasing, as if they really *were* young again, and Megan wanted to remind her that she had only just separated from her husband. It was nice to live in a fantasy for a few moments, though, even if Megan knew it wasn't true. Things had been so much simpler when they had walked to school together as sisters. When they didn't have to worry about husbands, bills, businesses, and everything else.

'What are you up to today?' Megan asked, changing the subject.

'I'll be at the new café. I'm there most days. There's a problem with the electrics and nobody who doesn't want to charge a fortune for a few hours' work.'

'Daniel was saying times were hard around here,' Megan said. 'I guess the new place gives you double the opportunity...?'

Megan wasn't sure what she was asking. The real question was how, if business was hard, her sister was able to afford a second site.

'Something like that.'

The mood had shifted and Nicola opened her laptop once more. She put on her glasses and started sipping her coffee, before telling Megan they'd have to head off soon.

'Or you can take the bike in,' she added. 'You can leave it behind the café.'

The suggestion felt marginally better than walking, assuming it really *was* true that the gears were good enough to get up the hill. A part of Megan wanted that feeling from years before of freewheeling down.

Without Megan actually replying, Nicola took the lack of a 'no' as an acceptance. 'I'll show you it,' she said. 'It cost two grand.'

'The bike?'

'Ben reckoned it was cheap.'

It didn't *sound* cheap.

The bike itself was black and pink and looked much like any other bike, other than that, when Megan picked it up, it had a feathery lightness about it.

After a couple of mouthfuls of coffee, and a hunt for vaguely appropriate clothes, Megan pedalled along the back roads of Hollicombe Bay. She'd been unsure at first, but the old saying about never forgetting to ride a bike was apparently true.

There was a salty tang in the air, and the gulls howled as they circled. Across the sea, the merest hint of a reddy-purple clung to the horizon. Megan took her time to take it all in, before freewheeling down towards the café on the far side of town. Given her inability to pass a driving test, she wondered if she should have taken up cycling years before.

She left the bike in the enclosed courtyard at the back of the café, which was hidden from the road. There was no lock and no rack – but Nicola said it would be safe. At least if someone nicked it, Megan couldn't be to blame. She tried the back door, marked 'staff only', though it was locked, which left her traipsing around to the front.

Pam had already opened up, and was busy sipping her own drink while sitting at one of the tables. It wasn't quite opening time as she browsed something on her phone. When she spotted Megan, she blinked, half in wonder. 'You're back then,' she said.

'Is that a surprise?'

Pam thought on that for a moment, and it felt as if she had been in on a conversation that Megan had missed. 'Lakshmi's gonna be a bit late today,' she said, as if the previous part of the conversation hadn't happened. 'So you'll have to work the till.'

Megan wasn't sure why Pam wasn't going to do that herself, although, from what she'd seen the day before, Pam didn't appear to do much of anything.

'I left a bike in the courtyard at the back,' she said. 'Nicola said I could. Do you reckon it'll be safe?'

'Nobody's nicking bikes round here.'

Megan didn't push on why. Either there was little to no crime – which felt unlikely – or people were busy stealing things more obviously in the open. Megan thought on it for a moment, then added: 'I tried coming in the back door but—'

'It's locked.' Pam's eyes were suddenly narrow with apparent suspicion. She'd spoken so sharply that Megan took a half-step back.

'I know, I suppose—'

'Just come in the front,' Pam added, with a forced brightness. She eyed Megan for a few seconds too long, and then pushed herself up. 'Time to work,' she said, before heading to the front door to turn around the open/closed sign.

The first forty-five minutes were a blur of customers, and trying to remember how everything worked. Lakshmi's arrival gave respite – and then the morning continued much as the previous had. There were drinks to make, tables to clean, and food order receipts to put through the kitchen hatch. Megan hadn't thought too much about it the previous day, but it was an odd system of pushing scraps of paper into the oversized letterbox space whenever somebody ordered food. She had to ding a bell to let the kitchen staff know a new order had arrived. Then, not long after, a plate or two would appear in the same space, and the bell would be sounded in response. There was some sort of board on the other side of the gap, meaning there was no way to see into the kitchen. Megan didn't even know how many people worked in there.

Pam had apparently forgotten her annoyance from first thing, and was back into her pattern of chatting with customers while Lakshmi and Megan did the work. Pam took her break first, not that it made much difference to the workload.

It was while she was out that something went wrong with the hatch. The board on the other side had collapsed forward, blocking the spot to drop off orders. Lakshmi was busy with a line of customers, leaving Megan unsure of what to do. A door marked 'kitchen staff only' was to the side of the hatch, with a pushpad lock on the wall. The door, like the one at the back, was locked – so Megan knocked, hoping to get somebody's attention. When none came, she tried again.

There was a faint mumble of voices from the other side, definitely a man's, but perhaps someone else's too. There was a click and a clunk, which sounded like a lock being opened.

That was why Megan was in the process of trying the handle one more time when a hand gripped her shoulder and spun her around. Megan yelped from the way she'd been pinched – and she turned to see the wide eyes of Pam.

'What do you think you're doing?' she hissed.

THIRTEEN

Customers were watching, although Pam appeared oblivious. She was glaring, demanding a reply, a different person. Megan wasn't sure what was happening, and couldn't remember the last time somebody had actually put their hands on her. Her shoulder throbbed slightly.

'The hatch is broken,' she managed, pointing towards the wall.

Pam scowled, keeping her attention on Megan for a few seconds before shifting her gaze to the side. 'Move,' she huffed.

Megan stepped away as Pam shielded the pushpad with one hand and typed a series of numbers into it with the other. The door popped outwards and Pam swiftly stepped through it, closing it behind her. There were more sounds of voices and then a *thunk*. Whatever had gone wrong with the hatch on the other side had been fixed, with the space to place and pick up orders restored.

When Pam re-emerged from the kitchen, she clicked the door back into place and then forced a smile. 'Sorry about that,' she said. 'All fixed now.'

Megan turned from Pam to the hatch and back. 'Is everything all right in the kitchen?' she asked.

'They just don't like being bothered while they're working. I thought Nicola might have told you that?'

Megan tried to remember what had happened the day before. Nicola had said something about there being no need to go into the kitchen and to use the hatch, but it had been more throwaway than anything else.

When it became clear Megan had no idea what Pam was talking about, the other woman lowered her voice and added: 'I'll tell you later.'

A gentle murmur returned to the café as customers went back to whatever they were doing.

Megan stared at Pam for a second or two longer, and then returned to the counter, where Lakshmi was taking orders. The incident had lasted barely a minute and the pain – if it could be called that – from Megan's shoulder was already gone.

Lakshmi went on her break and work continued as if nothing odd had happened. Megan took orders and money at the counter, then made drinks and picked up food from the hatch. The main change was that Pam cut down the gossiping by a good eighty per cent, and cracked on with actual work.

When Lakshmi returned, it was Megan's turn to head into the sunshine. She had no particular plans for how to spend her time, though considered texting Nicola to ask if there was something weird going on with the kitchen. Or Pam. Or both. It had been such an explosive, surreal reaction to a mundane thing that she had to remind herself it had actually happened. In the end, she figured that if she was going to mention it, then in person would probably be for the best.

The air conditioning of the café provided quite the contrast to the warmth of the day. The high street was a swarm of bare legs and bare arms, with the smell of sun cream sitting on what little wind there was. Megan didn't want to settle among the throngs, where it was hot and cramped, where children were screaming their delight at the day, so she headed around the back of the café. The bike was untouched where she had left it in the courtyard, so Megan dragged it onto the pavement and started cycling away from town. She craved the peace.

The salty breeze brushed her skin as she pedalled into it, not following any particular route, other than avoiding the steepest hills. Within minutes, she was out of the centre, surrounded by low hedges and banked emerald fields. Megan had never experienced the outskirts of town in anything other than a car or a bus, yet there was a beauty to it all that was so easy to miss when zipping past at national speed limit.

Megan slowed to a near stop, maintaining the balance as she looked up past the swaying grass to the dilapidated church on the top of the slope. Decades before, on otherwise quiet Sundays, parishioners' hymns would drift through the town. Christmas carols would herald the festive season. Now, there was a large hole in the spire. The white walls that had once been lit to create a beacon of fellowship were brown with dirt and age.

The slope around the field was gentler than the hill that led to Nicola's house on the other side of town. Megan cycled slowly up, using the gears as her sister had said. She had no plan, other than enjoying the solitude of it all, though it was impossible to ignore the church when she reached it.

It was a sad, neglected sight of boarded-up doors, and missing roof tiles. The words 'This Sunday' could vaguely be recognised on a service board that was on its side and half buried in mud. It looked like a building abandoned in a rush; something from a zombie apocalypse TV show. There was a second church in the town itself, and Megan didn't know anyone who was religious. The bigger surprise was that this place had survived so long. It was too far out of town for most to walk.

Megan had left the bike by the rickety gates – and she was about to pedal back to the café – but then, from nowhere, she *did* have a plan. Perhaps she had all along. Trevor's farm was on the other side of the road and he was somehow connected to everything. Nicola had said it wasn't a farm any longer – and Megan could see that from the state of the place. An old barn was in the distance, along a rubble path, and it was in almost as bad a state as the church. There were holes in the roof and a stack of rotting pallets resting against the side.

The farmhouse itself, near the road, wasn't a lot better. There were more missing tiles, and the single-pane windows had a grubby, waxy sheen, like slime on the back of a draining board.

Megan crossed the road and stood at the end of Trevor's drive, staring towards the dark SUV that was parked in front of the farmhouse. The vehicle that had been at the back of the sweet shop the night before was easily the newest thing she could see. It was the one which had dropped off Helena and the others.

'Get on with it,' a voice had said.

There was nothing in particular to see, certainly nothing out of the ordinary.

Except that Megan still had Trevor's front tooth wrapped in a sock. He had to have been near that stream where Megan found the body.

She was already a dozen steps onto his property when she realised what she was doing. A barbed-wire fence ran along one side of the gravelly path, while the other opened out onto piles of tyres, and various pieces of broken machinery.

A part of Megan wondered if she should simply knock on the door and ask Trevor if he knew anything about the woman in the stream. She didn't have to let on that she had his tooth. Perhaps there would be an innocent reason? Or maybe he'd lie and it would be so obvious, she'd know something was up?

He might not be in, but, if he was at work, his vehicle wasn't. Unless he had more than one.

Megan suddenly realised she didn't know anything about him. Perhaps he was married? Maybe he had children, lots of them, and some were in the farmhouse now? They could be watching her.

She was still continuing along the length of the drive, almost level with the house as she passed the SUV. If someone came out now, it would be hard to explain why she was there. It was also hard for her to turn around.

It was as she pressed on further that a flash of colour caught her eyes. The SUV wasn't the only car parked on the drive – there was a second vehicle, hidden behind the house itself.

A maroon Mini that very much belonged to Megan's sister.

FOURTEEN

Megan stared. Nicola had told her to take the bike to work because she was at the second café in a neighbouring town all day.

Except she wasn't. She was at Trevor's farmhouse instead.

It was an odd thing to lie about, though perhaps it wasn't a lie? Maybe Nicola had got sidetracked, or... what?

Ben had done the cash-and-carry pickup in place of Trevor the day before, so it might be something to do with that? Were the local businesses doing each other another favour?

Megan couldn't figure out if this was strange, or whether she was reading too much into things. Much like Jessie's missing friend, who'd turned up doing a late-night kitchen shift, there was nothing specifically *wrong* – and yet things didn't feel quite right either.

If Megan hadn't found that tooth, and Trevor hadn't had emergency surgery the day before, she wouldn't even know who he was. She certainly wouldn't be standing on his land.

The buzz from her bag made Megan squeal. She half expected to see Nicola's name on her phone screen, asking her what she was doing. It wasn't. It was an unknown number, marked: 'Maybe Pam'.

Where ru?

Megan eyed the farmhouse and her sister's car, then decided it would be weirder to knock than it would be to leave. After the disappearing body, Nicola already thought there was something going on with her. Seemingly stalking her in the middle of an afternoon, when Megan was supposed to be working, wasn't going to help.

She typed out a quick 'on my way', before hurrying back to the bike. She was going to be late back for a second day in a row.

The ride back was easier than the one out. Megan free-wheeled down the deserted slope, away from the farmhouse and church, and then coasted back to the café. She left the bike in the courtyard and headed back inside via the front door.

Pam was leaning on the end of the counter, chatting to one of the local mums. She made a point of looking to her wrist, even though she wasn't wearing a watch, but didn't say anything.

A couple was on one of the circular tables, sharing a pair of toasties; while a small family were slurping milkshakes over by the window. Lakshmi was at the other end of the counter, thumbing something into her phone. There were no other customers, leaving Megan to wipe down a few already clean tables to make it seem like she was doing something.

As Pam continued talking to her friend, Lakshmi told Megan about her philosophy degree, and how her dad thought it was a waste of time. 'He wanted me to be a doctor,' she said, although she didn't sound too down about it. 'He still thinks I'll end up switching courses if he goes on about it enough.'

Megan tried to say the right things. A part of her wished her own father had taken a similar amount of interest in her adult life, although it hadn't mattered so much when she was happily married. She thought she'd had someone in her life with whom to share those burdens about what the future might bring. And now... she didn't.

'...Have you always worked in a café?'

There had been a few seconds in which Megan had switched off. She'd been daydreaming of Whitecliff again, and her life there. She realised Lakshmi had asked a question.

'I was working behind reception in a gym up until a week or so ago,' Megan replied.

'Oh...?' It sounded like a question, which it probably was.

'It was supposed to be a temporary thing but I'd been there for almost two years. Me and my husband were trying for a baby...'

She hadn't meant for that to come out but it was hard to explain why else she was closing in on forty without a career to speak of. It wasn't really the thing to share with someone barely out of college, and almost half her age.

Megan could sense Lakshmi struggling for what to say. *Where was her husband? Was there a baby? Why was she working for her sister?* All legitimate questions, all with awkward replies.

They were saved by the door opening and closing to reveal Chrissy with the pushchair and the whybrows. Chrissy bumped the buggy into a series of empty tables and then waved to Pam, before approaching the counter to order 'the usual'.

The rest of the afternoon continued to be quiet, with Pam locking up ten minutes before the official closing. She never had got round to that promised explanation about what had gone on with the kitchen.

Megan cycled back to an empty house and sat in the attic bedroom with the angled window open as far as it would go. She checked the socks in her case, making sure Trevor's tooth was still there, wondering what to do with it, and whether it meant anything. She didn't have an answer. The window to tell the police had closed and she wasn't sure they would believe her anyway. Once a suspected fantasist, always a suspected fantasist.

Nicola got home after around an hour. She called upstairs, asking if anyone was in, and Megan headed down to sit with her in the kitchen. If Pam had said anything about Megan's double lateness, then Nicola didn't let on.

'How's the second café?' Megan asked.

'I've been there all day,' Nicola replied, which wasn't quite what Megan had asked. 'It's coming along but you have to supervise every little thing.' She sighed and batted away a yawn. Megan didn't challenge her on the 'all day' part. She'd spent her time upstairs trying to think of a way to bring up the incident with Pam.

'Something weird happened at the café today,' Megan said.

A frown crept onto Nicola's face. 'Like what?'

'The hatch broke. It looked like something fell down on the other side. I was at the door to go in, the one with the keypad, when Pam yanked me away.' Megan squeezed her shoulder, playing up the point a little.

She wasn't sure what she expected. Perhaps surprise that one member of staff had put hands on another, even if it was fairly gently? Perhaps bemusement? Instead, Nicola pouted her lips for a moment, thinking.

'They don't like being bothered in the kitchen,' she replied.

'That's what Pam said.'

'They're very focused on their work.'

Megan must have raised an eyebrow, or something similar, because Nicola's features shifted a fraction at her sister's scepticism.

She sighed. 'Look, we don't make a big deal of it but not all of the wages go through the, um... well, you know. It's easier to pay cash sometimes and, because of that, we don't want any customers to start poking around, asking how many staff we have...'

She stared at Megan a moment too long, in a similar way to Pam. Ben had talked about cash-in-hand the previous day and Megan started to nod slowly. Assuming Pam knew what was going on, it explained her alarm at Megan opening the door to the kitchen.

'How many do work in there?' Megan asked.

Her sister blinked, not expecting the question. 'A few. What does it matter?'

There was an inkling of irritation, which probably wasn't a surprise. If the people in there were being paid cash, there was a good chance they were getting less than minimum wage. Numerous laws were being broken.

'Why don't you just pay them normally?' Megan asked.

Nicola slapped her own head exaggeratedly. 'Why didn't we think of that?!' She sighed again, then added: 'Because Covid messed everything up and things aren't back to normal yet. It's hard running a small business. Our heating bills tripled last winter. It's not forever. We're trying to stay afloat. Not only that, it's better for them. They take home more money at the end of the day.'

She was exasperated, and Megan didn't particularly blame her. It was a different world from her life. Her *old* life. Everyone was struggling. Cost of living and all that.

Nicola moved on, ignoring the 'yanked' part of what Megan had said previously. 'Jess said she'll go to the Bake Off on Saturday, so thanks for asking. She listens to you more than she does me.'

There was a momentary hint of resentment.

Megan needed a moment to compose herself, still stuck on

the cash and broken laws part. 'You're her mum,' she managed. 'I'm her cool aunt.'

A sigh. 'Ben's dad called her this morning. She didn't pick up because she says she doesn't answer calls. Apparently nobody her age does. He called *me*, so I texted her, telling her to pick up next time, and they've apparently figured it out.'

There was a part of Megan that enjoyed hearing the minor drama. It was better than finding young women dead in streams, or walking out on husbands. Something normal among a sea of not.

Nicola glanced over Megan's shoulder and gulped. It felt as if something awkward might be coming. 'Are you going to Daniel's book club later?' she asked.

'Probably.'

Megan replied a little more quickly than she'd meant to. From the moment he'd asked, she was always going to go, despite her pretend indecision. She expected a little more teasing, following on from the morning's. If anything, it was the opposite. 'It's just... I was talking to Ben earlier and he reckons Daniel's a bit, um... *problematic*.'

It felt like a deliberate choice of word and, not for the first time, Megan sensed her sister had been discussing her when she wasn't there.

'What does that mean?' Megan asked.

'Just that he's divorced. Fairly recently, as well.'

'I'm still *married*. It's just a book club. What do you think's going to happen?'

That got a slightly raised eyebrow. 'I'm just saying that maybe he's not the best person to be around...?'

Megan thought of her sister's car, parked outside Trevor's farmhouse. A man she still hadn't met, yet someone who seemed to be dominating her thoughts. She didn't even know what he looked like, having only seen him in the dark. Was he something to do with Nicola's quick change of heart towards Daniel? Something had certainly changed since the morning.

'Are you saying *I'll* be problematic if I get divorced?' Megan said.

'Obviously not. There are other things.'

'Like what?'

'I don't know... Ben was worried about you. We both are.'

It was hard to argue with that. Nicola *did* sound concerned, not that Megan wanted pity. Nicola was also flustered all of a sudden, picking up a salt shaker from the table, looking underneath for some reason, and then putting it back down.

'I suppose I'm just saying you should be careful.'

Megan considered a sarky reply. It was this sort of thing that made Jessie come to her aunt more than her mother. Except she *was* staying in her sister's house, and it really did seem like sisterly worry.

'I'll be careful,' Megan replied. 'It's just a book club. There's wine and cheese. How bad can it be?'

Before she could say anything else, Nicola's phone started to buzz across the table. She grabbed it and muttered, 'Ben', before hurrying through the back door, and closing it behind her.

Megan left her to it and returned upstairs to the hot bedroom. She lay on the bed, listening to the whispering trees and the faint chirp of the gulls. She played on her phone as doors opened and closed below. She thought she heard Jessie's voice, maybe Ben's as well, though nobody bothered her.

She considered replying to the messages that had been building up. There were those from her colleagues at the leisure centre, wondering why she'd disappeared with only an email to her boss saying she wouldn't be coming back. There were a handful of friends who'd heard what had happened between her and Paul, and wanted to make sure she was OK. Lots of concern, though Megan didn't know how to reply to any of it.

Doing that would mean acknowledging what had happened between her and her husband.

There were plenty of messages from him, too, although the numbers had dropped off over the past day. As Megan checked the time and counted down the minutes, she wondered if, perhaps, that meant he was finally getting the message.

The Labour Club was a couple of streets away from the hustle of the high street. Paint was peeling from the blackboard at the front, although someone had written 'Meat raffle, Sunday, 7pm' in scrawled chalk.

Megan had left Hollicombe Bay not long after she was legally allowed to drink, so the town's pubs and social clubs had never been her thing. She had vague memories of being at someone's birthday party when they were nine or ten. They'd booked one of the side rooms of the club, and had played skittles while getting high on cake and full-fat Coke. The party had ended abruptly when the birthday boy had kicked over the skittles and burst into tears because he'd lost.

As far as she could remember, it was the one and only time Megan had been inside the club.

Not that inside contained anything unexpected. The ceilings were low, the carpet sticky, the noticeboard filled with posters for tribute acts, and the dartboard surrounded by old boys who'd been parked there since the three-day week. Groups of women were packed into booths around the side of the lounge, cradling half-pints of lager as Diana Ross squeaked from the dodgy PA system. It was the sort of place that would have been filled with smoke when Megan was growing up, with a black ceiling and coughing bar staff.

Megan hovered in the middle of the room, scanning for where to go. She spotted Daniel off near the pool table, eagerly shaking the hand of a pensioner. They laughed about something and then the woman disappeared through the adjacent door. When Daniel spotted Megan, he waved and beckoned her across.

'There's wine and tea through here,' he said, nodding into another room.

'Is that the skittle alley?' Megan asked, now remembering where it had been.

'That's long gone,' Daniel replied. 'They ripped it out about ten years ago. I think someone tripped on it.' He glanced past her, waving to someone else. 'You can head on in,' he added, talking to Megan again. 'We'll start soon but I'm waiting on a couple more.'

As the newcomer approached from behind, Megan passed into the next room. The déjà vu hit so strongly, so instantly, that Megan was left standing a little inside the door, staring and blinking. Back then, a table for presents had been set up on the far side, where a television was now pinned to the wall. There had been a second table filled with jelly, cake, and sandwiches in front of the fire exit. Different times, and all that. The skittle alley had lined the longest wall and there had been a steady *clunk-thwick* of ball hitting alley, and pins.

It was almost thirty years since it had happened, yet Megan could still smell the dust of the carpet and baked-in stench of cigarettes.

'You all right?'

A man was suddenly in front of her, frowning with concern. Megan knew why. She was standing in the middle of the floor, wide-eyed as if trying to remember where she'd parked at the Big Tesco.

'You look like you've seen a ghost,' he added.

'No, I'm, uh...' Megan stumbled over a reply, taking in the man properly. He was taller than her, though stooped, like he was checking to see if there really *was* a pound coin on the ground. He was burly and balding.

No, not burly. That wasn't the polite way to say it. *Stocky.*

His cheek was swollen, with the hint of a purply-grey bruise. His top lip had ballooned, and there was a scabbed cut across his bottom.

'I'm Trevor,' he said, as he offered his hand to shake.

FIFTEEN

'It's Megan, isn't it?' Trevor added. 'I know your sister – and Ben of course. Good friends of mine.'

Megan realised she was shaking his hand, although she didn't remember offering hers. His fingers were sausages, wrists like her thighs. Up close, he was even bigger than he had seemed as a silhouette the night before.

'Yeah, uh, Megan,' she managed. 'Sorry, I don't think I know you...?'

That got a grinned shrug, like a creepy uncle about to slip an arm around a niece's waist for no reason. 'No matter. I was chatting to your sister today. She said you were staying with her for a while and that you might be here.'

He paused as if expecting a reply, though Megan didn't know what to say. She'd assumed Nicola had been talking about her – and it was now clear she had. Was that a problem? She didn't know.

'I own the chip shop,' he said. 'And the sweet shop. I heard you've been doing shifts at Nic's...?'

'Right.'

He bobbed on his heels a little as Megan realised he was

trying to start, and maintain, a conversation. She was giving nothing away. He didn't know she had his tooth – though he *might* know she'd found that woman in the stream.

'What happened to your lip?' Megan asked, narrowly stopping herself from asking directly about his *tooth*.

Trevor touched it momentarily, seemingly without thinking. 'Accident at home,' he said, and it felt like a politician parroting a line.

She wasn't sure why, but Megan suddenly felt bold. 'What sort of accident?'

The reply again came instantly: 'Tripped over one of the dogs and clipped my tooth on the stair rail. Gave 'im a right rollicking. Always under my feet, that one.' Trevor paused and then added: 'I'm at the age where people start calling it a "fall"!'

He laughed and Megan gave a weak smile. It might've been true but it sounded rehearsed, even down to the chuckle at the end. Make a joke and move on.

There was no chance to add anything else because Daniel had appeared at Megan's side. He clapped his hands and waited until the murmured conversations had finished.

'I think we're all here,' he said. 'It's our biggest turnout yet.'

Megan did a quick count – and there were fourteen including her. A couple of older women were in their Sunday best, and a man in a suit was hovering near the toilets. A pair of girls, probably no older than seventeen, were standing awkwardly next to each other, next to the cheese.

'Feel free to help yourselves to wine and snacks,' Daniel said, pointing across to a table that Megan had missed. It was where the skittle alley used to be, with three boxes of wine lined up next to a row of paper plates.

Daniel paused a beat and then nodded across to the younger girls. 'I did ask your mums and they said you could have one glass if you wanted. If not, there are soft drinks next door...?'

He got a mumbled reply that Megan didn't catch – and then they were off. Someone started unstacking the chairs and they all helped arrange them into a circle.

It was immediately clear that the two younger girls knew the book better than anyone in the room. They brought up themes and some of the language that stood out to them, as others nodded along. The age of landline phones and no internet clearly seemed stone-age to them. Gary Oldman did not get a mention, and neither did Alec Guinness, although one of the older women did talk about 'the lighting', before correcting herself.

Nobody seemed to mind and it wasn't long before talk moved on to general issues around town: the weather, the tourists, some roadworks, the bookshop and its erratic opening hours, the quality of the night's wine and cheese, whether grapes were better seeded, and whose turn it was to buy crackers.

Megan didn't say a lot, listening and watching instead. Although it was seemingly Daniel's group, he also didn't talk too much. He caught her eye a couple of times, smiling and nodding at various points.

Trevor had a pristine copy of the book on his lap. He was either one of those who didn't like cracking book spines, or he'd not read it. There were moments in which it felt as if he, too, was looking her way – except, every time Megan glanced towards him, his eyes were elsewhere.

As the boxes of wine were finished and it became clear they were no longer talking about the book, there was a vote for the following month's read. Someone suggested *The Green Mile* and nobody objected. Megan overheard a whispered 'I have the DVD' from one of the older women to another.

People began to drift away: the younger women first, and then the suited older guy. A few headed into the bar area, where the click of pool balls rattled around the murky walls.

Trevor had been hanging around close to the fire exit, and, from the way he kept eyeing Daniel while pretending to be looking at his phone, Megan had the sense he was waiting for the other man to be alone.

Eventually, it was only the three of them. Megan helped Daniel clear what was left on the tables and, when it became obvious she wasn't going anywhere, Trevor ambled across. 'I've gotta head off,' he said, as he shook Daniel's hand. 'It was a good night. Big turnout.'

They ended up thanking each other amiably, before Trevor drifted through the fire exit and into the night.

It was only Megan and Daniel left in the Labour Club lounge. The faint sounds of The Jackson 5 crept through the closed door that led into the bar. An orange haze spilled through the only open window as the sun began to set.

The two of them moved across to the window without needing to talk about it. The view of the ocean was obscured by a couple of buildings but V-shaped shadows of gulls bobbed across the reddening sky.

'What did you think?' Daniel asked.

'I think it was a pretty good excuse to drink wine and eat cheese.'

'I did tell you that!'

Daniel laughed to himself as they stood side by side, facing the window.

'Can I ask you something?' Megan said.

'Sure.'

'It's about Trevor. I asked him about what happened with his lip and his tooth. He said something about tripping over his dog but... I mean... it sounded like a lie...?'

The question lingered, unanswered for a moment, as Megan wondered if Daniel would be curious about why she was asking. Why should she care? Last night she had felt like telling Daniel everything. But now, she didn't want to explain

Trevor's tooth being wrapped in a sock back at her sister's house, let alone where she'd found it.

If Daniel was wondering about her motives, he didn't say. He snorted quietly under his breath. 'Of course he's lying,' he said.

SIXTEEN

Megan turned to face him, though Daniel continued to look through the window towards the glowing horizon.

'If you're drunk and fall over, you don't want to *say* that,' Daniel added. 'Much easier to blame a dog.'

He spoke as if pointing out that cows went moo and sheep went baa.

There was a part of Megan that thought he might be right. Nobody particularly wanted to own up to their own stupidity or drunkenness. Much easier to blame an animal.

Except she had what she was sure was Trevor's tooth – and she had found it nowhere near the stair rail of his house.

Daniel was still talking. 'I've never really liked him, to be honest. One of those types who thinks he knows everything. He's on the business association with Ben, Nicola, me and everyone else. Always wants it to be his way. He's sixty-odd and he's never been married, never had any kids. He's lived on his own since his dad died. What does that tell you?'

It didn't feel as if he was after an answer and, though Megan knew what he meant, *she* was almost forty with no children and now, probably, single. As far as she knew, it was the same for Daniel. Nicola had said he was recently divorced and apparently 'problematic', whatever that meant. She considered asking, except there was no polite way to bring it up. Nothing she had seen made her think that of him.

They stood together for a moment and then Daniel turned to her once more. 'Do you want a drink? Or we can go for a walk?'

The draw of the hazy warm evening was too much of a pull. The season never seemed to last long and then the lashing rain and howling wind would be back.

Megan said the sunset looked too good to miss, so they headed out into the cosy embrace of the midsummer evening. They didn't talk about a route, didn't talk about anything. Instead, they ambled through the streets towards the seafront. The beer gardens were largely full, though there was none of the menace that Megan sometimes felt while walking in White-cliff. There, it was bigger and busier. One football result going the wrong way might see a series of sunburnt men in three-quarter shorts rolling around in the gutter for some reason. Hollicombe Bay was families and kids. Unlike other seaside towns, nobody ever came to this beach for a stag do and there weren't groups of women carrying around six-foot inflatable penises.

Within minutes, Megan and Daniel were at the sea wall. The horizon was a blushing fusion of purples, reds and oranges. They sat on a bench, watching at first, not needing to speak.

'I've seen worse,' Daniel said, with a gentle laugh.

Megan took a breath, closed her eyes momentarily, and then squinted back into the light as she re-opened them. She'd not planned to tell him but there was something about the calmness of the evening, not to mention the sunset. A droplet of safety and sanity among the lake of upheaval that had overtaken her life.

'I saw something on Sunday night,' she said. 'I was in Nicola's house and there was a scream. I went out to the woods at the back and there was a girl in the stream. A woman, really. Nineteen or twenty, something like that.'

Daniel shifted on the bench and turned to look at her. Megan continued watching the horizon. 'What do you mean?'

'I tried chest compressions but she didn't come round. I was so sure she would. People always do on TV...'

Megan tailed off, remembering that moment in which she'd been certain the young woman would burst upwards gasping for air and clutching her chest. It had been such a clear vision, Megan sometimes had flashes that it actually happened. That everything was OK.

'I didn't have my phone,' she added. 'I had to go back to Nic's house and then I couldn't get reception. I had to go out front to call the police. They wanted me to flag down the car, so I waited on the street. We all went into the woods together and she was... gone.'

Someone had twisted the dimmer switch a fraction and the oranges of the sky had become reds, the reds were purples, the purples black.

'How do you mean "gone"?'

'She wasn't there. We walked up and down that stretch of stream and there was no sign of her.'

The pause lasted a fraction too long and it was hard to tell whether it was scepticism or curiosity. 'You mean she was sleeping and woke up, or...?'

'She wasn't breathing when I found her. I tried to bring her back, I really did, but it didn't work.' She paused, gulped, and then added: 'Someone must've moved her body.'

It was the first time Megan had specifically said it out loud, although it was the only explanation.

'What did the police say?'

'They talked to me for ages afterwards. I think they thought I was wasting their time.'

That wasn't *all* they thought. After Nicola had spoken to them, they probably believed Megan had gone through some sort of breakdown.

Daniel had been quiet for too long and Megan sensed him searching for the right words.

'I know how it sounds,' she added.

'I suppose it's that we don't get many bodies around here. Not since the fire.'

When Megan glanced down, Daniel's hands were on his knees. His palms were down but she had already seen the scarring.

The fervour of the setting sun had faded so quickly that the street lights were beginning to turn on.

'Shall we walk?' Daniel asked – and Megan wasn't going to refuse. She'd had enough of sitting.

They set off in much the same way they had the first time. They wandered towards the bottom of the hill as a silty, newly chilled breeze wafted from the ocean.

Neither of them had spoken properly for a minute or two. Megan had nothing else to add – and she couldn't blame Daniel for not offering an explanation.

'D'you know tourism was down for nine years in a row after the fire,' he said. 'We were too young to know what any of that meant but Hollicombe Bay went from being this cosy little holiday resort to being the place with the fire and the schoolkids. Easy to see why people didn't want to come.'

'How do you know the figures?' Megan asked.

'When I took over the arcade, I was going through Dad's books. It was almost a decade until we got back to the point we'd been at before the fire. I think it was probably the same for everyone around here. We coasted for a few years and then Covid hit. We went another eighteen months or so where, basically, nobody came.'

Megan thought about what her sister had said, with the cash

payments and hidden kitchen staff. This was someone else saying the same – and she wondered why he'd shifted the conversation onto this. Then Megan realised what she was missing. After the school fire, the town had struggled in all sorts of ways. The last thing it needed was a new investigation. More attention of the kind nobody wanted.

'Maybe that's a reason to cover up a dead body?' she said, partly to herself, unsure if she believed it.

'I didn't mean it like that,' Daniel replied. 'I was just thinking out loud. Perhaps she was drunk and woke up? I don't know what to say.'

'She wasn't drunk.'

Megan struggled to hide her disappointment, mainly because it sounded like Daniel didn't believe her. Or maybe that he did, but not the part about someone moving the body. Except Megan had placed her hands on the woman's chest and pumped to the rhythm of *Stayin' Alive*. She'd left those handprints. Nobody would have slept through that.

'Do you think you'd recognise her if you saw her?' Daniel asked.

'I suppose.'

'This isn't a big town. I don't know if you've been out much during the day, but, if she was sleeping, something like that, maybe you'll see her around?'

As unlikely as it all felt, Megan figured it wasn't the worst point to make. She was wavering from minute to minute. The young woman *couldn't* have simply been sleeping. And yet, perhaps, if Megan *did* spot her on the beach, or working in one of the shops, things would fall into place?

Then Daniel had to say it.

'There must be a lot of stress involved in being back...?'

He phrased it as a concerned question but Megan knew at what he was hinting. It had been similar with her sister.

'I know what I saw,' Megan said firmly. 'I *touched* her.'

They were halfway up the hill – but stopped at the same corner they had the night before. Perhaps they'd been walking slower than she realised, because the evening had slipped fully into night. They sat on the same wall from not quite a day before and stared across the rippling black ocean.

'That's me,' Daniel said, nodding across to a slightly ramshackle bungalow three doors down. On their previous walk the night before, Megan had somehow forgotten it was the house in which he'd grown up. When she was a teenager, she would often go out of her way to walk past, hoping she might spot Daniel coming out. She dreamed of them striking up a conversation and then, hey, Mrs Daniel Clarkson here we come.

The lights were off in the house and a decade-old Ford was parked on the cracked driveway. Megan wondered if this was his way of inviting her inside. She considered what she'd say. A part of her, that teenager who'd never quite grown up, would have barely believed her luck. The other pictured her husband back in Whitecliff. They were still married, despite everything.

Separated, a silent voice reminded her.

A couple passed on the other side of the street, having a shouting match about who was more toxic: the husband or his sister-in-law. His drinking was apparently out of control, while she was always 'sticking her oar in'. Daniel and Megan listened and watched as the couple weaved their drunken way into the distance.

When the entertainment was over, Daniel stood and brushed something from his trousers. 'Shall we carry on?' He nodded up the hill towards Nicola's house and Megan joined him as they set off at their tortoise pace. 'How are things at your sister's café?' he asked.

Megan almost told him about Pam's over-the-top reaction, plus the dodgy under-the-counter workers in the back, but decided she was better trying to forget it.

'Quieter than I thought it'd be,' she said. 'I didn't think I could say no when she asked if I wanted to do some shifts. Not with me staying at hers.'

It was another thing Megan hadn't admitted out loud until that moment. She really didn't want to work in the café but felt obliged.

'She's not paying you in Bay Bucks, is she?' Daniel laughed.

'Cash in hand. *Real* cash.'

Daniel didn't seem surprised. 'A few places are doing that in town,' he replied. 'That and the Bay Bucks thing. Trying to keep as much money in the community as possible. Buy local, spend local, all that.'

There was a firmness that Megan didn't think had been there before. It felt a bit us versus them, and perhaps it was? Even on the coast, Hollicombe Bay was the poor cousin. White-cliff had its Bay Burning at Christmas that pulled in visitors, Steeple's End had its harbour and indoor market, and Hollicombe Bay had... what? A tragedy that had driven people away for a decade.

They walked for a few minutes more, until they reached the junction where the stream dipped and disappeared into the pipe that went under the road. There was still a person-shaped dent in the hedge from where Megan and the officers had followed the brook into the woods.

'I'm making a habit of walking you home,' Daniel said.

'Not really home,' Megan replied, instantly regretting the unnecessary correction. She didn't know quite where home was any longer.

They were standing a little away from the street light, enveloped by shade. There was a moment, maybe longer, in which she wondered what it might be like to kiss him. In years before, in another lifetime, she had thought about it so often, for so long. Even though it was a long time before, the intensity of those feelings never truly disappeared. Not completely.

What would he do? Would he pull away? Press into her? Would he want to? Did she?

She had enjoyed the two walks and it could spoil all that. Daniel was recently divorced and she was separated. They'd not really talked about that but they were – *technically* – both single. She could push onto her tiptoes and he was right there. Was he thinking about it?

Except...

Megan had still been sleeping in the same bed as her husband a little over a week before – and she wasn't that sort of person.

'Thanks for the walk,' Megan said, and it was hard to mask her glimmer of reluctance about the night ending. 'And the cheese.'

If he'd been having similar thoughts to her, then Daniel said nothing. 'It's been fun,' he replied. 'I'll catch you around.'

They hovered for a moment, neither quite sure how to say goodbye, and then he turned and started to saunter back down the hill.

Megan watched him for a moment and then headed for her sister's place.

The house was quiet as she let herself in. There was nobody downstairs, and the lights were off. A hint of music bled from the other side of Jessie's door, though there was silence behind Nicola and Ben's.

Megan eked her way up into the attic and pulled the hatch closed. She had left the window open a little, though immediately stripped off to escape the sweltering, grasping heat. It was so much warmer inside than out.

Megan checked that Trevor's tooth was still safely wrapped in her sock, and then lay on the bed and closed her eyes, waiting for the dream of the woman and the stream to take her.

SEVENTEEN

WEDNESDAY

Ben was in the kitchen as Megan yawned her way downstairs. Despite worrying what her dreams might bring, Megan had slept until the alarm on her phone had woken her. From the furnace of the night before, the attic now had a chill that had left her snuggled underneath the bedcovers.

'Sleep well?' Ben asked, which was the ultimate small talk. Did anybody *actually* care whether someone else had had a good night's sleep?

Megan batted away another yawn, which was an answer of sorts. That wasn't what Ben wanted to talk about anyway.

'I heard you were at book club last night,' he said.

'I didn't realise it was such big news.'

Ben didn't laugh. A spoonful of his overnight oats was halfway between the glass and his mouth, but he lowered it. 'I don't want to tell you what to do, it's just...' He paused and Megan knew he was about to tell her what to do. 'It's just...' he repeated. Another pause, and then: 'I know you've had a bad time of it recently and, er, Daniel's a bit problematic.'

'That's what Nicola said.'

'Right. We were thinking, that maybe he's not the best person to be around at the moment...?'

He spoke quickly and then jammed the spoon of oats into his mouth and started to chew, avoiding any swift reply.

It was no coincidence that both Ben and Nicola had used the same word to describe Daniel. They'd definitely discussed it and decided on a party line.

'What does problematic mean?' Megan asked.

Daniel swirled a hand near his mouth to indicate he'd answer when he was done chewing. His breakfast looked like something that might be dispatched into a toilet bowl while someone's hair was being held back by a close friend.

'Just that he had a bad divorce,' Ben said, with a gummy mouth.

'What sort of bad divorce?'

Ben wasn't doing well under the questioning. He dunked his spoon back into the goop and swirled it around. 'People talk around here.'

'I still don't know what that means.'

Megan was trying, probably failing, to hide her annoyance. If there was something for her to know, what was it?

Ben was saved at least some of the awkwardness as Nicola arrived, towelling her wet hair. Something was in the air as she stood at the end of the table and turned between them with a curious look on her face.

'Everything all right?'

'I was telling her about Daniel,' Ben said, though he was looking at the floor as he spoke.

'You didn't tell me much of anything,' Megan remarked.

Nicola was instantly at her husband's side. 'Daniel had a bad divorce,' she said, parroting her husband. It was a far cry from the playful teasing about him from the morning before.

'Nobody's explaining what that means.' From nowhere, the

frustration that had been building was out. 'First you tell me I'm seeing things, now you're telling me who I can be friends with.'

It had come out louder and fiercer than Megan meant – and Nicola took a half-step back. Her fingers were on her husband's shoulder and Megan watched them tighten a fraction.

'It's not like that,' Nicola said. 'We're just worried about you. This is all a big change in your life, with Paul and the break-up and...' Nicola's body twitched a fraction and Megan was sure her sister had nodded towards the woods at the back.

'What's the problem with Daniel?'

Ben took a breath, though it was clear he was waiting for his wife to answer. Nicola hesitated as well and Megan had the sense they'd gone over this in bed either that morning, or the night before. Or both.

'It's not one thing in particular,' Nicola said. 'But his wife left town in what felt like a hurry and people have been speculating ever since.'

It felt like an endless loop of never quite getting the answer.

'Speculating about what?'

'Why she left. Why they divorced. Nobody seems to know.'

'Why is it anyone's business but theirs?'

That got something close to a shrug as Nicola leant across and flicked on the kettle.

'There was a fight a month or so back,' Ben added. 'I heard he broke someone's nose on the seafront.'

Megan thought on that for a few seconds. '*Whose* nose?'

'I don't know. That's what I heard.'

It had a *because I said so*-vibe, and they all knew it. Megan couldn't hide her obvious disbelief as she rolled her eyes.

'You know what the town is like,' Ben said, defensively.

Megan started to reply and then bit her lip. It was all insinuation and innuendo. Someone heard something from someone, who heard it from someone who claimed they saw it. Plus, if

Daniel's wife *did* leave town in a hurry, how was that different than Megan herself escaping from Whitecliff?

Escaping.

She hadn't thought of it in that context before. She hadn't left her husband and her house, she'd *escaped* them.

'Thanks for your concern,' Megan replied firmly. Perhaps she meant it? She wasn't sure – and she wasn't going to hang around for more of a lecture.

Megan excused herself and then headed upstairs to get dressed properly. She retrieved the bike from the shed and wheeled it around the house. The morning was cooler than those before, and a gentle mist clung to the ocean. Megan was running early for once, so cycled down the hill nearest her sister's house, ending up on the seafront. The dewy air was heavy in her lungs as she pedalled past the closed shopfronts. A black lab was off its lead, trotting along the beach as the owner walked behind, staring at her phone. On the other side of the road, a gull was sitting on top of a bin, pecking at something by its feet.

The mist thickened as Megan reached the other end of town. She had an arm out, wobbling slightly as she signalled to make a turn. From nowhere, a pair of parked police cars spiralled from the cloud. They were parked on the beach side of the road, shrouded in fog.

Megan braked and checked her shoulder, before swerving onto the wrong side of the road and pulling up next to the police cars. Half-a-dozen people had massed near the barrier, overlooking the rocks that stretched out towards the sea. Murky grey blobs shuffled aimlessly in the gloom, perhaps on the beach, or maybe on the rocks themselves. The tide would be on its way in soon and it wouldn't be long until nobody could be out that far.

A woman turned to take in Megan. They didn't know one

another, yet there was a glint of excitement or intrigue in the woman's eye.

'What's going on?' Megan asked.

'They've found a body.'

EIGHTEEN

The memory of the disappearing young woman from the stream was at the front of Megan's thoughts. The woman was there, then she was gone – and now she was... *here?*

Who else could it be?

There was no siren, not at this time of the morning, but whirring blue lights surged through the mist as an ambulance pulled in behind the police cars. A pair of paramedics climbed from the front and headed for the steps that led down to the beach.

Megan checked the time on her phone, knowing she was going to be late – again. She wasn't going to go anywhere until she saw the young woman being brought up from the rocks. She'd be able to tell her sister and everyone else that she hadn't imagined things.

'Do you know what happened?' Megan asked.

'Only that someone found a body,' came the reply. 'I think it was a dog walker.'

'Is it a woman...?'

'No idea.'

One of the other members of the small crowd was on their

phone, telling someone on the other end to get down to the seafront because something was happening. As that was going on, others were being drawn to the barrier as they spotted the police cars and the crowd. The morbid fascination of it all felt uncomfortable to Megan – but she wasn't going to be the first to break and head off. She continued to watch the vaguely people-shaped blurs bob back and forth through the mist. She presumed it was police officers securing the scene, but it was like trying to focus on something through a dirty window.

The next time Megan turned back to the crowd, there were twenty or so people trying to look around each other, out towards the rocks. Some were taking photos on their phones, even though it was too foggy to see anything definitive.

Time passed and the crowd swelled to thirty, more, as piercing shafts of morning sun began to arrow through the dissolving mist.

And then the dark shapes drifted into focus as they moved closer to the wall. The tide was returning and the officers were running out of time as they carried the paramedics' stretcher. A cream blanket was stretched across a person-shaped lump as the officers scrambled over the rocks, trying to keep everything as steady as possible. The paramedics followed, while, in the distance, the other officers appeared to be taking photographs of a spot hidden by the shape of the cove. There was a flash of someone in a white coat, or perhaps simply wearing white. It was hard to tell from so far away.

Megan focused back on the group with the stretcher, who had reached the sand as they headed for the steps. The sheet was flapping as the mist was replaced by a fizzing sea gust. Megan could taste the salt as her hair was whipped backwards. She was so busy trying to pull the hair from her eyes, to blink away the sting of the wind, that she almost missed what happened next.

As the officers continued to carry the stretcher, the breeze caught a corner of the sheet and flipped it up and over. The officer somehow managed to catch it, while continuing to balance the stretcher – but there was a second or two in which the face of the person underneath was uncovered.

It wasn't the young woman from the stream.

It wasn't a woman at all.

There was barely a glimpse, and Megan was at a distance – but it was clearly a bald man, probably in his fifties or so. Maybe older. People were still taking photographs but Megan felt a growing wave of shame as she slipped through the crowd and retrieved her bike.

She had been so sure the body would be the young woman from the stream. So desperate for vindication. And, in the end, all she'd done was stare at a private moment she had no right to see.

And be late for work.

Megan pedalled the short distance to the café and left the bike in the courtyard at the back. She was almost fifty minutes late as she headed through the front door but there was none of the morning rush. Lakshmi was serving a customer as Pam wiped down a table. When Pam looked up, there was something closer to surprise in her eyes than there was anger. She glanced up to the clock over the door but Megan cut her off before she could say anything.

'They found a body on the beach,' she said.

Pam's mouth was open, halfway through a word Megan didn't catch. Her lips bobbed and closed like a fish and then she started again: 'A body...?'

'There were police and paramedics. The tide's on the way in, so they're working quickly. There's a bit of a crowd.'

Pam glanced around the nearly empty café. 'Guess that explains where everyone is. Any idea who it is?'

'A man. I don't know other than that.'

Pam stood up straighter and let out a long, low gasp. 'I

wonder what happened? There was a guy who fell over the wall last summer. He was trying to do a video on his phone and went straight over the edge, do you get me? Cracked his head open. They were saying he was lucky the tide was out, or they might not have been able to get him back.'

It was probably the most animated Pam had been since Megan had met her. Any tardiness had been forgiven in the face of fresh gossip about a dead body. Pam spoke with such relish that it sounded like she had a thing for people cracking their heads open. Probably a YouTube playlist marked 'LOL' that featured a load of people Humpty Dumptying off things and landing with a splat.

She did have part of a point though. When Megan had been growing up, everyone seemed to bang on about quicksand to the point that she was terrified of going on *any* wet sand. There were always vague stories about someone walking out too far and then getting swallowed by the quicksand and unable to escape as the tide swarmed. Megan had nightmares about it. She had never even heard the word 'apocryphal' back then. Then, at some point in the 2000s, it was as if everyone collectively decided it was a load of old guff, and nobody ever spoke of it again.

Throughout the day, as customers came and went, there was whispered news and rumours about what had happened. Apparently the body belonged to someone who was staying at one of the caravan parks on the edge of town. His wife had reported him missing the night before. Somebody else reckoned he'd last been seen in a pub near the seafront, which left Megan wondering if she'd walked past him when she was with Daniel the night before.

Later still, and someone reckoned the man had been having an argument with his wife. He'd gone one way, she'd gone the other. She'd made it back to the caravan, he hadn't. Nobody knew for sure what happened but he'd ended up on the rocks, which was where he'd been found by a dog walker that morning. Perhaps he fell, or maybe he'd gone for an overambitious scramble across the rocks in his drunken state? Megan pictured the ranting couple from the night before and their argument about a sister-in-law. She wondered if he was the victim. It felt like such a waste.

For a short while at least, the image of the woman in the stream was shunted from the front of her mind as she tried to remember what the arguing man had looked like. She'd have to ask Daniel to see if he remembered. They hadn't swapped phone numbers but he owned the arcade, so would probably be there at some point. She might go looking for him on her lunch break.

But then the thought of everything that had happened with Megan's husband was back – and it was hard to see Daniel as anything other than a distraction.

There was something else about the evolving story of the body. The wife had reported her husband missing, even though they'd apparently been arguing. Megan had found that woman in the stream – and surely, if she really *had* been dead – someone would have noticed? She'd have parents, or friends. Maybe a boyfriend, or girlfriend? A brother or sister? It wasn't possible that someone that age could simply disappear without anyone noticing.

And yet... that's what Nicola had been saying the whole time, wasn't it? With all the insinuations that Megan had imagined everything. If she really *had* found a body, if there really was a dead young woman, why hadn't anyone reported her missing?

Megan tried to think her way around that as the day continued. She took orders and gave change. She made drinks and cleaned tables. She shuttled food from the kitchen hatch, and dirty dishes back the other way.

The rumours were winding down as the afternoon wore on

and customers decided caffeine wasn't the best thing for the time of day.

Yet Megan couldn't stop thinking about the wife reporting her husband missing. That's what people did when someone disappeared.

Could she *really* have been mistaken about what she saw in the woods?

It was as she was lost in those thoughts, doubting herself, when Megan realised she was being watched. Something prickled at the back of her neck and she turned to see a woman standing in the doorway, blocking the way as she stared across the café.

Their eyes met and Megan saw the years that had gone by. The holidays they'd had together, the nights out, the times they'd shared a bed or a blanket.

Lucy was her best friend. She was also the woman who'd stolen her husband.

NINETEEN

Lucy hurried across, arms wide as if she was going to try to hug Megan. She wasn't sure it was actually going to happen but, in case it did, Megan sidestepped behind a table and held up a hand.

'We've been so worried about you,' Lucy said.

'Are you joking?'

'You just left. You didn't say where you were going and you're not replying to anyone's messages. Your phone doesn't even ring.'

'That's because I blocked your number.'

Lucy had been halfway through a word but stopped herself and settled on a sorry-sounding: 'Oh.'

The table was already clean but Megan gave it a wipe anyway for something to do with her hands.

'Can we talk?' Lucy asked. She was leaning on the back of a chair, wearing a summer dress that she and Megan had picked out together a couple of years back. Megan wondered whether Lucy had forgotten that, or if she had chosen the outfit as an attempt to remind her of the better times they'd had as friends.

Pam had noticed something going on and was hovering at

the end of the counter pretending to be looking the other way as she nosily angled herself towards the conversation.

Megan didn't want to talk to the other woman – but if she said that, the back and forth afterwards would be unavoidable. And it would all be in front of Pam with her *do you get me?* and her LOL playlist of people getting horrendous injuries.

'I'll be done in twenty-five minutes,' Megan said. 'Wait outside and we'll talk after.'

Lucy had likely been prepared for a lot more pushback, if not outright anger. She let out a long sigh of relief and then muttered a 'see you soon', before heading back out of the café.

Time dragged, which was fine with Megan. She gave everything an extra-long clean and made sure not to hurry any customers, even though they were closing. She told Lakshmi to head out, and finished counting the day's takings with Pam, then asked if there was anything else to do.

By the time she left work, forty-five minutes had passed. Megan hadn't expected Lucy to give up and go home, although she enjoyed the small victory of making her wait. That's all she had left, really: those pathetic wins that counted for nothing. Everything else had been taken away.

Lucy was sitting on the wall across the street, her legs bobbing freely as if on a swing. She was typing on her phone, thumbs a blur, as some sort of sixth sense made her look up and take in Megan. She stopped and stood as Megan waited outside the café, wanting Lucy to come to her. No reason to make it easy for her.

Lucy crossed the street and then hovered a fraction off the kerb. There was no traffic coming, unfortunately. 'Is there somewhere we can go?' she asked.

'What's the point?'

'We've been so worried you might've... done something.'

'Like what?'

Lucy squirmed, not wanting to say, even though they both

knew what the 'something' was. A car grumbled around the bend, so Lucy stepped onto the kerb and pointed along the road, towards the beach and the ocean. 'Shall we look for a bench?'

Megan didn't reply, but Lucy didn't wait – which really was *just* like her. The absolute cow.

Lucy set off along the street, pausing until Megan was at her side. They reached the corner and waited for a break in traffic, then crossed to the benches that were a little back from the sea wall. They were only a few paces from where Megan had stood that morning, watching the poor man be carried away on the stretcher. All signs of that had now gone. The mist had long since lifted, leaving the blue of the ocean to filter into the lighter blue of the sky.

Closer to shore, floats had been set up to form a squared perimeter. Screaming kids were bashing hired bumper boats into each other as a bored-looking lifeguard pretended he wasn't staring at his phone.

Lucy was sitting and Megan slotted in at her side. They sat silently for a minute or so, watching the boats and the kids.

'We called the gym,' Lucy said. 'They told us you'd quit and nobody had heard from you. We went out around Whitecliff during the day looking for you, then at night. We tried the hockey club in case—'

'I've not played in years.'

'I know – but we didn't know where else to try. Paul thought you might've come to your sister's but he didn't have her number. I tried finding her on Facebook but she's either not on there, or she's blocked him and me. We were going to call the police but then he remembered your sister had a café. The idea was to find her and see if she'd seen you. I didn't know you were working there.'

It had all come out as a frantic monologue. Megan wasn't sure how to reply, so she didn't.

It took Lucy a few seconds to catch her breath and then she was off again. 'I've been walking around town. I've not been here in years. Someone was saying they'd pulled a person out of the sea overnight and I was worried it was... well, you...'

'What would you have done if it was?'

Lucy started to say something and then changed her mind. She held up her phone instead. 'I've been texting Paul to let him know I found you and that you're OK.'

Megan snorted at that. 'It's a bit late to care now.'

'Of course we care!'

'I must have missed all that caring when you were busy shagging each other.'

Lucy must have expected it. She slumped a little lower, though all that did was make her dress ride up and bunch around her middle. Just enough to see the beginnings of the bump. If Megan didn't know it was there, she likely wouldn't have noticed.

Except she *did* know and she *had* spotted it.

Lucy saw the sideways glance and straightened her dress, gently touching her belly as she did.

Lucy spoke much more quietly now. 'I'm really sorry but I don't know what else to say. It's horrible and it's not fair on you – but we can't take it back. It happened.'

She touched her bump again, maybe subconsciously, maybe not. It probably didn't matter either way. Lucy was right, of course. It *had* happened, it was horrible and unfair – and it couldn't be taken back.

The pregnancy was one of the reasons why Megan had to leave Whitecliff. She wanted that white-hot rage. She wanted to lash out and break things, and yet a tiny voice within almost understood what they'd done and why. She wished it wasn't like that but what could she do?

Like with the girl in the woods, when Megan had been convinced those chest compressions would make her leap up.

She'd seen that on TV, in movies, just as she had seen scorned husbands and wives going crazy. When it came to infidelity, Megan thought it would be shouting and throwing things.

Except there was a part of her that understood Lucy and Paul's choices.

She hated that part.

'What do you think it's like,' Megan said, choosing her words, 'when you and your husband spend years trying for kids. And then you get the tests and find out *you're* the problem. Not him. *You.* You can't have children – and then, just as you're coming to terms with it, you find out your best mate is pregnant. You're desperate to be happy for her, and you sort of are. But then you find out it's your husband's baby. What do you think that's like?'

Lucy didn't answer, because what answer was there?

The two of them continued to sit watching the bumper boats bounce off each other. The lifeguard had put down his phone and was scanning the beach, though his attention appeared to be more on the group of bikini-wearing teenage girls than anywhere else.

A minute passed, probably more. Megan didn't want to be on the bench and she certainly didn't want to be next to Lucy – but she couldn't quite force herself to stand and walk away.

'It's so nice here,' Lucy said, quietly, and largely out of the nothing. 'Whitecliff's so busy at this time of year and you forget what it's like down the coast.'

Megan didn't reply. They might have made this sort of cosy small talk a month ago but they were way past that.

'Are you OK here?' Lucy asked. 'Are you staying with your sister, or...?'

'I'm fine.'

'I know you're angry and that I can't make it better. I suppose I wanted to say that it was never about you.' Lucy leant forward and pinched her nose. 'Not that. That's not how I meant it to come out.'

She swirled her hand, searching for the words as Megan focused on the boats. A group of three boys were in separate vessels, seemingly trying to bash each other hard enough to knock someone in. The lifeguard shouted something towards them, not that they were listening.

'We fell for each other,' Lucy said. 'Paul and I. We didn't mean it to happen but it did. And maybe that makes it worse, but—'

'Can you stop talking?' Megan couldn't stand the sound of the other woman's voice any longer.

Lucy did as she'd been asked and they watched silently as the lifeguard came down from his chair to shout at the boys. It was already too late. By the time he got there, two of the three were in the sea. They were treading water, trying to drag the third bumper boat, so their mate would join them in the water. The lifeguard started whistling, while the boys acted like a dog with selective hearing being called away from sniffing the ground. There was a lot more whistling and then, eventually, the two boys in the water clambered back onto their boats.

'Is the baby OK?' Megan asked, surprising herself that she cared.

Lucy touched her stomach, then cradled the bump with both hands. 'We had a scan a week ago and it's all as expected. We should find out next week if it's a boy or a girl.'

There was far too much 'we' in that sentence for Megan's liking. That scan 'a week ago' had happened when Megan didn't know her husband had got her best friend pregnant. She wondered if it was that scan that had prompted her husband to tell her what was going on. If they were going to find out the gender in a week, that meant Lucy was somewhere around four months gone. It had happened sometime around Easter.

She so wanted to be angry. She was almost more furious about not feeling it. This was the life Megan wanted, the life she had tried for all those years before the final verdict came down that she was incapable of having children. She shouldn't be sitting on a bench having cosy chats with one of the two people who betrayed her.

Lucy held up her phone. 'Paul needs to talk to you about the house and a few other things.'

Megan's tone was calm now, though she didn't feel it. 'I don't want to talk to him.'

'He said he's tried texting—'

'I got them but I've not read them.'

'It's just, um...' Lucy tailed off and then tried again. 'I'll tell him you'll get back to him when you're ready. Assuming that's all right?'

Megan wanted to say that of course it wasn't OK. She shouldn't need a go-between to pass messages between her and her husband.

'Why did you do it?' Megan asked, not wanting the answer, but somehow needing it.

Lucy wriggled on the bench. She started a reply two or three times before finally settling on: 'I'm not sure if—'

'Just tell me.'

Lucy sighed and rolled her shoulders. Pumped herself up. 'It was not long after I'd broken up with Jordan. Paul picked me up because I was stranded in town. We got talking and I suppose we didn't stop. It wasn't planned.'

Megan didn't know if that made it better or worse. It had been in the week between Christmas and new year that Lucy had texted, asking if Paul could pick her up because she couldn't find a taxi. Megan had practically shoved him out the door, wanting her friend to be safe. Everything might have been different if she'd not checked her phone, or if he'd been drinking, or if Lucy *had* found a taxi, or if a hundred other small things had gone differently. If Megan had ever passed her sodding driving test.

Or maybe it would have all been the same anyway? Things had never quite been the same between her and Paul after it became clear they weren't going to have children together. They had tried to pretend it was fine but it was only ever a pretence. That was clear now.

The lifeguard was back on his high seat on the beach below as the bumper boats reverted to a standard level of collision. The trio of boys were nowhere in sight.

Megan got up to leave and hovered for a moment, standing over her former friend. Lucy made no effort to move.

'Are you living here now?' Lucy asked again.

Megan wafted a hand in the vague direction of her sister's house, before realising what she was doing. 'I don't know.'

'Paul said he'll move out of the house if that's what you want. You can have it to yourself. That's what he's been trying to text you.'

'I don't know what I want.'

It had been less a week since she had left. But now there was the implication that, if Megan wanted to stay at the house, then Paul would move in with Lucy. Everything was changing so quickly. It was inevitable, she supposed. Lucy was having his baby, so of course they'd move in together. Megan couldn't stand the thought of them living *in her house*, but she couldn't see herself living there on her own, either. It was the place she and Paul had bought to raise a family, not somewhere for her to live as some spurned spinster.

Why couldn't she be angry, for God's sake?

She knew why, of course. It was because he wanted a baby as much as she did. She'd denied him the chance and now he'd found another way.

'Don't come back,' Megan said, as she finally hauled herself away from the bench. 'Tell Paul not to come either.'

'It's just—'

Megan didn't wait for a reply. She was off the kerb and almost in front of a honking taxi before she realised what she'd done. She wanted to get away – and hadn't looked before trying to cross the road.

Lucy was there now, in that stupid dress, with her stupid concern on her stupid face. 'Are you...?'

'Just go,' Megan told her. 'And tell him to stop texting.'

TWENTY

Megan quickly returned to the café, where the sandwich board had been padlocked to the drainpipe, meaning they were closed for the day. She checked over her shoulder, almost expecting Lucy to be there but grateful that she wasn't. A part of her had probably anticipated one or both of Lucy and Paul showing up. She'd blocked Lucy's number and ignored everything from Paul. The unread messages he'd sent since she'd left Whitecliff on a bus four days before were into the hundreds. There was only so long a person could disappear without expecting someone to come looking for them.

Unless that person was lying motionless in a stream.

Nicola's bicycle was still resting against the wall in the courtyard at the back of the café where Megan had left it. She stood next to it for a minute or three, taking a breath and holding the air for as long as she could before letting it out. There was still no anger, but she could feel the ground rumbling.

She'd not had a panic attack in three years.

The first one had come on the morning before she'd failed her fourth driving exam. She'd been at home by herself and had put two slices of bread in the toaster, when the earthquake began. The counter was trembling and something had started screaming in her ears. Then she'd realised the only things quivering were her hands. Megan wasn't sure what happened after that. She'd found herself sitting on the floor, knees to her chest, wondering what the sound was, before realising the doorbell was ringing. Her driving instructor was parked outside, ready to go with her to the test centre. He'd been ringing the bell for three minutes, and she had two missed calls.

All of that had happened, somehow, without her realising. And then she went and failed her test.

The panic attacks had come steadily after that, sometimes triggered by obviously stressful events, others for no apparent reason. Then, without knowing why – although suspecting it was because she'd stopped trying to drive – they went away.

The attacks always began with an earthquake.

Megan clasped the bike's handlebars as it remained resting against the wall. She screwed her eyes closed and tried to count to ten. She never got past three and yet, with her eyelids shut, the quaking didn't get any stronger.

Please, she whispered to herself. *Please.*

A minute passed but maybe it was longer. Maybe a lot longer. When she opened her eyes, there were greeny-purple stars – but everything was still.

Megan gave herself another few seconds and then wheeled the bike away from the wall, towards the small cut-through that led to the street. She wasn't sure she could actually ride it, not at the moment, but she could push it.

An SUV was parked across the exit, half its wheels on the pavement, large dent in the bumper. Megan stopped, partially because she didn't want to squeeze through with the bike, but also because it was the vehicle she'd seen Trevor driving at the back of the sweet shop. The one that had been parked on his drive.

Why was it here?

For a moment, Megan thought the unwelcome rumbling was back. She readied herself, set to force it away, and yet... nothing was moving. Instead, behind her at the back of the café, the fire exit had been wrenched open with an echoing clunk. A young woman stepped blinking into the sun, before cupping a hand across her forehead to shield her view. She froze when she spotted Megan, who was similarly welded to the ground. The other woman lowered her hand and squinted to Megan, who stared back.

Perhaps stared was the wrong word? Megan ogled her, blinked, gawped, couldn't believe what she was seeing.

It was the girl from the stream.

TWENTY-ONE

The memory was so crisp of the way the young woman's dark hair had been splayed against the dirty ground. Now, at the back of the café, her hair was the same colour – except it was tied into a bun.

'*You...?*'

Megan realised she was the one who'd spoken. There was so much she wanted to ask, except anything more than that one word felt stuck. She'd been doubting herself, wondering if – perhaps – she really *had* seen the woman in the stream. Nobody seemed to believe her and yet, from nowhere, here she was.

She wasn't dead.

A large man stepped out from the fire exit behind the girl, lugging a big bin. He hauled it around and dropped it on the floor, before dragging it across to the larger wheelie bin in the corner. He lifted the main lid and emptied everything inside, before letting the top fall back into place with a clang.

It was only when he turned that he spotted Megan.

For a second or two, everything stopped. The gulls were silenced, the distant chatter of tourists ambling up and down the seafront was gone.

And then everything happened together. The larger man began to usher the young woman back into the café's kitchen, just as a young man stepped outside. He was around the same age as the girl from the stream, nineteen or twenty, standing in the doorway blinking into the light as the other man called something to him. It took Megan a moment to realise he'd spoken in a foreign language.

The two younger people were shuffling back inside when Megan called 'stop'. She was more surprised than anyone that everyone actually did.

Megan had taken a couple of steps forward, still clutching the bike, focusing only on the woman from the stream.

'I saw you,' she said. 'You were in the water.'

Megan couldn't quite bring herself to say the other woman was *dead* in the water. She wanted to ask why she hadn't responded after all those chest compressions. Or, maybe she had – after Megan had already left?

Where had she gone afterwards? Why was she here? So many questions.

It was the larger man who replied, his accent thick and, in the moment, unidentifiable: 'No English for her.'

The woman's eyes were wide with what Megan thought was recognition. It really had been her – and she knew who Megan was.

Megan turned to the man instead. He was standing next to the fire exit door, newly emptied bin in one hand as he beckoned the other two back into the café with the other.

'I saw her in the woods a few days ago,' Megan said quickly, before the pair could get inside. 'She was in the stream.'

The word 'dead' still didn't quite come. It sounded madder in her head now that the woman was standing in front of her. How could she have been so wrong?

'No,' the man replied, shaking his head. 'Must be someone else.'

How would he know?

Megan turned back to the young woman, with her dark hair in the bun. She couldn't think of another identifiable feature about the person she'd seen, other than that this was definitely her.

'It was her,' Megan replied, slowly at first, before twisting back to the girl. 'It was you, wasn't it?'

The young woman opened her mouth and, for a moment, Megan thought she was going to reply. Except she didn't speak English, and hadn't understood her. It was then that Megan noticed the gentle discolouration around her eye. Not quite black, more an olive green.

'Is there a problem?'

This was a new voice – and Megan turned back towards the cut-through, where Ben had appeared. He looked past her, or maybe over her, towards the bigger man – and Megan saw the recognition between them.

'Everything all right?' Ben added, although it was unclear to whom he was speaking.

The bigger man answered: 'She said something about Sophia and a stream.'

So that was her name.

Sophia.

Megan eyed the girl. She had shied further back into the door frame and was standing alongside the young man who'd followed her out.

Megan turned between Sophia and Ben, needing to be understood. '*That's* who I saw in the stream,' she said, talking to her brother-in-law. 'This is who I was telling you about. She's why I called the police.'

Ben's eyes darted towards Sophia and back again. 'She seems fine to me...'

It was a fair point considering Megan had told Nicola, him, and the police that she'd found a *dead* girl in the stream.

Megan felt herself deflating, unable to explain what she was seeing now, or what she had seen then.

Ben nodded to the other man. 'Are you ready?'

The large man didn't bother to reply. He ushered the other two out of the kitchen, dumped the bin inside, and then slammed the door. The pair led the way out of the courtyard as the man followed – and then, moments later, there was a *thunk* of what Megan assumed was the SUV's doors closing. An engine started and then roared as the vehicle pulled away in a hurry.

Megan was left standing in the courtyard, still holding onto the bike, as Ben hovered a few paces away.

'I know what I saw,' Megan said quietly – although she wasn't sure that she did. What had seemed like such a clear image of the girl on the bank of the stream, with those hand-prints on her pink top, now felt hazy and dreamlike.

The earth was beginning to quake and she gripped the handlebars tighter.

Moments before the fire exit had opened, she'd been on the brink of a panic attack and, now that idea was in her mind, she wondered if that was what had happened in the attic before she'd heard the scream. It had been so hot up there and every-thing back in Whitecliff really *had* been that stressful, like everyone kept saying. She'd been through a lot. And, maybe, there had been an earthquake then? She remembered thinking about panicking, wondering if she was.

Ben spoke slowly, and it felt as if he was choosing his words carefully. 'You probably saw her on the street at the weekend.'

Megan understood what he meant. She had got off the bus on Saturday and hurried through the streets of Hollicombe Bay to her sister's house. Everything *had* happened really quickly. And perhaps she *had* seen Sophia on the street and remem-bered her face for some reason?

Except...

'I know what I saw,' Megan said, but her voice was weak and it didn't sound convincing, even to her.

'But she isn't dead,' Ben said. He was stating a fact and yet it felt so devastating. The two things couldn't be true.

'I know what I saw...' Megan barely finished the sentence, because she *didn't* know. Not any longer.

'Do you need a lift back?' Ben asked, moving on. 'I can put the bike in the back.'

Megan was shaking her head.

'Are you sure you're all right?' he added.

'I'm fine.'

'It's just—'

Megan stomped past him, shoving the bike out in front. 'I'm fine!'

TWENTY-TWO

Megan was at the other end of town, near the bottom of the slope that would lead up to Nicola's. The bike was hooked over the back of a bench as she sat and stared across the ocean. An ice cream van was parked a hundred or so metres along the street as a row of children and families lined up tidily against the wall. Gulls circled, hoping there was a dropper. Megan watched for a while and the queue never seemed to shrink. As soon as someone paid and headed off towards the town or the beach, somebody new joined at the back.

A pair of teenage girls were now on the end, whispering into each other's ears as they clasped their phones tightly. They were maybe a year or two younger than Sophia, both with similar long, dark hair.

Megan had seen Sophia in the woods, dead in the stream. She had *touched* her. She'd left handprints on her top.

Except Sophia was alive and well, seemingly working in the kitchen of the café. Megan had somehow missed that part when they'd been in the courtyard. The only reason Sophia had been leaving the café was because she worked there. For three days, Megan had been worrying about who she'd seen by the stream when, quite possibly, that exact person was on the other side of a hatch.

It was hard to escape the conclusion that she had been wrong about it all. That, as Ben had said, she'd seen Sophia on the street and then transposed her face onto... what? A hallucination?

If that was somehow true, it would be the first time she had seen things that weren't there.

Aside from Paul, nobody else knew about the panic attacks – and even he didn't know of their extent. He hadn't known Megan was having any for around the first year. After that, she'd told him they had stopped a good few months before they actually did. Even so, she had never imagined people or scenarios. Instead, once the panic attacks were over, Megan was left with a low-level sense of worry about everything and nothing.

If things had somehow developed from panic attacks to making up dead bodies, then Megan had a far greater problem than she felt able to cope with.

'Oh, hello.'

Megan was lost to those thoughts as someone stopped in front, blocking the sun. They were a big dark blob until they edged to the side.

'Sorry about that,' Daniel said. He was holding a Mr Whippy 99 in one hand and moved quickly to lick around the edge of the cone as the ice cream started to drip. He was smiling gently as Megan fumbled for something to say. 'Do you want some company?' he asked.

Megan wasn't sure whether she managed a 'yes' but, regardless, he slotted in at her side.

'You look like you've had quite the day.'

'You could say that.'

'Did you hear about the guy they found on the rocks this morning? Someone said he was drunk but I don't think anyone knows for sure.'

'I thought it was going to be the girl I saw,' Megan replied. 'The one from the stream.'

Daniel polished off the ice cream from on top of the cone and pushed the flake down into the stem. 'I can see why you've had a rough day.'

Megan snorted a little at that. What an understatement.

'I saw her,' she said. 'The girl. She's alive and well, working in the kitchen of the café. She's called Sophia.'

It was only then it dawned on Megan that Sophia was one of her sister's cash-in-hand workers. Someone likely being underpaid. She wondered how much the young woman would be getting.

Daniel had been about to bite into the wafer cone but stopped. 'She's... alive?'

Megan blinked back to the moment: 'I talked to her.'

'What did she say?'

'Not a lot. She seemed a bit scared.'

Megan hadn't realised that until she'd said it out loud. There was a language barrier between her and Sophia – but the confusion on the young woman's face had been more than that. When Sophia had backed away into the fire exit, it was because she was frightened.

'Wouldn't you be scared if a stranger accused you of being dead?'

Daniel finally took that bite of his ice cream as Megan considered that. The answer was a definite 'yes', assuming Sophia understood at least some English.

Or perhaps it was Megan's manic expression that had terrified the poor girl.

'How's the ice cream?' Megan asked, wanting to change the subject.

'Good as ever. I come down here once or twice a week. Can't help myself.' Daniel was halfway through the stem of the cone as he nodded towards the ice cream van. 'Do you want one? He's a mate of mine.'

Megan shook her head, even though the truth was that she probably did. Above that, she felt relief that Daniel wasn't treating her like a lunatic.

He polished off the rest of the cone and then licked his fingers. He stood and stretched high, arching his back until something clicked. 'I need to get back to the arcade,' he said. 'Do you want to come? I'll show you around.'

Megan was back to hanging around in the arcade as a teenager, wasting her coppers on those two-pence machines that never paid out. The rushing déjà vu was such a pull to happier times.

And then she remembered. 'I've got my sister's bike,' she said.

'Bring it with you. You can leave it in the office if you want the grand tour.'

Suddenly, there was a sliver of light in the bleakest of nights.

They walked along the pavement together, Megan pushing her bike, as Daniel carved a path through tourists with a series of 'just behind you, pal', 'steady there, mate', and 'coming through's.

Flashing lights ringed the sign across the arcade, while a cacophony of pops, pings and laughs echoed from the inside. Two dance machines were next to each other, close to the entrance, and there was a steady *thump-thump-thump* as a group of youngsters had what looked like a dance-off. Further in and four race-car cockpits were full as a quartet of thirty-somethings who should probably know better wrenched the steering wheels from side to side. Past that, there was a queue for the punching machine, with a group of largely overweight men throwing shadow punches – *doof-doof, one-two* – into the air while waiting their turn.

Daniel was wheeling Megan's bike now, weaving it expertly around the punters as Megan followed. When he stopped in the back corner, Megan was so taken with watching some sort of kickboxing game that she almost walked into the back of him. He typed 1-2-3-4-5-6 into the keypad and then opened the door, before ushering her into the office.

There were banks of monitors inside, as Megan realised every step she'd taken inside the arcade had been recorded.

Daniel left her bike leaning on the back wall and then slumped into a comfy-looking leather recliner. He nodded towards a similar one opposite, and Megan allowed herself to be swallowed by the chair.

'This place is so big,' she said. Usually, if something had seemed large as a child, it would appear smaller once grown up. The arcade felt the opposite

'Dad had a lot of dead space in the way he'd set things up,' Daniel replied. 'I had a few walls knocked through – and the place next door had been condemned, so I bought that and fixed it up. There's still a big storeroom at the back but, other than that, everything's full.'

Megan spent a few seconds watching the monitors. Another half-dozen people had joined the crowd to watch the dance-off at the front of the arcade.

'They're here every day,' Daniel said. 'I always leave some discount vouchers at the caravan park and they come down in the afternoon.'

It felt like such an obvious thing to do in an attempt to draw an audience already in town. Still, even with the most obvious things, someone had to think of it first – and, seemingly, it had been Daniel.

Megan stared at the monitors for a moment, before remembering the other stuff. She needed to talk to someone properly – but it couldn't be a member of her family.

'My old best friend came to see me today,' she said. 'Lucy.'

Daniel had been looking at his laptop but he spun to face her. 'That's good!' He must have seen something in her face because he instantly added: '…Isn't it?'

'It would be if she wasn't pregnant with my husband's baby.'

It felt almost freeing to say it so openly. The only other person Megan had spoken to was her sister – but even that hadn't quite reached the point of opening up about the pregnancy. Nicola knew Paul and Lucy had had an affair but nothing more.

'Oh,' Daniel said, which was quite the understatement. There was a considered pause and then: 'I guess that explains you being separated.'

He sat, listening, as Megan told him how she'd only found out the previous week. It had begun with Paul uttering the immortal words, 'We need to talk'. The four words from which nothing good ever came. He'd told her they'd grown apart, which had Megan convinced he was simply leaving. Then the double bombshell. BANG! He was 'in love' – not having an affair – with Lucy. BANG! Lucy was pregnant.

Paul wasn't one for sugar-coating. He'd gone full jugular.

Megan didn't remember what she'd actually said to him, only that he'd left the house to give her space. Perhaps she'd slept that night but probably not. One day blurred into the next. She'd quit her job at the gym the next day, but maybe it was the one after that. Then she'd talked to Nicola and arranged to stay with her. There was a bus, and then she was back where she grew up, and the attic was really hot. Then there was a girl in the woods. Except there obviously *wasn't* a girl in the woods because Sophia had been standing right in front of her a little over an hour before.

Nicola had been right all along, things really *had* been too much for her.

Daniel listened, giving her his complete attention. He didn't interrupt, didn't ask any thicko follow-ups, or try to make it about him. Didn't say he knew how she felt. That would be the worst. *Oh,* your *husband got* your *best friend pregnant, did he?*

'I'm sorry,' Megan added at the end. There was a tissue in her hand that she didn't remember being given. Her eyes were raw and she realised she'd been crying at some point. Somehow, that had happened subconsciously.

'You don't have to be sorry,' Daniel said. 'You haven't done anything wrong.'

Megan was hunched in the seat, almost doubled over as she dabbed her eyes with the tissue. She didn't want to talk about Paul, Lucy, the baby or Whitecliff any longer – though it really did feel as if a tiniest part of the burden had gone.

'Ben says you're problematic,' she said, laughing as it came out.

'*Problematic?*'

'Nicola said the same.'

Daniel shrugged: 'I suppose I can see why he said that.'

Megan looked up to where he was still watching her. 'I thought you'd be annoyed, or try to deny it?'

That got a second shrug. 'It's very like Ben to talk in that way. It's the same at the business association meetings. It's all black and white. An idea is bad or good. No greys.'

Megan considered that for a moment and realised he was right. That was always how she'd thought of her brother-in-law, even though she had never articulated it in such a clear way. When Megan had told Nicola and Ben that the results were back and she couldn't have children, Ben had pouted a lip and said 'probably for the best'.

'I'm not exactly popular around here,' Daniel said. 'I tried to get longer hours for this place, so we could open until 1 a.m. on Fridays and Saturdays – and you'd have thought I'd sacrificed someone's gran. Plus this place is always noisy, and kids hang around. It's everything a town full of old people don't like.

Sometimes, I think I'm completely out of the loop on what gets done. Like they've already made decisions before anything ever gets to a vote.'

He paused for a moment and glanced at one of the monitors, where the crowd for the dance machine was now close to twenty. 'If you wonder why it's so hard to get phone reception around here, it's because there's only one mast up on the hill, near the church. The council keep voting down any plans to build another. It was only last year that someone tried to burn down the only mast, 'cos they'd watched some video about 5G giving them Covid.' He rolled his eyes. 'It wasn't even a 5G mast.'

He shook his head and sighed in frustration.

'People believe everything they read on Facebook,' he added. 'There was this big outcry because someone reckoned a paedo had moved in up the hill. Turned out he drove a black Corsa – and someone had been arrested for child sex offences up in Newcastle, who also happened to drive a black Corsa. Completely different person. It's a good job nobody lynched him.'

Daniel twirled a finger close to his ear – and he wasn't done.

'I've been trying to push ideas for years to turn the town around. There's this place in Canada, where goats live on top of a shop. There's grass up there, a pen, and the goats go about their business – but thousands of people come to see them. They buy things in the store, they eat in the cafés, they stay in the local area. And it's just one simple idea. A whole community built off this one silly idea.'

For a brief moment, Megan was living in Daniel's world – which was a relief because it wasn't her own. 'You want to put goats on top of the arcade?'

A laugh. 'Not really. Maybe. What's wrong with that? You should see the pictures. That one idea fuels a whole town. That's what we need here. Not necessarily goats – but *some-*

thing. Except people don't want to be told. They like the caravan parks and the fact everything's closed at four. They wish it was like the old days, even though most of them are too young to remember.'

It was as passionate as Megan had seen him, or probably anyone for a long time. Suddenly, the idea of sticking farm animals on a roof didn't seem as mad. She knew what he was talking about, too. The number of old people who banged on about the war as if they'd lived through it was ridiculous.

'Anyway,' Daniel added. 'I'm "problematic" – and I'm fine with it. People 'round here want things easy. They'll say things like, "Why can't we just get seasonal workers for three months?" And I try to tell them that nobody wants to come to the middle of nowhere to work for minimum wage for three months, especially now everyone from Europe needs a visa. But they don't get it. They just say "Nobody wants to work anymore", as if anyone can afford to live here when they get paid eight quid an hour.'

Megan pictured Sophia back at the café and wondered how much she was being paid to work in the kitchen. Megan herself was being paid cash in hand, and she imagined the immigrants, legal or not, being paid in bank notes by Ben or Nicola. It wouldn't be above board and Megan figured she should probably bring it up with her sister again. She'd more or less accepted the dodgy employment arrangements that morning but putting a face to things – *Sophia's face* – made it feel worse. More exploitative.

Then she remembered something else. Despite everything he'd said, there was another reason why Nicola and Ben had insisted Daniel was problematic.

'I heard your wife left unexpectedly,' Megan said.

Daniel didn't miss a beat. 'Not really, although it might've seemed like that to other people.'

'I also heard you broke someone's nose on the seafront...?'

That got a bit of a snigger, with a hint of a shrug. 'Did the person who told you that actually see it?'

'No.'

'Funny that. There *was* no fight, and I definitely didn't break someone's nose.' He held up his palms, showing off the scaly scars. 'You know what it's like round here, with the rumours.'

Megan *did* know. After the fire at their school, she'd heard so many stories about what had happened inside that classroom, even though she had *actually* been there.

'My ex-wife is Becca,' he said. 'Her brother's Jamie – and he got the wrong end of the stick when we separated. The break-up was more or less mutual. Becca wanted to sell up and leave town. She was sick of the seaside and how small everything was. She wanted to live in a city.'

'You didn't?'

Another shake of the head. 'You can't really reconcile two people wanting to live in two different places. Anyway, Jamie somehow got it into his head that there was more to it than that. There was rugby on, something like that, and he'd been drinking all day. I came out of the arcade and he was waiting for me. There was a bit of shouting and pointing, that sort of thing. Definitely no fight, let alone a broken nose. Except, somehow, by the time it went around town, we'd been rolling in the road and he'd ripped my shirt, then I'd broken his nose.' He rolled his eyes. 'Seriously, ask anyone if they *actually* saw it, and you'll always hear that they heard it from somebody else. Everyone thinks I had some massive fight, and then they turn up to book club as if nothing happened. It's such a weird town.'

Megan couldn't argue with that. That's the sort of place Hollicombe Bay was.

Daniel didn't finish with any sort of pleading. *You believe me, don't you?* Megan *did* believe him and she didn't need to be asked.

Something buzzed and Daniel picked up his phone from the side of his laptop. He glanced at the screen and frowned. 'I'm going to have to deal with this,' he said. 'Sorry, I didn't mean to unload on you and then turf you out.'

'You're turfing me out?' There was a *hint* of mock indignation to Megan's tone.

He smiled. 'You can stay and watch the monitors if you want – or I can give you some tokens for the machines – but I've got to head out for a while.'

A part of Megan wanted to stay to while away a wasted evening playing games she would be bad at. She might have done if it didn't feel as if everyone in the arcade outside was either half her age, or an overweight bloke trying to punch a machine.

'I should probably get back myself,' Megan said, as she stood and crossed to the bike.

Daniel walked her out, leaning into the 'just behind you, big man' and 'careful there, fella'-spiel as people moved out of the way. When they reached the pavement, the clamouring bustle of earlier had shrunk to a quieter evening. People were in restaurants or the pubs, else heading back to their campsites.

They said a goodbye, with a bonus 'see you around', which was feeling more literal by the day.

Megan walked the bike to the end of the high street, remembering clearer than ever why she'd left town in the first place. It was precisely because of those whispers and the rumours. The way nothing ever seemed to change and, on the rare occasion it did, older people went ballistic over it. She had walked away from Whitecliff a few days before because she couldn't stand it any longer, but – in all likelihood – she couldn't take Hollicombe Bay any longer, either. What was there for her? A job she didn't like at a café owned by her sister? A sweltering attic bedroom, in which she crept around so as not to disturb the real inhabitants of the house on the floor below? It wasn't much.

Megan cycled slowly up the hill to her sister's house. She left the bike in the shed and then let herself in through the back door. She was never quite sure if and when the house would be empty, seeing as everyone kept their own hours.

This time, it definitely *wasn't* empty.

There was a slam of the front door a moment after Megan had entered the back. At almost exactly the same time, Nicola's voice bellowed from the living room. 'I've been waiting for you to get home!'

For a momentary second, Megan thought her sister was shouting at her – except, as she moved into the living room, she realised Jessie was in the opposite doorway, Nicola standing between them, unaware of Megan's presence.

Jessie's eyebrows were high, her eyes wide, as she stared in horror at whatever her mother was holding. It was a pen, or a thermometer or...

... A pregnancy test stick.

'You're seventeen!' Nicola shouted.

Suddenly, Nicola's previous complaints about Jessie being sick in the mornings weren't anything to do with a returning eating disorder.

Except Jessie's eyes weren't saying that. The poor girl was terrified, and definitely not ready for this conversation. Her gaze flickered momentarily away from her mum, focusing on Megan for the briefest second. That was all it took: a silent plea loud and received.

Help.

And Megan did help. 'It's mine,' she said.

TWENTY-THREE

Nicola turned from her daughter to her sister, the pee stick twisting in her fingers. 'I didn't know you were home,' she managed, which somewhat underplayed the situation.

'Just got in,' Megan replied. She risked the most transient of glimpses to Jessie, who was staring at her open-mouthed.

Nicola held up the pregnancy test higher. 'This is *yours?*'

It was too late now. 'Right.'

'But you can't get pregnant...?' It came out as something of a stutter – and probably harsher than was meant. Nicola gulped after finishing the question.

Megan was somehow speaking far more calmly that she felt. 'That's what I thought. I guess nobody knows for sure.'

As Nicola stared, Megan glanced to Jessie once more, where the teenager was resting against the door frame, seemingly with some degree of relief.

'I guess... congratulations?' Nicola said, although it sounded like another question.

'I'm not telling anyone yet, so please don't let Ben know.' Megan's sense that she would need to get out of this at some point suddenly hit and, in a moment of clarity, she added: 'I did a second one that said not pregnant, so I don't know. I'm waiting for a few days. It might be hormones.'

It was deliciously vague. If in doubt, blame something on hormones. Stomach ache? Hormones. Bit tired? Hormones. Start thinking a Tory MP is good-looking? Hormones. Dodgy pregnancy test? Hormones.

Nicola was chewing her lip, considering the reply, when she went for it: 'Is it Paul's?'

Megan stared her down, not flinching or wavering until, after a couple of seconds, Nicola backed off.

'You don't have to answer. I suppose when you said about him and, er, Lucy that I thought...'

The sentence went unfinished as Megan continued to stand much stronger than she felt.

The impasse was broken by Jessie saying she was off to her room. Before her mum could apologise or say anything else, the teenager was off up the stairs.

Megan took a couple of steps towards the door. 'I'm going up for a shower,' she said. 'Shall I take that...?'

Nicola was still holding the pregnancy test and looked to it as if she'd never seen it before. She stretched, passing it across, as Megan took it carefully, avoiding the peed-on end.

Upstairs, Megan knocked gently on Jessie's door. She called 'It's Megan' as quietly as she thought she could get away with. There was a shuffling from the other side and then Jessie pulled her door open. She looked to her aunt and then the pregnancy test and then started to say something before Megan shook her head, before pointing up to the next floor.

The two of them headed to the attic, where Megan dropped the test into the bin. They ended up sitting on opposite ends of the chaise longue, proving it was at least useful for something.

'I probably should've put it in a different bin,' Jessie said quietly. She had twisted to face the angled window.

'Do you want to talk about it?' Megan asked.

It got an instant shake of the head but then a slow, reluctant: 'I can't get him to reply. I did the test yesterday and sent him a message. Then another. Then I called.'

Megan rested a gentle hand on the teenager's back. 'Is it someone from school?'

Now it was Jessie's turn not to reply – and it was hard not to think of the times Megan had done everything she could to get pregnant. The calendars and ovulation charts. Lying with her legs up, or grabbing Paul because it was the optimal time. The mechanics, not the love. All that for nothing – and here she was next to a seventeen-year-old who'd seemingly managed it with no trouble, and without meaning to.

There was no justice.

Megan swallowed those thoughts and took a breath. It wasn't about her.

'You don't have to tell me anything you don't want,' Megan said. 'I'll be around if you want to talk – or even if you just want to sit with someone.'

There was another few seconds of silence and then: 'It's my drama teacher,' Jessie said quickly, not giving Megan time to consider things. From nothing, it all came out in one go. They'd been rehearsing through the summer for a play, which was where she was most days. He had keys for the studio, and a few of them had been running lines and discussing scenes.

The precise details weren't there, and Megan didn't particularly want or need to hear them. The rest was fairly clear. As with discovering the body, this felt like the precise sort of thing that should be dealt with by somebody who knew what they were doing. Megan tried to appear unflustered, as if this was the type of thing she figured out all the time. Inside, she was desperately trying to come up with the correct words.

'Have you told anyone else?' Megan asked, which got a shake of the head.

'What would you do?' Jessie replied.

It was such a tough question – not only because having children was a thorny issue for Megan, but because it wasn't really a question an aunt should be answering. For another thing, Jessie wasn't *technically* an adult. Much of the last decade of Megan's life had been thinking about having children but she couldn't comprehend being responsible for one when she was barely an adult.

'I don't think I can answer that,' Megan said carefully. 'I know you might not want to right now, but you'll have to talk to your mum at some point.'

'Then she'll know you lied.'

'I think she'll figure that out when a baby comes along – and it's not me giving birth.'

That got a soft, humourless laugh.

'If not your mum, there are nurses who can help,' Megan added. 'I know there's a clinic in Whitecliff. We can get the bus there together, if you want?'

There was no instant reply. There was a lot to think about.

They sat together for a minute or two, both twisting to face the window. The stupid chaise longue wasn't only in an odd place, it was facing the wrong way.

'I didn't realise it was so hot up here,' Jessie said.

'It's why I have the window open all the time.'

Jessie shuffled and fidgeted. 'This isn't very comfortable.'

'I still wonder how your parents got it up here. It's massive.'

Jessie hrmmed at that. It was something of a mystery as to why it was in the attic at all.

'Dad will go mad,' Jessie whispered. 'Especially if he knew about Lucas.'

It felt as if she hadn't meant to say the name. She went quiet and sucked in her cheeks. Megan didn't want to push, at least not right now. The poor girl had only just found out and, though it was not something she should go through by herself, she was going to need at least a little time to process it.

And then Megan found herself saying the words she didn't think she would. It might have been because she wanted to change the subject anyway, or her own unease at how the day had gone. Perhaps even that she simply wanted to share something with her niece. But it was there.

'Do you still want to hear about the fire?' Megan asked.

Jessie eked herself up. Her voice was croaky. 'Yeah... I mean, if it's OK.'

It had been a long time since Megan had spoken about what had happened in the school, even though it was never too far from her thoughts. One of the reasons she had left Hollicombe Bay in the first place was to get away from the people who wanted to talk about such things. From the head tilts and the *you know she was there* whispers.

'It was just after New Labour came in,' Megan said. 'Not that that means anything to you, I suppose. Me and your mum used to do orchestra after school.'

'I didn't know Mum played an instrument.'

The interest was a big switch from the despair of moments before.

'She used to play flute. She was really into it for a year or so.'

'What did you play?'

'Percussion.'

That got a moment of confusion and then the slimmest of smiles: 'You played the triangle?'

'Not *just* the triangle!' Megan allowed herself to laugh. 'I played the xylophone as well – although the school one never sounded quite right.'

Jessie was still smiling: 'A bad workman...'

There was a moment in which Megan was back to being that fourteen-year-old, struggling to read music and hit the right keys. Calling the club an 'orchestra' was probably pushing it a bit. They were all children trying to learn instruments – and only a few, like Nicola, had been tied to one in particular. It was more something to do.

'We always practised in a classroom on the upstairs floor of the school,' Megan said. 'I don't know if it's still there but the caretaker's office was right next to it. We were busy playing and paying attention to ourselves. What we didn't realise was that a fire had started in the caretaker's office. It burned through the cupboard and then, from nowhere, the door of our class was on fire.'

Megan remembered her eyelashes stinging from the heat, as if an invisible fly had been circling. She'd never felt anything like that before or since. Not just like opening an oven but being *in* the oven. A rippling shiver whispered through her and she was back in the classroom.

'What did you do?' Jessie asked, a fair question.

'I know it sounds like a cop-out – but I don't completely remember. There were people screaming and I know we were on the other side of the room, by the windows. Even if we'd wanted to jump, it was too high – but we couldn't open them properly anyway.' She nodded to the angled window that was cracked. 'They didn't open all the way.'

The attic felt even hotter than it had been and Megan wondered if Jessie could feel the same prickling she did.

'The flames kept coming closer,' she continued. 'There were desks on fire and I remember this kid's coat on the floor. It was green and new – but it shrivelled into a ball the moment the fire touched it.'

Megan wasn't sure if she had always remembered that, or if it had suddenly reappeared. She was staring at the gap in the attic window, linking it for the first time back to the school.

'There were sirens,' Megan said. 'They got louder and louder – and then the fire engine was right outside the window. I remember thinking they'd need a really long ladder – and they had one, of course.'

'Did they break the window?'

'Yeah... but by then, there wasn't anywhere for us to go. The fireman was waving us away to give him space to hit the window – but we couldn't move. He ended up breaking it anyway.'

'He got you out?'

'And your mum, with a few others.'

Not everyone though.

When Megan had found that young woman in the stream, she'd told herself she'd never seen a dead body before. It was true in a false kind of way. She'd never *specifically* seen the bodies but she had heard the screams. She'd seen her teacher and some of the other students swallowed by those approaching flames.

That's what Hollicombe Bay was to her. It was why she knew she'd never be able to call the town home again, even if she was living in her sister's attic. She'd never quite understood why Nicola hadn't left as well.

'I get why nobody wants to talk about it,' Jessie said.

They sat for a short while, neither comfortable on the seat, neither wanting to move. That wasn't the entire story – but it was enough for now. It was only then that Megan remembered the other thing she'd meant to tell her niece.

'I saw your friend,' she said. 'Helena. She was working in the kitchen at the back of the sweet shop.'

Jessie blinked back into the attic. 'I guess she got a summer job.' A pause. 'At least she's all right. I wonder why she doesn't come out any more?'

'I saw the girl from the stream, too. She's called Sophia. She works in the kitchen of the café.'

That got the merest hint of a frown. 'It was only a few months ago Mum was saying they couldn't get anyone to work in the kitchen. Dad reckoned they might to have to close because there weren't enough customers. Now they're opening a second café. I don't know what's going on.' She twitched and then stood. 'I can't believe how uncomfortable this sofa is.'

Jessie had been clutching her phone the entire time they'd been in the attic. She glanced to the screen and then away.

'Has he messaged back?' Megan asked.

Jessie's twitching eye gave the reply before she did. 'No.'

TWENTY-FOUR

Megan spent the rest of the evening in the attic bedroom, mainly to avoid any sideways questioning stares from her sister. Even though she'd asked Nicola not to tell Ben about the pregnancy test, Megan was almost certain it had already happened. Probably as a text message as soon as Megan had left the room. Nicola and Ben didn't seem the sort of couple who kept much in the way of secrets from each other – although Megan had once thought that about herself and Paul.

Problems were coming.

Megan had covered for her niece because she'd seen the horror in the poor girl's face as her mother had been holding the test. It couldn't last forever, but would hopefully give Jessie enough time to get some sort of response from Lucas the drama teacher.

Megan googled him, along with the school name. Lucas Fernandes had that 'well actually, Hoover is a brand name' kind of face. He was thirty-seven and his Facebook photo showed him wearing sunglasses with his face smushed into a woman's of a similar age. The rest of his profile was hidden, though it seemed likely he was married. Either way, he was definitely twenty years older than Jessie.

No wonder he wasn't answering his phone.

The age of consent was sixteen, Megan googled that too, although she was sure there was something about abuse of trust when it came to teachers getting up to no good. She thought about calling the police and asking, though things hadn't gone too well the last time she'd spoken to them. She could contact the school – but Jessie definitely wouldn't appreciate it.

Either or both of those options were still open, but for another day. What she mainly felt was rage against this Lucas fellow. This teacher who had taken advantage in the worst way. He would have to be held accountable one way or the other, but Megan wasn't sure how to reconcile that with her niece's wishes.

Megan continued swiping on her phone. The local news was full of stories about the man who'd died on the rocks. It felt like such a long time before that Megan had stood in the mist and watched the body be carried across the beach, even though it was only that morning. Most of the rumours heard across the day appeared to be true. He'd had an argument with his wife and, while she'd headed back to the caravan park, he'd remained out. The next thing anyone knew, his body had been found by that dog walker. The police were asking for witnesses, although it seemed unlikely that the truth of what had happened could be known for sure.

Sophia was never far from Megan's thoughts. The big guy at the back of the café had said she didn't speak English but perhaps she could understand some? Either that, or Megan could use Google Translate to try to talk to her. She wanted to ask if she'd been in the woods on Sunday afternoon. Had she been in the stream? What had happened before and after?

And, if she hadn't been in the woods, that left bigger questions, almost all of which were about Megan and her state of mind. That was a place she definitely didn't want to go.

The problem was how to talk to Sophia without the big guy being around. That more or less ruled out anything around the café and the kitchen, considering he apparently worked there as well.

What Megan *really* needed was to find out where Sophia lived. She wouldn't simply turn up at the young woman's door, she wasn't a maniac, but she could engineer an *oh, it's you* moment if she *just so happened* to be in the area.

One option was to ask Nicola or Ben about Sophia and where she lived, and probably about how much they were paying her, too. Except that would involve a conversation that could easily be swung back to her claimed pregnancy.

Megan wondered whether there would be some sort of employment document. A contract, a payslip, something like that. It felt unlikely, given the whole cash thing – but perhaps not impossible. There could be an application letter, something with an address.

Megan lay on the bed with the window open, listening to the sounds from the floors below. There was a TV on and Ben laughing. Then some clanging around in the kitchen as one of them loaded the dishwasher. The rumble of pipes had become familiar over the days Megan had lived in her sister's house – and she listened to the water flowing as someone took a shower.

Megan remembered something from the early days of when Nicola began seeing Ben, when her sister said that he watched *Newsnight* every night. It was a little joke back then, mainly because it felt like such a grown-up thing. It came in handy as Megan heard movement on the stairs not too long after eleven. A door opened and closed, there was a quiet murmuring of voices and then... quiet.

Twenty minutes passed and the house was silent. Megan gave it another forty, just to be safe, and it was almost half-past midnight when she crept down from the attic. In the few days she'd lived in Nicola's house, Megan had become used to the squeaky floorboards near the handrail, plus the one that bounced a little near the top of the stairs. She slipped around those and tiptoed to the ground floor, where she waited in the hallway, listening to the hush.

Into the living room, and Megan headed for the cabinet underneath the television. She shone the light from her phone across three drawers, all of which *could* have been filled with papers and documents, none of which were. Instead there was a series of spaghettified cables, random pens, a game controller, batteries, packs of tissues, and a book entitled *Think Yourself Rich*. The sort of guff that had only made one person rich: the charlatan who got it published.

The next cabinet was full of booze; mainly the kind of rum, ouzo and vodka that people brought back from holiday, only to abandon for the next two decades.

The kitchen drawers had the expected cutlery, random utensils that nobody used, foil, cling film, and boxes of sandwich bags. The exception was the drawer nearest the back door, that was packed with papers. Megan paused for a few seconds, listening for any sign of a creak from above. When nothing came, she pulled out the wedge and began to finger through it. Most of them seemed to relate to Jessie's school. There were letters from years back about dates for parents evenings and school trips. Some of her reports were in there, along with posed photographs, two swimming certificates, and some sort of rosette that might've been from a sports day.

Nothing useful – and Megan felt a bit grubby for snooping as she slipped the cluttered pile back into the drawer.

Megan wasn't sure where else to look. She returned to the living room and edged around the sofa and armchair again. She didn't really know what she was looking for, but whatever it was hadn't been in any of the obvious drawers or cupboards. She was ready to give it up as a bad idea and head back to bed when she noticed the television unit wasn't pushed all the way to the wall.

There was an obstacle course of wires to get around the side. She expected more wires, perhaps an abandoned fireplace, or something. Except, more or less in plain sight, a boxy black metal safe was sitting on the carpet, almost waiting to be found. It was wedged neatly between the back of the unit and the wall. Once noticed, it seemed impossible that Megan had never seen it before, especially as she had sat on the sofa facing it. Almost the perfect hiding place.

The safe was locked, with a pushpad on the front. Megan knew she shouldn't – except speaking properly to Sophia was the only thing that was going to answer the questions she had about what she'd seen in the woods.

It was a guess, but an educated one. Megan and Nicola had signed up for bank accounts at the same time, and received their cash cards in the post. They'd gone to the cashpoint in town and each changed their PIN one after the other. Megan's hadn't changed in the twenty-plus years since and she doubted Nicola's had either.

She tapped 7-7-2-7 into the safe and there was an instant *click-clunk* as the lock disengaged. It almost felt too easy. It definitely didn't *feel* right.

That didn't stop her.

The safe was full of papers and Megan lifted them out as she sat on the floor and started to sort. There were contracts, though mainly for the delivery and provision of equipment relating to the café. There was a title deed, a marriage certificate, and...

Something squeaked from the stairs.

There was no way Megan could stuff everything back into the safe in time. She turned off the light from her phone and continued sitting, holding her breath unconsciously and listening. A minute passed. More. Then there was another elongated *eeeeeeeeek.*

The scrape hadn't come from the stairs, it was from above. The footsteps were too heavy to be anyone other than Ben. He thumped across the landing into the bathroom and there was a click of a door. The quiet lasted a minute or two and then the door re-opened and the footsteps backtracked to the bedroom.

Paul had been a late-night flusher and Megan wasn't sure whether that was more courteous, or if it was better with the silence.

She waited, holding her breath, phone light still off, as the bed frame creaked above. Then it was quiet.

Megan turned the light back on and continued flitting through the pages. There were a couple of contracts for workers – but nothing recent, and certainly nothing for anyone named Sophia.

Megan edged around the side of the TV unit again, reaching towards the back of the safe, where there was a little under £300 in cash, which didn't feel unusual. None of it did. On the bottom of the safe, underneath the pages Megan had already read, was a transparent document wallet. The sort of thing in which Megan used to hand in her homework back in the day. She returned the other papers to the safe as she removed the wallet. There were a couple of dozen pages inside, most with the logo of a bank in the corner.

None of it was anything to do with where Sophia lived – none of it was anything Megan had been looking for.

It was much worse.

It took barely a few glances to see that Nicola and Ben owed almost a million pounds. The amount was spread across more than one mortgage, loans, and credit card debt.

Megan read the pages once, twice, and then again, because the numbers were barely believable. She wondered if there was a decimal place or two missing – except it was all there. Her sister owed a staggering amount of money – and she was clearly behind with at least some of the payments.

Megan kept going. Beneath those pages there were more bank statements – but not in either Nicola or Ben's name. Megan shone her light closer to the page, not quite able to believe what she was seeing.

Her father's name and their childhood address was listed. There was a phone bill, too, plus a chequebook buried in the wallet, all with their dad's details. The cheques themselves had been pre-signed by her father, either that or the signature was a good forgery.

That wasn't all. A quick scan of the stubs and there it was in scribbled blue ballpoint.

A little over two months before, Nicola had taken almost £70,000 from their father.

TWENTY-FIVE

THURSDAY

Megan was up early the next morning, before either of Ben or Nicola could bother her about the pregnancy that wasn't.

She retrieved the bike from the shed and wheeled it along the back of the house, ready to ride down the hill towards the café. It would be easy to waste a bit of time before her shift started. Except Megan didn't see how she could spend a day serving customers and pretending everything was fine. She had returned to Hollicombe Bay to escape the drama of her husband getting her best friend pregnant – and yet there was a different kind of drama in her hometown.

The mist was back for a second morning, sitting low in the gully at the bottom of the hill. The tops of the shops were barely visible as the clouded quilt stretched far out to sea. The blinking lights from bobbing buoys flickered somewhere in the distance and the air had a spiky chill.

Megan knew where she was going. She'd made the decision while sitting on her sister's floor the night before, and then spent the rest of her waking hours trying to think herself out of it.

She cycled away from the new estate on which her sister

lived, navigating the alleys and back roads until she reached the old part of town. In the distant past, Hollicombe Bay had been a fishing town. The harbour was long since gone, as was the market and any semblance of industry. All that was left was the collection of houses and cottages that was once the centre of town.

It was where Megan and Nicola had grown up – and where their father still lived.

Megan hadn't spoken to him in three years, since the misplaced phone call about her birthday that she'd described to her sister. Her dad hadn't made any attempt to contact her since, not that Megan had tried. He knew nothing about her separation, or anything from her recent life.

The lawn at the front of the house in which Megan had grown up was filled with knee-high yellowy-brown grass. The path to the front door was speckled with weeds and moss, as parts of the long grass had collapsed across. Curtains were pulled across the downstairs windows and the only sign of life was the faded 'no free newspapers' card taped to the inside of the front door.

Megan left the bike in the grass and tried the bell. When nobody answered, she knocked on the glass, and then flicked the letterbox flap a few times. The sound boomed, though there was still no reply. Not that Megan was surprised.

She unhooked her keys from the inside of her bag and tried the one she'd had since she'd turned eleven.

It was somehow both predictable and not that it worked. There would have been no desperate need to replace the door or the lock – and it didn't seem as if many other things around the house had been changed in the couple of decades since Megan had left home.

The hallway was dark and dusty. A light fitting hung with no bulb, and the raised border that stretched along the length of the wall was coated a crusty grey. Megan could taste the house as much as she could see it. Like opening an old, old book. There was the hook on the wall where she used to hang her coat but it was upside down, hanging from a single screw. It was familiar, yet not. A disjointed memory of something that once was.

'Dad...?'

Megan's voice bounced around the house, unanswered.

She closed the door and edged along the hall, finding herself spluttering as she partially inhaled a cobweb that stretched from one side of the hall to the other. She palmed it away, coughing as she tried to get it out of her mouth. There were more webs across the entrance to the stairs, plus a balled threaded mass in the corner above the door to the kitchen.

Another call of 'Dad...?' went unanswered, not that anyone inside could have ignored her coughs.

The old landline phone was on the wall, near the kitchen door. Megan used to stand in the cubby, talking to her friends – and, perhaps because of that faded postcard of a thought, she picked up the receiver and listened to the long hum of the dial tone.

It was impossible to ignore the creeping sense of unease. This was the part of the horror movie where Megan would be telling the lead to get out and run.

The kitchen sink was full of grubby plates, welded with grime. A saucepan was on the stove, filled with tomato sauce that hadn't been liquid in a long time. Greeny-white mould crusted the rim, with a metal spoon poking from the grimness.

The living room was dark and empty. Megan tried the dimmer switch but nothing happened. The light from her phone told her that the fittings were as empty of bulbs as the one in the hall. She touched the back of the armchair, only to come away with a palmful of dust. The room had been given over to the spiders and, as Megan backed out, she figured they were welcome to it.

The stairs creaked so perfectly that it was as if it was a sound effect. The school photos on the walls had been there since Megan and Nicola were girls – and hadn't been replaced. If it wasn't for the dust, it could have been two decades in the past.

Megan shivered. She didn't want to press on, but what choice did she have?

She could have checked her father's room first but didn't like where her thoughts were going. Instead, she opened the door to her old bedroom. She hadn't entered since she'd left home, though a part of her still expected the walls to be covered with posters covering up that light pink. There would be the stick-on heart she'd put in the window after winning it in a radio giveaway. The small television with a built-in video player would be on the shelf above the bed.

Except none of it was there. Instead, rows of unmarked boxes lined the walls and, even though she'd shown no interest in the years since she'd left, it was hard for Megan not to wonder what had happened to all her things.

Not that she dwelled too long.

Nicola's room was empty, the floorboards exposed, the sockets unscrewed as wires hung dangerously loose.

Next was the bathroom, which Megan couldn't bring herself to enter after opening the door. The walls were speckled with spiralled greeny-grey mould – and the bath was brown. The ick gave Megan the shivers.

One room to go.

Megan rested a hand on the door to her father's bedroom. There were always stories about people who died alone in flats and houses, and were found months later. There would be quotes from neighbours, saying they'd not seen that person in a while. Or from somebody at a charity, saying how sad it all was.

Always questions over why nobody had noticed sooner, or what the family were doing.

She could call the police, of course. Have them open the door. But Megan knew she wouldn't. She was the one who hadn't spoken to her dad in three years and there was nobody else to blame. She closed her eyes, took a breath – and opened the door.

TWENTY-SIX

The room was empty. Bedcovers were largely on the floor, as were the pillows. More cobwebs covered the curtains, plus the table next to the bed, where the water in a glass had gone brown.

It didn't seem as if anyone had slept in the house for a while.

'Dad...?'

Megan turned in a circle, peering through the gloom. He had to be somewhere.

She headed back down the stairs and checked the living room once more before returning to the front door. She was going to have to ask Nicola about the last time she'd seen their father.

Back outside, Megan closed the door and picked up the bike from the grass. She was about to set off when she noticed that, unlike everything *inside*, the bushes at the side of the house *had* been disturbed. The grass was long and unkempt but the shrub was squashed tight to the property line, as if it had been pushed past harshly and frequently.

Megan put the bike back down and swept her way through

the grass until she was at the side of the house. She followed the row of squat bushes past a dilapidated gate that could be stepped over and into the back garden.

She and Nicola had spent hours splashing in a paddling pool when they were really young. Megan had vague memories of a swing set near the back fence, and someone falling off and landing on the concrete. Was it her? Nicola? Did it happen somewhere else? At all? So many of those reminiscences felt incomplete and fuzzy.

There were no swings now, no paddling pool. Instead, almost incomprehensibly, a caravan was sitting on a stack of breeze blocks. It looked far too big to have made it into the space. There were no wheels, although a pile of tyres was stacked at the back. Much of the casing was rusty and, even to Megan's untrained eye, it wasn't level. The rear hung slightly lower than the front, as if there was something very heavy at one end. Ratty curtains were pulled across the windows, at least two of which had moss growing from the rubber seals.

Megan had never seen the caravan before.

She crossed the crumbling paving slabs and knocked on the door. It rattled in the frame and, for a moment, Megan thought it was going to spring open.

Nothing happened, so Megan open-palmed it a second time.

'Dad...? It's Megan.'

This time, there was movement. The caravan rocked from side to side as a grunt echoed from the inside. Megan took a couple of steps backwards and, a moment later, the door sprang outwards.

The dark thoughts of minutes before were gone as Megan stared up at her father.

'Dad! God! Will you put some clothes on?'

Megan's father blinked down at himself, and the pair of

light brown Y-fronts he was wearing. Aside from a single sock, it was the *only* thing he was wearing.

He craned in and squinted. 'Megs?'

'It's me, Dad. Can you get dressed?'

His pepper-pot stubble was uneven, his hair frizzier and greyer than she'd ever known. There was much more grey across his chest, like a massive brillo pad.

'D'you wanna come in?' he asked, nodding backwards towards the caravan. There was a hint of a slur to his voice and, though it was an innocent enough question, Megan could see the scraggle of bottles and binbags behind him.

'We can talk out here?' she said, more of a question than a command as she turned to a pair of plasticky garden chairs. They had once been white, and, though now covered in a green dusting, were better than nothing.

There might have been a nod, it was difficult to tell as Megan's dad headed back into the caravan. He left the door open as he stomped towards the end that was angled higher. It rocked back and forth, even more precariously.

Megan scooched on one of the chairs and tried to avoid looking towards the caravan.

A metal catapult sat on the ground at the side, alongside a pile of rocks each a little smaller than a golf ball. She wondered what her father needed it for, though the spread of nicks and chips in the brickwork at the back of the house gave her some idea.

There was a series of clinks and thumps from the caravan and then Megan's father eventually stumbled down the steps towards the spare seat. He was in jeans that had holes in both knees, plus a checked shirt on which he'd misaligned the buttons while trying to do it up. As he slipped into his chair, he took a sip from a grubby white mug – and Megan didn't need to ask what he was drinking. It certainly wasn't tea.

They sat for a while as Megan realised she had no idea what

to say to him. He was wriggling and tugging at the shirt, unable to figure out what he'd done wrong. His haggard skin and sunken eyes made him seem so old.

'How long have you had the caravan?' Megan asked, as she struggled to know what to say.

Her dad took another sip from the mug and tried to focus on her. There was something glassy and distant as he replied with, 'Alf. You know Alf, don't you?'

Megan didn't – though it wasn't worth saying so, and it wouldn't have made any difference anyway. He began a long-winded story of the aforementioned Alf, whose brother was trying to get rid of a caravan, except it wasn't his brother – and maybe it was his friend? And maybe he wasn't trying to get rid, he was trying to sell.

The story rambled through a cast of characters, frequently contradicting itself, and never once answering the question of when he actually got it. Megan let it all go. This was one of the reasons why she'd not visited in so long. Why she didn't answer the phone if it showed a landline number with a Hollicombe Bay 01 number.

She'd zoned out as his story drifted to an end. He had a gulp of his drink and then added: 'Have you seen your sister?'

'I'm staying with her for now,' Megan said. 'I broke up with Paul.'

He nodded along, though lacked anything to indicate he understood. She could have told him anything and got the same reaction.

'Do you know Nicola has one of your chequebooks?' Megan asked. There had been no build-up but she doubted it would matter.

It took her father a few seconds to react at all. He had been staring aimlessly at the ground, or maybe the catapult.

'She has a café,' he said. 'Did you know that?'

'I know, Dad. I've been helping out there. I'm asking if you know she has one of your chequebooks? All the cheques have been signed and I'm wondering if you did it.'

He was nodding, though that didn't mean much.

'She also has bank statements in your name, plus a utility bill. I wanted to make sure you knew.'

He had stopped nodding, but was still staring vacantly.

'The stubs make it seem like she's had thousands from you, Dad. *Tens* of thousands. I'm asking if you *gave* her the money?'

Megan's dad let out a long sigh and then started rubbing his eyes. 'Always about money with you two, isn't it?'

'I don't want your money, Dad. I'm asking if you gave Nicola your chequebook.'

Still, no answer came. He continued to stare at the ground to the point that Megan crouched and picked up the catapult. It was heavier than she thought, with a springy, rubbery pouch.

'What's with the catapult?' Megan asked.

This time, the reply was instant. 'Squirrels. Bloody things. The grey ones. They're killing off the red ones, do you know that?' He waved a hand around, presumably indicating the garden. 'They're everywhere.'

Megan passed him the catapult and he began twirling it in his fingers. As she watched, Megan shivered while a memory slithered around her mind. Something like this had happened before. Something with her father and a catapult. She'd been really young and they'd been near a river somewhere. It was all vague flashes, nothing clear.

'Do you ever see anyone?' Megan asked.

'Cliff,' he replied immediately. 'Takes me out on his boat sometimes. Down the coast to Whitecliff and back. Good as gold, he is. Only one who's ever stuck by me.'

There might have been a dig at Megan there, though there seemed little point in rising to it. Cliff was a name about whom Megan had more vague memories. He was 'Uncle Cliff' when she and Nicola had been younger and he used to bring them chocolate selection boxes at Christmas.

'Nicest guy in the world, Cliff,' her father continued. 'Do anything for anyone. He lives on his boat now.'

It felt as if another long-winded rambling anecdote might be on the way but, instead, it was as if a switch had been flicked and he was onto his next thought.

'How's Jessie?' he asked.

Megan's first thought was that she was pregnant via her drama teacher and that big decisions and big trouble was coming sooner rather than later.

She never said that. 'She's OK.'

That got a nod and, for the first time since they'd sat, Megan's father caught her eye. He'd been interested in the answer.

'I heard something about you pushing over one of her friends in town,' Megan said.

His eyes narrowed. 'Her friend was smoking! I told her to put it out.'

Megan sighed silently. She could picture how it had gone, with some weird, red-faced old man snatching a cigarette from a teenager. Regardless of whether he'd meant well, it had been a poor decision.

What Jessie couldn't have known was that her grandfather had a mortal enemy when it came to smokers and smoking. Everyone in town knew that the fire which had ripped through Megan's orchestra class had been started by a cigarette in the caretaker's office. Her father's best friend, Michael, had been caretaker at the school for more than fifteen years when he was sent to prison for manslaughter. It was all over the news after the fire.

It had led to her dad's childhood friend dying in prison barely four months after he'd been sent there. Nothing had been the same after that.

Which was why her father hated everything to do with smoking.

The only shame was that he hadn't turned against drink at the same time.

'I'll have a word with Jessie,' Megan found herself saying. 'I'll explain the smoking thing.'

He didn't deserve it, not really – but then Jessie didn't deserve to have two useless grandfathers in her life.

Megan had already told her about the fire itself. The way it started, and the link to their family, was simply another detail.

'The money's for her,' Megan's father said from nothing.

It took Megan a few seconds to realise he meant the cheques.

'Jessie gets everything when I go,' he added. 'I've never touched the life insurance from your mum.'

'What about everything Michael left you?'

That was the other thing about Michael's death in prison. Everything he owned went to Megan's father. From what Megan could tell, much of it had been drunk. Her father didn't deny any of that.

'She's going to Cambridge,' Megan's dad said. It was the most animated he'd been since Megan arrived.

'Who? Jessie?'

Her dad wasn't listening. 'It's expensive,' he replied. 'That's what Nic said. She needed money for tests, uniforms, fees, a place to stay. She asked if I'd sign the cheques so she could pay for Jessie without having to keep coming back.'

If nothing else, *he* believed it to be true. Except, if Jessie was going to Cambridge, wouldn't she have mentioned it? Or Nicola? Those who went to a prestigious university weren't known for playing it down, let alone their parents. In the conversations Megan had with her niece, university hadn't come up.

Megan glanced past her father, towards the open caravan

door. A bottle of Jack was lying sideways on the ground, a step or two past the entrance. As he picked up his mug and had another gulp, she knew there would be more inside.

'It would've been there for you, too,' he said. 'Was always for the grandkids.'

'You know I can't have children,' Megan said quietly.

'That's what they told your mother – and then she had you two.'

Megan closed her eyes, honing in on the distant screech of the gulls. It was much quieter in the old part of town, where most of the noise came from farmers and their tractors up on the hill. She stood and rubbed her eyes, the tiredness suddenly hitting her. There had been too many late nights and early mornings.

'I don't want to talk about this, Dad,' Megan said.

She took a step back towards the side of the house but he stopped her with a simple three words.

'I have cancer.'

When Megan turned to look at him, he continued talking.

'The colon and the prostate. Dunno if that counts as one or two cancers. Two for the price of one, huh?'

Megan wavered. Her life had started with tragedy as her mother gave birth to her. Then there was the fire, then the loss of her father's best friend had led him to the bottle, and Megan to leaving town. She'd thought she was going to start a family elsewhere, but then her husband had got her best friend pregnant – and here she was back where it all began.

She sat and cradled her head in her hands, massaging her temples. It was too much. Wouldn't any one of those things have been enough?

'How long have you known?' she asked, with a croak.

'Three months.'

'How's the treatment?'

When no reply came, Megan let go of her head and sat up

straighter. She'd probably known the answer before asking the question.

'Told 'em I don't want it. What's the point, huh? I've been lucky to last this long: we all know that.'

This time it was Megan's father who risked that glance towards the caravan and what was likely a mountain of glass within. There was no lie and they both knew it. He'd been pickling his liver for years.

'Does Nic know?' Megan asked.

'Why'd you think I gave her the chequebook?'

It was hard to know why Nicola hadn't told Megan about their father's cancer. Actually, it probably wasn't hard to know. If Megan knew, she'd have visited their dad, who would've likely told her about the money.

Megan slumped and felt unable to speak. Was there anyone in her life who would simply tell her the truth?

Her father pushed himself up with a grunted heave. He lofted his mug and grumbled his way into the caravan, before returning not long after. When he sat again, he went back to sipping the drink.

'Don't suppose you fancy going to the offy, do you?' he asked.

'No, Dad.'

Megan sat and watched him fiddle with the catapult, in among drinking whatever was in his mug. She tried to come up with the words – but didn't want to add to all the lies with more of her own. Was she sorry? She didn't know. Would she miss him? Maybe the father who existed before his best friend killed himself.

Except that person was a long time gone.

It was a few minutes until Megan stood again. She was three steps back towards the front of the house when her father called out.

'Will you... uh... visit again?'

'I don't know,' Megan replied.

He croaked and Megan didn't turn, even though she thought there was a hint of a sob there. 'I'm still your dad,' he said, with a rasp. 'If you ever need me...'

The sentence wasn't complete but neither was the sentiment. Megan *had* needed him many times – and for the past twenty years, he'd never once been there.

'Bye, Dad,' Megan said. And then she walked away.

TWENTY-SEVEN

The bus rattled around the country lanes, jumping in and out of potholes like a mobile bouncy castle. Megan had started the journey with her head resting on the window – but it hadn't been long before she'd accidentally side-butted the glass and given that up as a bad idea.

Megan had a double seat to herself and had something of a stomach ache as the green blurred past the windows. She'd taken the bike back to Nicola's, then headed for the bus stop, before texting her sister to say she wasn't going to be at the café that day. Because she couldn't think of a proper reason, Megan hadn't bothered to give one. She'd ignored the 'u ok?' reply, plus the follow-ups, and the missed call from the unknown number she assumed was Pam's.

A man up ahead heaved himself up by hanging onto the rail as he grabbed for the push button on the other side of the aisle. He ended up doing something of an impromptu pole dance as the vehicle clunked down and up across yet another patch of uneven tarmac. After dinging the bell, he straightened himself while staring straight ahead, pretending nobody had seen.

Cancer.

Her dad had cancer. Megan vaguely remembered a time when she was nine or ten and a kid from school's mum had cancer. There had been an assembly about it – and Megan had gone home terrified that cancer would strike down her father, leaving her and Nicola as orphans.

And now, thirty or so years on, it was true.

There was no terror any longer. Megan had always assumed she would get a call one day from Nicola, the police, or a hospital to say it had happened. Except it felt different now she knew that call would be on the way in months. That there was a definitive date.

There was a massive difference between *choosing* not to see a person – and not *being able* to see them.

Megan needed to talk to Jessie about any possible university plans, not to mention checking in to see how she was going with the pregnancy. Before that, she wanted to see whatever was going on with her sister's second café for herself.

The bus continued to rattle along the narrow lanes, stopping intermittently in what felt like the middle of nowhere. The town of Steeple's End was further along the coast, part-way between Hollicombe Bay and Whitecliff. In terms of distance, it wasn't far – though there was no direct road.

Megan sat with her thoughts for almost forty minutes, until the sea re-emerged into view and a row of cottages appeared. The bus pulled up at the harbour and Megan followed a family along the aisle. A woman was lugging suitcases from the rack as her husband stood on the pavement, phone in hand, turning in a circle. 'I think it's *that* way,' he said, pointing towards the centre as his kids hauled cases from the bus.

After waiting until they were off, Megan thanked the driver and then stepped into the heat. She'd spent much longer with her father than she thought, then more time waiting for the bus. It was early afternoon and the streets were rammed with families ambling up and down the seafront. Some had stopped to sit on the benches and watch the boats head out from shore; others were shuffling around the cramped beach, trying to find a free spot to claim. There were signs up for a sandcastle competition at the weekend and a craft beer festival towards the end of the summer.

Megan weaved her way through the throng. Nicola said they'd taken on a site near the market, so Megan followed the signs towards the centre. There were people sitting outside the tearooms, more in the beer garden at the back of a pub. Tourist numbers might be down in Hollicombe Bay – but its neighbour didn't seem to share many of the same problems.

As Megan was passing under the arch leading into the market, her phone started to buzz. There seemed little point in ignoring her any longer, so she found a quiet corner and pressed to answer Nicola's call.

A surprised, 'Oh, you're there,' came, before Megan offered a weak 'hi'.

'I was beginning to worry,' Nicola said.

'I'm fine. Tell Pam I'm sorry. I think I needed a bit of time to myself.'

It felt like a lie, even though it wasn't.

Nicola sounded as if she was busy. There was a mumble of something Megan didn't catch and then: 'Where are you?'

'I've gone for a walk. I'll be back later.' Megan waited for a response that didn't come, so she added: 'I don't think working at the café is for me. I need a rest from people.'

There was no instant reply and Megan checked the screen to make sure the call hadn't dropped. 'Maybe that's for the best,' Nicola replied, although she hadn't concealed the hint of annoyance.

'Where are you?' Megan asked.

Her sister sounded surprised by the question. 'At the new place in Steeple's End. I was late getting here because I had to cover the morning at the café.'

Perhaps she hadn't meant it to sound so spiky, though it had.

Megan almost told her she was around the corner, but there was something else in her sister's voice that Megan recognised.

It was a lie.

When they'd been girls, Megan had always been able to tell when Nicola was lying. It was hard to describe why, other than that her voice changed. Perhaps the tone was slightly higher, or the cadence a little quicker? Megan had largely forgotten.

It was never the big lies, always the inconsequential ones. She would tell people at school that she had size six feet, even though Megan knew they were four. She once said she'd seen Howard from Take That in town, but that thing with her voice had given her away.

Just like it had on the phone.

Megan said she was going to go – and then she did. She kept hold of the phone for a short while, wondering if there would be a follow-up text. When there wasn't, Megan headed into the market, and out the other side.

She didn't have to go far to find a closed shopfront with white paper blocking the windows. A loud grinding boomed from the inside as shoppers walked in an arc to avoid the escaping dust. Megan stopped next to the arch that led back into the market. A part of her had thought the whole idea of a second café might have been invented, especially considering Nicola and Ben's financial issues.

She was about to see if there was a sign in any of the windows to indicate if this was the place her sister had bought, when the door bumped open.

Trevor strode out, his lip still discoloured. He had a tape measure in his hand and his jeans were coated with sawdust. He walked quickly across the street, where he unlocked a car that was parked on double-yellows and got in. The engine growled and then he roared away before any eagle-eyed traffic warden came around the corner. It wasn't the same SUV as from the night at the sweet shop – but Megan was more interested in why he was there at all. Her sister had been at his farmhouse, and now he was at the shop she'd seemingly bought in a different town. There had to be some link between them.

With Trevor gone, Megan crossed to the worksite. There were raised voices from the inside, plus a muffled radio. Nothing particularly out of the ordinary. A small sign sat in the corner of the furthest window, with 'coming soon' in large letters and 'Nic's Café', underneath.

The front door had been closed since Trevor's exit but it smelled like a sawmill near the windows. The view inside was blocked by A4 pieces of paper taped to the inside of the glass. Everything was uneven, like a bad primary school project.

Megan was peeking through a gap into the café when a loud bang made her jump. There was a burr of machinery, momentary silence, and then shouting in a language she didn't know. The gap in the paper was slim but Megan shuffled a fraction sideways, which gave her a better angle towards what looked like a counter.

The large man she'd seen at the back of Nic's original café was there, pointing towards something Megan couldn't see, while shouting with such fury that spit was flying from his lips. He banged hard on the counter and balled his fist, screeching something else, before finally lowering his hands.

It was then that someone touched Megan on the shoulder.

'Fancy seeing you here.'

TWENTY-EIGHT

Trevor's top lip had started to heal – and his new front tooth gleamed unnaturally white. Megan wasn't sure how she'd missed it the other night.

He loomed over her, staring down curiously. It felt threatening, but it might have simply been his size. He must have re-parked the car somewhere else and doubled back to the worksite.

'I was in town and figured I'd come see how Nic's new café is coming along,' Megan said. It wasn't even a lie. 'She's always talking about it, so I figured I'd see for myself.'

The voices from inside the café had gone quiet, leaving only stifled eighties hits from the radio.

'It's a bit of a mess inside,' Trevor said. 'It's probably not safe, plus there will be all sorts of insurance things about who's allowed on-site and all that.'

Megan nodded along. She hadn't asked to look inside, but he'd taken it like that.

'Do you need a lift back to town?' Trevor asked, motioning in the vague direction of the seafront. 'I'm heading that way in a minute.'

'I'm fine,' Megan replied.

'No worries. I'd heard you don't drive, so—'

'Who told you that?'

Crinkles appeared in Trevor's forehead as he realised he'd misspoken. 'Didn't you say something about it at book club the other night?'

'I don't think so.'

Trevor feigned thinking about it. 'I'm sure you did.'

Megan knew she definitely hadn't. Unless she absolutely had to, she never told anyone about not being able to drive. Inevitably, they would then ask how many times she had failed her test. It meant Nicola or Ben must have told him – but there seemed little point in pushing it on the street.

'I guess you're right,' she said.

Trevor nodded along, grateful for the out. He angled towards the café, wanting to get around her but not wanting to ask her to move.

With a confidence she didn't feel, Megan stood her ground. 'I'm sure I saw you the other night...?'

Trevor had been looking past her but took half a step away and stared back. 'What do you mean?'

'At the back of the sweet shop. It was really late... well, early, I guess.'

His eyes narrowed a fraction and he rolled his jaw from side to side. That new front tooth beamed brightly. And then he was smiling.

'I've had a few issues with the noise of the machines during the day. It was putting customers off, so we've been experimenting with doing things overnight.'

Megan nodded along, though they both knew the machines weren't the point. If they were disruptively loud during the day, they would surely be the same at night when people were trying to sleep. Plus, even though Megan had heard the machines, they hadn't been *that* loud. Not up there with the general hubbub of a seaside town in the middle of summer.

'Who's the man inside?' Megan asked, pointing towards the café.

'You should probably ask your sister.'

The reply had come so quickly that Megan needed a second to absorb it. She managed an: 'I'll do that' as Trevor continued to stand over her for a few seconds more. It felt as if something had shifted.

She wanted to ask about his tooth that she'd found by the stream that was still in her sock. Had Sophia kicked it out on that bank? And, if so, why? The tooth was the only real thing she could cling onto.

After initially motioning to head inside, Trevor backed off. 'Lift's still on offer if you want it?' he said.

'I'll get the bus.'

'Suit yourself.'

Trevor's gaze lingered on Megan for a second too long and then he pulled a set of keys from his pocket. He removed his phone from the other and started walking towards the seafront, only pausing for a quick glance over his shoulder to see if Megan was still watching him. Which she was.

When he was out of sight, Megan checked if she could see any more through the gaps in the disjointed paper. Even the radio had gone quiet and there didn't appear to be anyone there.

A minute or so later and her phone started to ring, with Nicola's name on the screen. It felt a safe assumption that Trevor had called or texted her. Nicola would know her little lie about being at the second café had been exposed and would want to explain. Megan allowed the call to ring off as she headed back towards the harbour.

The chip shop had opened for lunch, with threads of salty vinegar drifting enticingly along the back alleys of Steeple's End.

Megan was on the slightly longer route around town as a youngster on a skateboard bolted off the kerb, raced across the road and kick-flipped up onto the other side. His mates cheered as one of them filmed. Past them, a woman was arguing with a traffic warden about the definition of an hour, while her husband hid behind her.

It was easier to see in person – but, in contrast, Hollicombe Bay really was as Daniel had described to Megan. It felt old-fashioned and at least two decades behind even its nearest neighbour – and that was before mentioning the single phone mast. Perhaps the residents were happy with the quaintness, but Megan could see why the town felt like it was at a crossroads.

A family of four were at the bus stop: two young children sitting on their Trunkis, the father impatiently sighing at his phone, the mother trying to convince one of the children to stop swinging his legs.

'You'll fall off,' she told him, despite evidence to the contrary.

Megan smiled amiably at the other woman as they waited in line and it wasn't long until the bus pulled in. After letting everyone off, the kids ran to the back seat as the parents followed. Megan took a spot near the front and closed her eyes.

It was hard to put the pieces together. Her sister had some sort of link to Trevor – and had, at the very least, told him that Megan couldn't drive. It felt unlikely that was the only thing they would have talked about.

And Megan still had his tooth.

She really needed to talk to Sophia.

The bus chuntered its way out of Steeple's End and onto the country lanes. A trickle of people stepped on and off at the various stops until they reached the out-of-town retail park, just off the bypass.

Megan was staring at her phone, trying to read an article for the fourth time while barely getting past the first paragraph, when someone stopped in front of her. Megan assumed they were going to ask if it was OK to sit next to her when she realised it was Jessie.

'You all right?' Jessie asked. 'You were miles away.'

Megan blinked up to her. 'What are you doing here?'

'This is the college stop.'

It wasn't only Jessie in the aisle, a group of a dozen or so young women had milled behind her. Megan had forgotten the retail park backed onto the campus.

Jessie's friends continued past, towards the back of the bus.

'Are you staying on 'til Mum's house?' Jessie asked.

'I think so.'

'Good. 'Cos when we get back, I've got something really important to tell you.'

TWENTY-NINE

Jessie joined her friends near the back of the bus as Megan went back to pretending to look at her phone.

The students exited the bus one or two at a time along various stops on the route back to Hollicombe Bay. There were waves and 'see ya's as the bus grew emptier. Eventually, it dropped onto the seafront and then grumbled its way back up the hill on the other side until it was time to get off.

Megan was up first, though Jessie joined her as they climbed down to the pavement.

'I didn't want anyone to overhear,' Jessie said, as the cloudy exhaust of bus fumes cleared. She was beaming, much happier than the night before.

'What's happened?' Megan asked.

'I'm not pregnant. I came on overnight. That test must've been a blip – or hormones, like you said.'

She was bouncing – and Megan didn't blame her.

She wasn't sure what to say, other than: 'As long as you're happy.'

'I texted Lucas and he messaged right back. Said he'd been away with no signal.'

It sounded suspiciously made up – but Megan didn't bother to point it out. There were bigger issues.

'I don't want to sound like your mum,' she said, which automatically made her sound like Jessie's mum, 'but, I mean... you're not going to continue seeing him in that way are you?'

She fought back the cringe at how she'd said 'in that way'. No wonder young people thought adults were repressed weirdos.

'No,' Jessie replied instantly, although the follow-up came almost as quickly. 'I mean, well, no.'

'It's just he's—'

'I know. Too old for me.'

There was something about the way she said it that made it sound as if she *didn't* know. Not really. Older men with teenage girls was something that had seemingly been a thing forever. Rarely the other way around.

'Thanks for everything with Mum and the test last night,' Jessie added. 'It's a good job I didn't tell her. Good job you were there.'

Until that moment, Megan had forgotten that her sister believed her to be pregnant.

'Can I ask you something?' Megan replied. 'Your mum told me you were having trouble with your food again. I don't want to—'

'It's fine,' Jessie said, as she squirmed and looked to the floor.

It wasn't particularly Megan's business and there seemed little point in pressing. Instead, she changed the subject: 'Do you know what you're doing *after* school?'

Jessie stopped twisting as she squinted into the sun. They were still at the bus stop. 'I don't know. About a year ago, Dad was trying to push me into aiming for Oxford or Cambridge. Mum reckoned that's what *his* dad wanted for him. I got eights and nines at GCSE but...' She tailed off and then, because of Megan's apparent confusion, quickly added: 'That's As and A-stars. But I don't think it's really for me. Britney's going to drama school and I wanted to apply there. They're already full but I was thinking about a year at art college and then try to transfer. Apparently, people do it all the time. Or Will's taking a year out to work at a turtle sanctuary in Ecuador. I was gonna suggest that to Mum but she'd go mental.'

Megan nodded along. There was something bizarre about forcing young people to make long-lasting decisions when they barely knew who they were.

Also, there was no apparent pressing need for the seventy grand Nicola had taken from their father under the pretext it was for Jessie's education. It didn't seem as if Jessie knew anything about what had been done in her name.

'I saw my dad earlier,' Megan said. 'Your granddad. I asked him about what happened with your friend. I heard he shook her, something like that?'

That got a curious nod.

'I'm not going to defend him,' Megan added. 'But there is a bit of context you don't know.'

They sat on the bench of the bus stop as Megan explained how her father's best friend had been the caretaker at the school when the fire had started in his room. He had killed himself in prison after pleading guilty to starting it.

'He was already on a warning for smoking at the school,' Megan said. 'And then his cigarette started the fire. Dad's had a thing about people smoking ever since. He recognised you and said he saw your friend smoking. Something in him just kind of snapped.'

Jessie nodded along and it was then that Megan realised her niece and her friends were too young to smoke even if it had happened right then, let alone a year or so before. The legal age had been younger when Megan was growing up, not that it had made any difference. Megan had once paid an older girl 50p to buy her a packet of cigarettes from the newsagent when she and her friends were fourteen or so. She didn't even like smoking and had given it up before she was legally allowed to start.

'I didn't know Granddad knew the caretaker who started it,' she said.

'No reason you would.'

She considered things for a moment more. 'He shoved her pretty hard.'

'I'm not saying Dad was right, just explaining that it wasn't as random and mad as it might have seemed. He's lucky you didn't call the police.'

'Why didn't he say something?'

Megan sighed at that. She could have spent her adult lifetime trying to justify why her father made poor decisions. 'You know he's an alcoholic – but he functions at various levels. A lot of the time, you wouldn't know – and he can even be charming and nice sometimes. At least, he used to be. But it's still there and that means he makes impulsive, bad choices, even on an otherwise good day.'

Jessie took a moment to think on it. Megan had read somewhere that young people weren't particularly into alcohol nowadays. This whole thing was probably bemusing to her.

'Is that why you and Mum don't see him anymore?' Jessie asked. 'She said he drinks too much but I didn't know more than that.'

Was it Megan's place to tell her more? She decided it was. 'Our mum died when I was a baby and your mum was only a year old. Dad raised us himself – but he leant on his friends to help. Then, after the fire, something changed. *He* changed. When his friend killed himself, it all got worse. His friend left him his house and money in the will but Dad was drinking all the time. So, yeah, me and your mum figured we were better without him in our lives.'

'That's why you moved to Whitecliff?'

'One of the reasons. It was clean break.' Megan didn't add

that it was also a break from her father. A completely new beginning.

'Why did Mum stay?'

It took Megan a few seconds to realise she had never talked to her sister about it. Her way of dealing with the fire and their father's descent was to get away; Nicola's had been the opposite.

'You'd have to ask her,' Megan replied. 'I don't know.'

A bus started to slow as it neared the stop and Megan waved and shook her head to say they weren't waiting.

'Let's get home,' Megan said, standing and leading her niece across the road.

They passed a few houses until they were at the gateposts of Nicola's house. Megan blinked and she was talking to the police on the phone, trying to remember the address. Another blink, and she was back.

'Maybe I can do something for you sometime?' Jessie said.

Megan looked at her for a moment, wondering if she'd missed something.

'Because of the test and Mum,' Jessie added.

'Don't worry about it.'

Megan wondered whether she should press the point about Jessie and her drama teacher – except she hesitated too long and her niece was already halfway along the path to the house. There was always the danger of pushing Jessie further towards him, and Megan needed Jessie to keep trusting her.

When they got inside, Jessie went for the stairs as Megan kicked off her shoes.

'Oh, you're back too,' Nicola called from the living room. When Megan entered, her sister was on the sofa, typing on a laptop.

There was a few seconds of a stand-off in which Megan knew her sister wanted to be annoyed at her for ditching work without any sort of warning. There was also an impasse in that

Nicola had needlessly lied about being in Steeple's End at the same time Megan had *actually* been there.

Nicola removed her reading glasses and sat up a fraction straighter. 'Are you all right?' she asked. 'We were worried you'd had some sort of... I don't know... *breakdown.*' She gulped and then added: 'Not a breakdown but, y'know...'

Megan wasn't sure she *did* know.

'Can you stop saying "breakdown"? I just needed a bit of time to myself.'

There was a twitch in Nicola's expression that meant there was more. 'I spoke to Paul this morning,' she said, unable to meet her sister's eye.

Megan almost thought she'd misheard the name of her husband. 'Why?'

'Well... I called him. I was worried about you. Everyone is. We already were – and then you took off this morning and you weren't answering your phone.'

'But why Paul? I told him not to contact me – and then you went and called him. You know what he did.'

Megan bit her lip to stop herself continuing. She'd already been accused of having a breakdown – and that was before she knew her sister had talked to her husband behind her back.

'Of course I know. It's not about that. But I didn't know who else to talk to. I don't want you to do anything *stupid.*'

It was clear enough what she meant by that – and Megan wondered if she'd really been that unpredictable. Binning off work and disappearing for a morning probably didn't help. That followed everything with the young woman in the stream and the police.

'Paul's worried about you,' Nicola said.

'Not worried enough to stop himself shagging my best friend.'

'I know. It's just he said your house is empty if you want to live in it while you figure out what to do. He's moved as much of his stuff out as he can. He's, um—'

'He's moved in with Lucy.'

Nicola squirmed slightly on the spot. 'Right. I mean— Yeah. And I know how hard it is for you to be back here, with the school, Dad, and everything else. So the option's there if you wanted to go back to Whitecliff.'

Megan wasn't sure if this meant she was being kicked out – and something in her expression must have said as much, because Nicola quickly added: 'You don't have to leave. You're welcome to stay.'

The words said one thing, though the way Nicola's eyebrows twitched said another.

'Do you want me to go?' Megan asked.

'Of course not, but you don't seem very happy. Ben said you'd met Sophia and you thought she was the girl from the stream. Then you ran off today. We want what's best for you. If that means going back to Whitecliff, where you have your support network, then we understand.'

It was probably innocent enough, except Megan's support network had been her husband and her best friend. It would be hard to return to the house she and Paul owned in Whitecliff to pretend nothing had happened. Not that it had been easy to return to Hollicombe Bay and live in her sister's attic. There were spectres everywhere.

'I didn't tell him about...'

Nicola patted her belly as Megan remembered, again, that her sister thought she was pregnant. She could put her right now, say that she'd taken a second test that was negative. Or copy what Jessie had told her at the bus stop, and say she had started her period overnight.

Her sister was staring, waiting for some sort of response, and Megan found herself sidestepping the previous night's lie about the test.

'I'll think about going back to Whitecliff,' she said. 'I need a few days. Maybe after the weekend?'

It was vague enough. Chuck in a few maybes and think abouts, and people would hear what they wanted.

'That's good,' Nicola replied.

'And... I'm not going back to the café. Tell Pam I said sorry and that it's been good working with her. Lakshmi, too.'

Nicola nodded along, although she didn't seem particularly happy with it. 'We'll figure it out,' she said.

'Maybe we can do something tonight?' Megan asked, trying to sound upbeat. 'Trip to the pub, that sort of thing? Me and you like the old days?'

Also a reason to ask properly about what was going on with Sophia and the rest of the kitchen staff. And about their dad's seventy grand.

She didn't want to specifically say 'No Ben' – but Nicola was shaking her head anyway. 'That sounds great but it's the business association meeting at the Labour Club tonight. All the owners in town have them once a month.' A pause. 'You and Jess will have the house to yourselves. Ben and I will both be there and we're never back before eleven. Might give you a bit of time to think about things. We'll do the pub another night.'

'Sounds good,' Megan replied, although that was suddenly the last thing on her mind.

If all the business owners were going to be in one place until at least eleven, that meant they definitely wouldn't be in their homes.

THIRTY

Cycling in the evening felt like floating. There was nobody at all, and certainly no drivers, on the dirt tracks at the back of Hollicombe Bay. The trails weren't quite roads and had been carved into the land to allow farmers to move across the vast expanses of green more easily. As farming had dropped off over the years, the tracks had been adopted by hikers and bikers as a way to avoid traffic.

Megan stopped at a stile for a minute or so and peered across the bay. The sun was on its way down and an orangey glow crescented across the lower half of the sky as dark winged dots of gulls circled the bay. Everything felt calmer up and away from the town itself. Megan was so transfixed that she had to remind herself she was out for a reason.

The white church came into sight as Megan reached a locked metal gate that blocked cars from using the path. She wasn't confident enough to cycle around using the narrow gap, so she clambered off the bike and walked it through.

Another couple of minutes on and she was pedalling past the graveyard to the side of the church. The lane opened out onto the road itself and, as it was so open, Megan left the bike in the shade of a tree in the corner of the graveyard.

She turned to look across to Trevor's farmhouse. There were no vehicles on the drive and no lights on inside the main building. From what Megan could see, there was nobody there.

She had thought on everything her sister had said that afternoon and was coming around to the idea that it might be better for her to return to Whitecliff after all.

Except, she couldn't forget seeing Sophia in the stream. She swayed from knowing it had unquestionably happened, to wondering if people had a point when they kept saying she'd been through a lot. The mini panic attack in the courtyard at the back of the café hadn't helped.

Megan's only link to something having definitely happened was seeing the girl in the stream, plus Trevor's tooth on the side of the bank, and his dental surgery. She didn't know where to find Sophia by herself – but she *did* know where Trevor lived, and knew he wasn't going to be home until at least eleven.

The last time Megan had been at the farmhouse, she hadn't thought to look for security devices but, this time, she zoomed in with her phone's camera. If there were any, then she couldn't see anything obvious pinned to the walls.

Megan crossed the road slowly, partially because she was still looking for cameras but also because she remembered Trevor said he'd tripped over a dog. The trip might have been a lie, but she suspected the dog, or dogs, was real. There had been no sign of animals when she had last trespassed on his land – and Megan hoped any were securely locked inside the farmhouse.

She became bolder as she continued along his drive. If there were cameras, they were well hidden – and the same was true of pets. If she didn't know better, she'd have almost said the farmhouse was abandoned. Some of the upstairs curtains were pulled but there was little sign of life.

Megan moved quicker along the driveway, looking for anything that might be of interest. She had no idea what she was searching for – but there had to be something that linked Trevor to whatever she'd seen.

The front door was locked, as expected. Megan tapped the glass, partly to see if Trevor might be inside.

Oh, what a surprise you live here. I didn't know. Anyway, I used to come to the white church as a girl and was wondering how long it had been closed.

That sort of thing.

There was a faint sound of a dog woofing somewhere inside, although it wasn't anywhere near the door.

Megan glanced up and around, still looking for cameras, before starting to hunt under the nearby rocks and plant pots for a spare key. She'd never seen herself as a breaking-and-entering sort, although she supposed nobody did. Technically, if she found a key it wouldn't be breaking, right?

It would be harder to explain being inside if she was caught.

Not that there was a spare key anyway.

The windows were coated with a grimy translucent brown on seemingly the inside and out. Megan tried peeping through but couldn't see much other than a hazy murk. A part of her thought Sophia might be living at the farmhouse, although she had no proof or justification for such an idea. Another part, the quieter one for now, was telling her this was desperation. That admitting nobody had been in that stream would mean conceding she really did have a problem.

The back door was locked, though the barking dog felt closer than it had at the front. Megan checked under the door-mat, but there was nothing there. There was an open window above and she found herself eyeing the drainpipe, before coming around, somewhat, to her senses.

That quieter voice was getting louder.

The rest of the plot was more run-down than the farmhouse

itself. A wide greenhouse was towards the other side of a soil patch, though, even from a distance, Megan could see half-a-dozen broken glass panels. It didn't look as if anything had grown inside for years.

A harvesting rake from the back of a tractor had been aban-doned part-way across another field, while a tatty, torn scare-crow was on its back not far past.

The only other structure of note was a barn close to the treeline at the end of the drive. Though Megan could tell it had once been a maroon red, much of the paint had peeled or scratched away to reveal a scuffed metal.

Megan spotted the SUV as soon as the darkness within the barn morphed into a greying gloom. The doors of the barn were open but the vehicle was tucked out of sight, unspottable from the road. She approached it slowly, just in case, but there was nobody inside the vehicle. The dent in the back bumper was as clear as the first time Megan had spied it at the back of the sweet shop. The same vehicle parked a little outside the café's courtyard when she'd seen Sophia. Megan had first seen Trevor driving it, and then it had been parked on his drive. Except it had been the big man at the back of the café who'd taken it second time around. The pair were linked, somehow. And so were Trevor and Nicola. Plus all of them and Sophia.

Megan hadn't expected anything to happen but she tried the passenger-side door anyway – and it clunked open. She froze, half expecting an alarm or flashing lights but there was nothing.

The vehicle smelled vaguely of something fruity, perhaps one of those vape juice things. There were sweet wrappers in the door compartment, more in the centre, underneath the handbrake. A phone mount was stuck to the windscreen, with a cable trailing to the cigarette lighter socket. There was a small crack in the windscreen that Megan first thought was on the inside until she touched it. In case of fingerprints, and probably because she'd seen too many crime shows, Megan rubbed the glass with her sleeve.

She clambered back out of the vehicle and checked the back seat, where there wasn't much other than a tartan blanket that had seen better days.

Megan fiddled with the boot, trying to find the clasp before it popped open. There were more blankets in the back and Megan was about to close it when she spotted the flash of pink. It was partially obscured by a blanket covered in dog hair. A part of her knew what it was before she picked it up. Her heart fluttered a fraction.

It felt so long ago now but, among the green of the forest, something had gleamed a different shade. Megan had touched it back then and, as she lifted the pink top from the vehicle, she saw it again.

Pressed into the centre of the material was a greasy handprint.

Megan's handprint.

THIRTY-ONE

Ah, ah, ah, ah. Stay-in a-live. Stay-in a-live.

Megan had made the marks on Sophia's chest when she'd been trying to revive her.

After all the confusion, all the people who said openly or privately that she was losing it, or having a breakdown, here was proof that it had happened.

The material was smooth, some sort of imitation silk or satin. Megan pressed her hand to the shape of the print and could see how it matched the size of her hand. Her own palm presumably having touched the dirt at the time. She'd had those visions of the woman leaping up and gasping for air – and then Megan would promise to clean her top and everything would have been fine. Except none of that had happened. The woman, *Sophia*, had simply disappeared.

Megan checked underneath the dog blanket, but there was nothing other than more hairs. The inside panels were crusted with crumbs and some sort of gum that Megan ignored.

No matter. She had the top. Everything that she'd seen in the woods had really happened. Now she had to find Sophia to ask what had gone on.

Megan closed the doors of the vehicle and took a step back towards the main entrance. It was as she clipped her toe on what turned out to be a large hinge that she realised something was built into the floor.

The barn itself was covered with a dusty mat of straw or grass. There were hay bales in the corner, stacked into a cube and everything smelled of wet fur, even though there was no sign of animals. The part of the floor on which she was standing had a sunken spring to it. Like stepping on an unripened peach.

Megan trod carefully across the floor until it felt more solid, then she scuffed away some of the straw until she realised she'd been standing on a hatch. The light was fading fast – and, with the ground covered in hay, it was hard to see how large it might be. It was probably some sort of winter store, especially if it had been a working farm at some point.

Except the lure of the hidden door felt too much, even as Megan told herself it *wasn't* particularly hidden. If it wasn't for the lack of natural light in the barn, she'd have probably seen it before she felt it.

Now that she had noticed it, Megan realised there was some sort of hum coming from below. She was still clasping Sophia's top and rubbed the material between her fingers, reluctant to put it down, even as she felt the urge to investigate. The whirr was more something she *felt* than heard. A low-level rumble underneath her feet, inside the hatch, like a generator, or—

Something white flared across the front of the farm, swaying in an arc across the driveway. Megan was standing partway into the barn, in the middle of the open doors, as the centre of the beaming headlights focused directly on her.

THIRTY-TWO

There was a crunch of gravel and the rumble of an engine. Megan froze as the lights passed across, continuing to move as a vehicle swung onto the drive. Whoever was driving crunched the gears as they put the vehicle into reverse, and raced backwards towards the house. With a crunch of the brakes, they stopped out of sight – and then the farm was dark.

Megan didn't risk lighting up her phone screen to check the time. She had no idea how she'd managed to miss how late it was. It didn't feel as if she'd done much and yet it was dark.

Car doors slammed and then men's voices were talking over each other. Megan crept out of the barn, still clutching the pink top, as she allowed herself to be stolen by the shadows. Two figures were standing to the side of the main farmhouse, shrouded by dusk. A spark flashed as the larger one lit a cigarette and took a puff. The other was leaning on the vehicle, arms folded. Trevor was stooped in the way he had been when Megan first met him, scuffing a foot on the ground.

Megan was almost certain the big man was the person she'd first seen at the back of the café. He had ushered Sophia back inside and told Megan she didn't speak English. He'd been at her sister's second café, too, shouting at someone Megan hadn't seen.

'They just don't get it,' Trevor said. 'I told you it'd be like that.'

His voice was gruff and faint. Megan didn't want to risk moving any closer to hear more clearly. She wanted to retrieve the bike from the graveyard and get back to Nicola's.

The reply was lost to the night. Megan sensed the accent in the bigger man's voice, the same as she had at the back of the café. She hadn't placed its location then and certainly couldn't now. Probably Eastern European, not that that narrowed it down much.

Whatever he said, Trevor snorted in response. 'True. Ben gets what's at stake. He—'

The sound of her brother-in-law's name had Megan craning closer, not daring to move her feet, though desperate to hear whatever came next.

Trevor was interrupted by something from the larger man – whose voice was annoyingly soft. When he was done, Trevor continued.

'His missus is on top of that. That's what he said tonight anyway. He's always come through before.'

There was more mumbling as the other man continued smoking.

Megan wondered what Nicola was apparently on top of. Something to do with the second café?

Trevor started speaking but had barely got through a word when he stopped and held his face. 'Bloody tooth,' he fumed. The other man must've asked what was wrong because the fiery reply was instant: 'I told you: that bitch kicked me in the face.'

He swore and cracked his jaw back and forth with his hand – but it was something that Megan had suspected ever since she'd found his tooth. Sophia had kicked him in the face for some reason – almost certainly on the banks of the stream where Megan had seen her.

'You're gonna have to sharpen up,' Trevor said after the bigger man had replied. 'She shouldn't have been out there. What am I paying you for?'

The other man dropped his cigarette to the ground and stubbed it out with his foot. He shuffled and switched so that he, too, was leaning on the car.

'Is Dan a problem?' he asked.

They were the first words of his that Megan had heard clearly. His accent was such that she needed a second to decode it. Another to realise he was talking about Daniel. *Her* Daniel.

He'd told her after the book club that he'd never really liked Trevor. That Trevor was one of those who knew everything.

This was more than that. There was menace to the question – and Trevor was doing nothing to dispel it. If anything, it seemed like he was properly considering it.

He was chewing on something, though it was probably the inside of his mouth. 'If he is, I'll deal with him.' Trevor paused, then added: '*We'll* deal with him.'

Megan realised she'd been holding her breath and almost choked as she tried to let out the air. Trevor's reply had been a clear threat.

She eased herself a half-step backwards until she was pressed into a pile of tyres. The pink top was still in her hand as she barely dared breathe.

A minute or so later and the two men said they'd see each other the next day. Trevor headed for the back door of the farmhouse as the bigger man ambled towards the barn. There was something about the way he walked: maybe not a limp but a slight drag of the leg as he moved. As if he'd had a knee injury at some point. He was whistling quietly to himself as he hunted through pockets, though Megan felt his gaze wander across her as he walked. He surely couldn't see her, but that didn't stop her trying to shrink into the ground.

Lights swelled from the farmhouse as a dog started to bark louder. Meanwhile, the bigger man continued into the barn. The SUV's doors *thunked* open and closed, before the engine started. Headlights lit up the driveway as the vehicle pulled out of the barn and accelerated. Megan glowed in the glimmering rear red lights and didn't dare shift. If the driver checked his side mirror, there was a chance he would see her – but he didn't stop, didn't even slow, as he thundered along the rocky drive towards the country lane.

Megan counted to ten, took a step and realised her legs were jelly. She continued on until twenty and then her body started to obey. She looped across to the other side of the barn where a low wire fence traced the route of the drive. It was unlikely Trevor would be watching but Megan clambered over the fence, waited next to a clumped hedge – and then sprinted for the road.

It wasn't a long way and, at first, Megan thought she'd turned into some sort of super athlete. She could run at that speed forever, do a full marathon, something like that. Except reality hit as soon as she passed the gate. Her chest exploded and her head swam. How did people willingly run? *Why?*

Megan was at a slow canter as she crossed onto the graveyard. She'd left her bag by the bike and stuffed the pink top into that, before picking up the cycle. It was too dark to take the trail across the top of town, especially as there were no lights on the bike.

The freewheel down the hill gave her some time to get back her breath, even as her knuckles stung from clasping the brakes. She cruised along the centre of the road, hoping it would make it easier for any drivers to see her in the dark.

Not that there were any cars.

She allowed herself to relax slightly as she reached the

street lights of Hollicombe Bay. Megan walked for a bit – and then continued up the hill towards Nicola's. Except she never got that far. Megan stopped on the corner where she had twice paused with Daniel, and then turned and headed along the street.

There were lights on inside his house as Megan left the bike in the front garden and approached the door. She knew he'd be awake, even if she wasn't certain he'd be in. The doorbell sounded and Megan waited, still a little short on breath. She clutched her bag tight to her side, feeling the near weightlessness of Sophia's balled-up top inside.

A light clicked on in the hallway and a shadow loomed towards the door. A lock dinked into place and then Daniel was standing in front of her. He frowned slightly, confused at why Megan was there.

'Are you OK?' he asked.

'I think you're in danger,' Megan replied.

THIRTY-THREE

Daniel led Megan into his living room. A row of horror movie posters lined the longest wall, with one of the biggest televisions she'd seen on the other. A soundbar sat on a shelf underneath, next to a games console.

He seemed somewhat bemused by the news he might be in danger – and instead set about asking if she wanted anything to drink. When they eventually settled at opposing ends of a sofa, Megan's initial panic had faded somewhat. It was perhaps because he was so calm, because she was now somewhere safe – or even because the clown from *IT* was staring over her from one of the posters.

She told him she'd been up exploring the white church when she'd heard an engine. Trevor had got out of a car on the edge of his farm and he'd had a conversation with a big man who had an accent. It was sort of the truth, even though searching around a derelict church and graveyard made her sound like something of a nutter. Better that than someone sneaking around Trevor's farm for no discernible purpose.

'The guy with the accent asked if you were a problem,'

Megan said. 'Then Trevor told him he'd deal with you if you were.'

Daniel had been pressed back into the sofa but he angled in, sitting on the edge. For the first time since Megan had arrived, it felt as if he was looking at her.

'Are you sure you heard them properly?' he asked.

'Definitely. They called you Dan – but it had to be you, didn't it?'

Daniel nodded along. 'There was a bit of a falling out at the business association meeting tonight. The usual stuff.' He'd been talking to himself but looked up and caught her eye. 'There are always disagreements. Never anything *really* serious. I don't know why he'd say he'd deal with me.'

Megan remained quiet, letting him think.

He scratched his head and ran a thumb across that day's stubble. 'I suppose I can picture him saying it.'

'There's more,' Megan said, as she opened her bag. She took out Sophia's pink top and passed it across. Daniel turned it over, before holding it out in front of him.

'What is it?' he asked.

'That's her top. The girl from the stream.'

'I thought you said you'd seen her in town?'

'I did – but she was still there in the stream last Sunday, and so was Trevor. She kicked out his front tooth. I heard him say that, too. That's why he needed the dental surgery.'

Megan wondered whether she should take the top to the police. Could she convince them it belonged to the girl she'd seen at the stream? They hadn't believed the other stuff.

Daniel ran the top through his hand and turned it the other way around. 'Why would she do that?'

Megan wasn't sure how to answer.

It was hard to explain why Sophia being the person in that stream was so important to her, other than that nobody appeared to believe her.

'I don't know,' she said quietly. 'But something's going on, isn't it? I saw Sophia in the stream. She was dead and then she wasn't. She disappeared completely. That's her top and those are my handprints.'

Megan took back the top and held her hand over the muddy marks on the front, showing how they were the right size.

'Something is happening with Trevor and the guy with the accent,' she added. 'Plus Sophia. She might be in danger? Then they threatened you. And I think Nicola might be involved. Maybe she's in trouble too? I saw Trevor and this other bloke at her second café in Steeple's End today.'

It was all coming out. A stream of paranoid consciousness. Megan could hear the desperation in her own voice. Why couldn't she let it go? She almost told Daniel about having Trevor's tooth but that sounded madder than the rest. This is why she hadn't gone to the police: it sounded *mad*. *She* sounded mad.

'I want to talk to Sophia,' Megan said, unable to stop. 'But when she's on her own.'

Daniel was biting his bottom lip, probably weighing up saying something she didn't want to hear. 'I don't know how to make that happen,' he said, before pointing to the clothing. 'I don't know who she is, or where she lives. Where did you find the top?'

Megan faltered. She'd fudged the part about how and where she'd overheard Trevor.

'Up by Trevor's farmhouse,' she replied.

Daniel bit his lip again, and Megan didn't blame him. She'd borderline admitted to the trespassing without any explanation for why she was there.

'Do you know who the big man is?' she asked.

Daniel replied slowly, ponderously. 'Sort of. I've seen him around. I assumed he was some sort of handyman or contractor. I think he's called Oleg.'

Megan rolled the name around her mouth. 'I know he's doing work for my sister,' she said, although it all felt a bit murky. Perhaps Nicola owed him money? Or she owed Trevor, who was paying Oleg? Or maybe it was nothing like that?

'Did they see you?' he asked.

'No.'

'That's one thing.'

Daniel was thinking silently to himself as Megan wondered if he was actually concerned for his safety. He'd not heard the tones of voice when Trevor and Oleg had been talking. None of it sounded like a joke but it was hard to get that across. She was going to have to tell him at least some of the rest.

'There's a hatch in the floor of Trevor's barn,' Megan said.

'You were in his barn...?' Daniel's bemusement was back.

'There was something underneath. A hum, or a buzz. I thought it could be a generator but I don't know.'

Megan couldn't meet Daniel's eyes any longer. She was in too deep as a trespassing conspiracy nut.

'What do you think's under there?' he asked.

'I don't know. It's so remote, you could hide anything. Nobody's going to hear or see.'

Daniel was rubbing his chin. 'That's true, he's about a mile away from anyone. But I suppose I'm not really sure what you're saying. I get that you saw someone in the woods who disappeared. I don't really know how any of this links in.' He stopped and clucked his tongue – and then he said the words she'd been waiting to hear from anyone all week. 'But I believe you.'

It was another thing that Megan felt more than she heard. Like a heavy object being put down with a *whump*. She didn't know how to explain everything that had been going on, and there were still things like Trevor's tooth and her father's money that Daniel didn't know. Except it all felt linked – and Megan had an enormous sense that none of it was connected in a good way.

'Thank you,' she managed, relieved. Somebody finally believed her.

Daniel stretched and squeezed her hand. His fingers were warm and she let him hold her. She felt the scaling from the scars across his skin. Parts were smoother than others.

'I think there might be people under that hatch,' Megan said, letting those dark thoughts come. Letting her imagination speak. Letting it all out. 'I know it sounds mad but I wonder if he keeps people like Sophia under there. She might've been trying to escape when she kicked out his tooth. And he makes them work in places around town.'

It wasn't fully thought through and, even as she said the words, Megan was doubting herself. But it might explain why Pam and Nicola had been so keen to keep Megan out of the café's kitchen, and also why Oleg had ferried Sophia and the young man directly from the kitchen into the SUV she'd seen parked in the barn. Plus why Oleg had been at the second café, apparently shouting at someone who wasn't doing a job properly. They were keeping workers underneath Trevor's barn in the middle of nowhere, paying them a pittance.

'You said yourself Hollicombe Bay is struggling for people to work here,' Megan said, though it still didn't sound quite right. As if she was trying to convince herself more than Daniel.

'I think I'd have noticed if something like that was going on.'

'You said you're out of the loop.'

Daniel had started to reply but stopped. He *had* said that. He'd also said he felt like decisions were made without him before there were votes.

'I suppose it can't do any harm to check if there's anything under the barn,' Daniel said. He had let go of her hand at some point and she wondered for a second if he might be humouring her.

'What about the police?' he added, sounding slightly unsure.

Megan understood why. She knew how it all sounded – and the only proof she had of anything was a tooth and a pink top. It wasn't evidence, not really. It was a theory, and what if she was wrong? Her sister was already convinced Megan was having a breakdown. Word was already around town that Megan had caused that first police call-out. She might not be an outcast as such, but she would never escape those sideways looks from everyone as they whispered about her.

'Not yet,' Megan said quietly, suddenly doubting herself, and trying to remember the roll she'd been on. 'I won't know when Trevor's out,' she added. 'Or when he might be back.'

Daniel blinked, taking a second to absorb it all. Megan wondered again whether he was humouring her. 'I found out last year that the arcade is on the same electricity breaker as his chip shop,' he said. 'I'll shut everything off and then he'll get called down to have a look. He already thinks I'm useless at stuff like that, so it won't be a surprise. It should get you an hour.' He smiled gently.

'Won't you have to shut the arcade while your power's off?' Megan asked.

'We'll live.' He took a breath and then: 'Do you really think I'm in danger?'

'It sounded like it.'

'I just don't want *you* to be in danger. I can text to say when he's away from the farm – but that doesn't mean nobody else will be around.'

Megan already knew that was true. There was only so much she could control – but the important thing was that one person believed her.

She allowed herself to sink into the sofa.

'I don't think I can go back to my sister's,' she said quietly.

It was the unknown of it all. The apparent theft of their

father's money and the unexplained ties from Nicola to Trevor and Oleg. Not to mention the way Nicola and Ben had made her feel after she'd seen Sophia in the stream. She knew she wouldn't sleep in that attic. Not tonight.

'I can take the sofa,' Daniel said. 'It's more comfortable than it looks.' He stood and took a step towards the door. 'I'll get some clean sheets and you can have my bed. It's—'

'I just want to be next to someone,' Megan said. Daniel stopped and stared towards her. 'If that's OK,' she added.

Another soft smile: 'It's OK.'

THIRTY-FOUR

FRIDAY

It was almost half-past nine when Megan woke up: the longest she'd slept in a while. Daniel's mattress wasn't too soft, like the one in the attic. His pillows weren't too hard. Everything was comfortable. The two of them really had *just* slept, until Daniel's alarm had gone off at eight. He'd told her to stay where she was and, the next thing, another hour and a half had passed.

Her teenage self wouldn't have believed it and yet, after the evening before, Daniel wasn't that fantasy figure to her any longer. He was something more mature and comforting: the person who believed her.

Even with that, the previous night felt dreamlike and Megan doubted herself more than before. The hatch in the barn *would* be a store, which was what she'd thought in the first place. She'd misheard the threat about Daniel because she was too far away. The money Nicola had taken from their father could be explained.

Except Sophia's pink top *was* in her bag, at the side of the bed, where she'd left it. It was real.

As Megan staggered around the landing, looking for the bathroom, Daniel appeared on the stairs.

'I'm heading off to the arcade,' he said. 'I'll get Trevor where I can see him from about one o'clock. I'll message you when he's there.'

'You don't have my number.'

Daniel laughed at that as he offered her his phone. 'We can fix that.'

Megan typed her number into the device and passed it back.

He tapped something onto the screen and then looked up. 'I've texted you, so you've got my number.'

A sleepy fug crawled around Megan's thoughts as the late-night excursions caught up to her. She yawned and batted it away. She was in an oversized NFL sweatshirt that Daniel had in his cupboard, and she tugged at its shapeless form in an attempt to make it fit better.

'If you're wondering where it is, I moved your bike into the back garden so it doesn't get nicked,' Daniel said. 'Feel free to eat anything you can find in the kitchen. Hang around as long as you want. The front door will lock itself when you leave.'

It all felt so civilised and calm.

'Poke around if you want,' he added, pointing towards the door at the end of the hall. 'You might've figured it out already but I'm a horror movie fan. There's a bunch of memorabilia in there, so you might see some action figures.'

Megan smiled down to him. 'They're not boxed, are they?'

He took it with the spirit it was intended: 'They are, actual-ly!' He nodded towards the front door. 'I have to get off – but I'll be in contact. Stay safe.'

Although the lure of poking around his house had been strong, if only out of sheer nosiness, Megan had left soon after Daniel. She made her way back to her sister's house.

If Jessie was home, then she was keeping quiet in her room.

Nicola had seemingly assumed she'd been in bed the night before and hadn't known she'd stayed out – which was one thing. At least she'd not still been pushing the idea that Megan was on the brink of a breakdown.

Megan made some toast and then rechecked the safe in the living room, where the papers in her father's name and his chequebook remained. Megan was searching for a reason that she could be wrong, that the money hadn't been stolen, but it was hard to see anything other than what was in front of her.

Daniel messaged at half-past twelve, saying he was getting ready to turn off the power, which meant – depending on where he was – Trevor could be anything from five to thirty minutes away. Megan took the cue and retrieved the bike from Daniel's back garden, then cycled along the trails as she had the night before.

By the time she reached the tree in the corner of the graveyard, there were more messages waiting. Daniel said that the girl from the chip shop had come over to ask if their power was out – and that its lunchtime opening had been delayed. Trevor was going to be there within five minutes. That last message had arrived four minutes before, and Megan had no intention of messing around.

She ran along Trevor's drive, heading for the barn. The hatch was easier to see in the daylight, as she'd suspected the night before. The ground was still a thatched pattern of yellowy-brown hay.

Megan listened, trying to tune back into the hum she'd heard the night before. She knelt and pressed her hand to the springy door, trying to sense the vibrations – which would confirm the previous night hadn't only happened in her imagination.

There was nothing – not that it mattered. She would simply open it and look.

Megan followed the edge of the hatch around the floor, looking for a handle that didn't appear to be there. She did two loops and then tried digging her fingers into the crack, hoping to lift it. A wide metal edging ran the perimeter of the hatch and the harsh surface scratched at her fingers, which she could barely get into a groove underneath, let alone be strong enough to pick it up.

It had felt so simple when she'd spoken it over with Daniel the night before. He'd distract Trevor, she'd get to the farm and look underneath the hatch.

Except Megan couldn't even lift it.

That quiet voice from the night before was back, telling her she was wrong. But it was worse than that. Not only was she wrong, she'd allowed someone else to hear her wild thoughts and speculation.

No.

She simply needed something with which to lever open the hatch.

Megan hunted around the barn, checking behind the hay bales and in the corners, where she found a spindly looking stick. She jammed it into the gap between hatch and floor – and lifted, only for the stick to snap into three. She needed something stronger.

There was still no noise from underneath. No hum, no voices, no anything.

Megan checked her phone. It had been fifteen minutes since Daniel's last message and she had no idea how long it would take Trevor to put right the minor act of sabotage. Probably not long – and, although that didn't mean he'd be heading directly back to the farm, Megan couldn't risk hanging around when she didn't know his location.

She hurried out of the barn, towards the farmhouse. It had seemed so much more imposing the night before. Then she'd seen a desolate haunted house in the middle of nowhere. Now, it was more of a mess. The broken entrails of something that had once been.

Megan searched the piles of tyres, hoping for something narrow, long and strong. There was a wood pile towards the back of the house, next to a wheelbarrow and axe; then the end of a rake on the ground – but no handle. Megan picked up the axe, wondering if she could jam the blade into the gap around the hatch, before figuring she wouldn't be able to lever it enough anyway.

With nothing else immediately outside the house, Megan crossed a patch of newly shovelled land over to the greenhouse. It looked abandoned from a distance, with the broken glass and open door – but there were rows of plants on a low bench, plus a hosepipe pinned to the roof with a series of small holes dotted along its length. Crucially, there was also a pair of soil-caked shears resting in the corner.

Megan rushed back to the barn and dug the blades of the shears into the gap and pushed. The hatch eked and creaked, allowing the blades to slip underneath – and then, with an unexpected yelp of her own surprise, Megan managed to lever it up and out of the slot.

She noticed the handle as soon as it was up the air. What she'd thought was part of the metal lining that ringed the door was actually a circular handle that slotted into the fascia. The hatch wasn't even that big, perhaps a couple of metres square, leaving Megan to wonder why she'd struggled so much. Not that she had time to dwell.

There was darkness below, with concrete steps leading ominously into the abyss. Megan put down the shears and took out her phone, shining the flashlight into the murk, only to see the white evaporate into nothing.

'Hello...?' Megan hissed into the blank, without reply.

It was another moment in the horror movie where she'd be urging the lead to turn and run. Nothing good ever came from walking down a set of steps into a blackened pit hidden under a barn.

And yet that's what she did.

The light from her phone offered just enough to see the next step as Megan descended into the space underneath. Her second 'hello?' was more of a whisper, something to reassure herself. She stumbled on the bottom step and steadied herself by reaching towards the wall, where she found a switch. She swung her phone light around to follow a cord up the wall, and across the ceiling towards a light bulb.

Then there was light. The bulb was one of those dim yellow things that probably broke all sorts of laws around energy efficiency – and yet it was enough to illuminate the space.

It was smaller than Megan had thought – and nowhere near as deep. She'd pictured a pit and a web of tunnels, but it was one room. The space wasn't as wide or long as the barn above and someone who was six foot-plus would struggle to stand.

A rusty rake, shovel and hoe were leaning against one wall, next to a bucket – and there was what looked like a generator in another corner. There had to be power somewhere, considering the light worked – but no cables were connected to the generator.

Megan knew little about farming – but it seemed like the sort of stuff that might be left in an abandoned storeroom.

She walked around the edge, craning into the darker corners and looking for something – *anything* – that would make this trespassing worthwhile. When she had been talking to Daniel the night before, she'd been so certain this farm was the centre of something awful and yet, now, there was nothing.

Megan had to remind herself that she'd found Sophia's top in the SUV directly above where she was standing – except even that seemed like something of a leap. Even if it was, so what? Megan had seen the young woman in the woods but had clearly been mistaken about whether she was breathing. She had needlessly tried to revive someone, who had taken off not long after.

Another lap of the space and there was still nothing to see. Megan presumed the hum she'd thought she'd heard the night before was either the electricity supply, or imagined. It didn't matter which. This had all been for nothing.

Her phone buzzed as she reached the steps once more – and Daniel's message was predictable enough. Trevor had finished fixing things and she needed to get out.

THIRTY-FIVE

The aisles of the arcade were pinging and popping, with everything in full swing. The dance machine had a similar audience to the last time Megan had been there, while groups of young men continued to crowd the punching ball.

Daniel led her through the crowd and out the front, before they crossed the street towards the sea. The tide was half-in, half-out, apparently unable to make up its mind. For the first time since she'd arrived, the sky was a gloomy murk, almost as if reflecting Megan's mood.

Gulls were fighting over a discarded packet of chips on one bench, so Daniel led them along the front towards a quiet spot that overlooked an empty boat ramp. With the breeze crisper, not many were bothering with the beach, leaving only the diehards camped on the sand.

'There was nothing there,' Daniel repeated as they sat. Megan had already told him that once in the arcade.

She tried to stop herself squirming. A part of her had wanted to leave town to avoid this conversation. It wasn't only hard to admit she was wrong, it was embarrassing.

'There was a generator but it didn't look as if it's been used any time recently,' Megan said.

'Is that what you heard last night?'

Megan couldn't quite bring herself to say no, so went with a sorry-sounding: 'Maybe.'

They sat and watched a kayaker round the curve of the sea wall and paddle confidently towards the ramp. He was one of those people for whom it seemed natural as he expertly slipped onto dry land and levered himself out in one crisp motion.

'Was Trevor weird with you?' Megan asked.

'No more so than usual.' A pause. 'No threats.'

He meant it innocently enough, except Megan understood the undertone.

'I don't think people around here are bad,' Daniel added. 'A bit stuck in their ways, maybe simplistic sometimes in wanting easy answers to complex questions.' He held his hands up. 'That makes me sound like a right twat.'

'No, it doesn't.'

He shrugged. 'It does but... I think it's easy to forget we all went through a trauma.'

Daniel was holding her hand again, his fingers warm, even as hers were ice. She felt the sliced lines of his scars.

'*Multiple* traumas,' he added. 'You especially. The town's never quite got over what happened with the fire. They should've knocked down the school and started again – but it's still there. I think that's partly why people never seem ready to move on. The thing we all want to forget is always around. People send their kids there, knowing there was a day twenty-odd years ago when children just like them never came home. How is a community supposed to deal with that?'

He swallowed as the man in a wetsuit dragged his kayak up the ramp and along the path towards the car park.

'There were those years where tourists would come *specifi-*

cally to look at the school,' he added. 'Where they'd stand and have their photo taken. They still come, but not very many now. It's like how people have heard of "Lockerbie" and it's not because it's a small Scottish town.'

It was hard to know how to reply to that. He'd said what was in Megan's heart. Even without her father's slip into drink, she would have left town as soon as she was able. Hollicombe Bay wasn't a charming coastal resort and hadn't been in a long time. It was a byword for a catastrophic fire that she'd seen as closely as anyone.

As she thought on that, Megan wondered if – maybe – her sister was right. If everyone was right. She shouldn't have returned because she'd left for a reason. If Sophia *had* been in that stream, it didn't matter much because she was fine now. If her sister *had* stolen money from their father, call it an early inheritance. It's not as if Megan wanted it. She hadn't been back a week and had somehow managed to make anyone who knew her think she was having a breakdown.

For the first time, Megan wondered if she was. There were those beginnings of the panic attack that she'd fought away at the back of the café – and it was hard to deny her decision-making had been erratic. She couldn't quite remember why she'd agreed to work for her sister in the first place. Then she'd been late over and over, before simply not showing up.

None of that was normal, even though she'd told herself at the time that it was.

Megan slipped her hand away from Daniel's and used it to stifle a yawn. The tiredness was back, and the optimism had gone.

'Thank you for listening last night,' Megan said.

'It was good to see you.'

'Thank you for believing me.'

'Why wouldn't I?'

Megan could think of a few reasons, primarily because of how mad she sounded. The police hadn't believed her.

'What are you going to do?' he asked.

'I'm not sure,' Megan replied. 'First, I need to talk to my sister.'

THIRTY-SIX

As Megan arrived at the cafe, Nicola and Pam were locking up. They were chatting amiably until they turned and saw Megan. Pam's lips twisted as her eyes narrowed. It felt as if she was going to say something but, probably because Nicola was there, she settled on a muttered 'bye' and then turned to head off.

'How did you know I'd be here?' Nicola asked when it was just them.

'A guess.'

'Someone had to cover you...' It could have sounded harsh but it didn't. Nicola gave a small smile. 'Me and Ben have been filling in here all summer as and when.'

'Sorry,' Megan replied – and maybe she was.

'We left you in bed this morning,' Nicola said. 'Reckoned you could do with the rest.'

Megan nodded along, though it felt as if her sister might've checked the attic and already knew she'd been a dirty stop-out.

Neither of them had suggested it but they were suddenly on the seafront, walking along the curve of the bay. Megan had done a lot of walking and talking along the same streets in recent times. She'd lost track of days but crews were up the lamp posts, stringing bunting from side to side in preparation for the summer festival the next day. Signs and directions were being pinned to various posts, poles and shopfronts, advertising where people should go.

'Where does all the bunting come from?' Nicola asked.

'There must be a supplier somewhere who ships industrial levels of bunting from town to town all summer long.'

The two of them slowed as they reached the green, where three men were struggling to put up the marquee. One of them was trying to hold down a corner as the others tugged at various canvas flaps. One wild gust would send the whole lot off into the ocean.

Nicola and Megan looped around the park, pausing as they neared the lookout point. A boat was moored not far from the bay and a man was lying on the deck, top off, showing off a carpet of grey hairs. He was wearing sunglasses, his bare feet on the side of the boat as if it was a scorching day.

Megan hadn't seen him in decades but his raggedy mop of curly grey hair was enough to bring back the memories. 'Is that—?'

'Dad's mate, Cliff,' Nicola replied.

They stopped to sit on a bench underneath a pagoda, where a tall row of bushes protected them from the wind.

'They go out every now and then,' Nicola added. 'At least that's what Dad says. I'm convinced he's gonna end up overboard one of these days.'

'When did you last see him?' Megan asked.

Nicola had already given an answer days before – and yet she didn't repeat the lie, instead taking a breath. A simple gesture, nothing really. Something she'd have done millions of times and yet it told Megan precisely what she was thinking.

'I know about the money you've had from Dad,' Megan said. They both knew this part of the game was up. 'I saw him yesterday, in the caravan.'

If Nicola was surprised, or defensive, she didn't let on. When it came to their father, there was only one question that came first.

'How was he?' she asked.

'He answered the door in his underwear and he was swigging Jack Daniel's from a mug. But he was broadly coherent.'

That's what they'd come to: broadly coherent was as good as it got.

'He said he has cancer,' Megan added, her voice cracking halfway through the C-word. It felt more real out loud in her own voice. 'He said he only has a few months left.'

Nicola rubbed her eye. 'You know what he's like. His liver's somehow lasted all these years. He'll be around a fair while yet.' She laughed humourlessly, though her voice had cracked too. They had spent years expecting this and, now it seemed close, it wasn't how they thought it would be.

'Why didn't you say?' Megan asked.

Nicola sighed. 'I figured we each have our own relationship with him.' She rubbed her eye again, as if trying to massage the reason. 'I think I was probably trying to pretend it wasn't real.'

There was such truth that it ached. Megan's last twenty years with her father had been about pretending things weren't happening. It was going to end the same way.

The sisters sat together not speaking, because what was there to say?

A minute or so later and an older man strolled past, with a younger blonde woman at his side. He pointed to the lighthouse in the distance and said something about 'taking the Jag'.

Nicola waited until they were gone before leaning closer to her sister: 'Daughter or midlife crisis?'

Megan snorted at that – and for a moment, only a moment, it was the relationship she had lost. There was a time when she and Nicola had been so close. Megan had imagined them growing old and laughing together like this.

And then reality was back.

'Dad said he gave you signed cheques for Jessie and university. He thinks she's going to Cambridge.'

'It sort of *is* for university.' From nowhere, Nicola sounded defiant, although it felt forced, as if she was trying to convince herself. 'Look, if the business goes under, there's no money for anything. We don't just lose the café, we lose the house. There *was* a time she was thinking about university and maybe Cambridge. She had the grades. That's all expensive.'

'If you have money issues, why are you opening a second café?'

Nicola flapped a hand towards the centre. 'Because this place is dying. There are more people in Steeple's End. More tourists. Ben ran the numbers. He reckons we can make enough there to help us write off money here. It's a tax thing.'

Megan had no idea whether that was something that could happen. It sounded vaguely plausible... especially when using seventy-grand of someone else's money to get the second café open. She also had a point that, if the business failed, the house could be on the line. That wouldn't be good for Jessie, who hadn't done anything wrong. She wouldn't be moving out any time soon. No amount of snubbing avocado toast was going to help young people afford a mortgage.

In the moment, Megan decided to let it go. It wasn't like she wanted the money for herself. They sat quietly for a short while, taking in the view, perhaps both wishing things were different. That they'd done this more. Been better friends. Better sisters.

'I know who I saw in the stream,' Megan said quietly.

'Ben said.'

It wasn't much of a surprise. Ben had been at the back of the café, in the courtyard, when Megan had *almost* had the panic attack.

'He said you seemed a bit confused by everything,' Nicola added.

'I wasn't confused.'

'You told us you'd seen a dead girl in the stream, then you changed your mind and said it was Sophia.'

That was hard to deny. It was exactly what had happened.

'We don't know what you're trying to say,' Nicola added, and, for some reason, the 'we' was incredibly irritating.

'I'm not sure I do either,' Megan replied.

She thought of the tangible proof: Trevor's tooth still in her sock and Sophia's pink top with the handprint. Something had certainly happened, even if she couldn't quite figure out what.

'Do you want to meet her?' Nicola asked.

Megan sat up straighter and turned to her sister. 'Who?'

'Sophia, of course. I can take you to her, if you want? Assuming she's in. Her English isn't great which is why she prefers to keep her head down. I'm sure you can make it work if you want to ask her something. Maybe she'll tell you if she was in the stream? Maybe not? Either way you'll get some sort of answer.'

It felt as if an '...and then you'll stop going on about it' was going to be tagged onto the end, though it didn't come.

Even though it was exactly what Megan had told Daniel she'd wanted, now it was on offer, she was hesitant. What if Sophia said she'd not been in the woods, that she'd never been there? As long as Megan didn't know, she could rationalise what she had seen. If there was a definite answer, she'd have to face the fact that maybe she was having some sort of breakdown.

Perhaps everything with Paul and Lucy, with returning to Hollicombe Bay, really *was* too much for her.

'I don't know,' Megan said.

'I just want you to be happy,' Nicola replied. She reached across and squeezed Megan's hand momentarily. 'Especially in your condition. *We* want you to be happy. Ben, too. We appreciate you speaking to Jess the other day, too. It's been good to have you around. I know Jess has enjoyed it.'

Nicola didn't know the half of it – and she still thought Megan was pregnant.

The disappointment of finding nothing underneath Trevor's barn and the fact her theories had come to nothing left Megan with the sinking sense of melancholy. Hollicombe Bay really did offer very little for her. If she could let go of the money that Nicola had taken from their father, and Megan was fairly sure she could, then the only thing left was Sophia.

'I'd like to meet her,' Megan said.

THIRTY-SEVEN

Nicola stood up from the bench and brushed down her front. 'We can go now if you want?' she said.

Megan stood as well. 'Now?'

'It's obviously been on your mind since the weekend. We can clear everything up.'

Megan wasn't sure why but she'd expected more of a build-up. But it felt obvious that Sophia lived somewhere in the town. Of course they could just visit her now.

'I'll text and make sure she's home,' Nicola said. 'I think she's better with written English than spoken.'

She took out her phone and thumbed in something quickly before they started to walk back around the green. Their father's friend, Cliff, was no longer cloud-bathing on his boat deck.

'If she's not in, we'll head home,' Nicola said, although, the moment she'd spoken, her phone dinged. She checked the screen and then: 'She's home and says we can go over. It's not far.'

It felt very real now.

Megan followed her sister back towards the town centre as a

spiralling sense of dread began to flow. She was about to be shown up in front of her sister. Sophia would say she hadn't been in the stream. Or, maybe worse, she'd say she was – but she obviously wasn't dead. She and Megan had actually had a conversation, that Megan must have forgotten. It didn't feel as if anything good would come from them talking and Megan couldn't remember why she thought it would be a good idea. What was the best that could happen?

But it was too late to say any of that.

The centre was close to being fully decked out in its summer festival finery. The bunting was now largely up, while wide banners had been draped at either end of the high street. A row of Portaloos had appeared near the steps that led down to the beach and a street-sweeping crew were litter picking up and down the street.

Megan wasn't sure where they were going, though Nicola came to an abrupt stop outside the chip shop. It was early evening and a line stretched out the door as the smell of batter, salt and fat wafted tantalisingly.

There was a door next to the shop and Nicola pushed it open, before holding it for Megan. In front was a set of stairs and the two of them headed up into a dark hall, with a door on either side. Nicola's phone lit up the space as she checked her messages while turning between the doors.

'This one,' she said, before knocking on the door with a '1' pinned to the front. The sound echoed along the tight corridor as Megan felt a stifling sense of self-awareness. This was really happening. No going back.

It took a few seconds until the door was opened, revealing... someone that took up much of the frame. Oleg poked his head into the corridor and squinted to take in Megan.

'This is Oleg,' Nicola said – as the man offered his hand. 'Oleg, this is my sister, Megan.'

Megan found herself shaking his hand, if it could be called

that. His hands were so big, she could have shaken just one of his fingers.

He held the door open for them, and, as the sisters entered, Nicola continued talking. 'Oleg does some work for us in the kitchen but he's also been helping out as a handyman at Steeple's End. He's a bit of an electrician, a bit of a mechanic. Good with everything.'

Oleg closed the door behind them and didn't respond to the compliment. He seemed the sort who would react to insult or praise with exactly the same, unmoving, face.

The flat itself looked like the sort of place that an estate agent would describe as 'wonderfully minimalistic', in the sense that there wasn't much there. A sofa covered in pink and cream flowery canvas was pressed against one of the walls. The sort of thing that should've gone straight from the factory to the tip. There was a small coffee table, a lamp, and not much else.

The three of them stood awkwardly in the near-empty living room.

'Sophia is Oleg's daughter,' Nicola said. 'They're over from Slovenia.'

Oleg turned towards the doors at the back of the room and called 'Soph.' There was a shuffling and then she emerged into the living room.

Sophia.

Her arms were folded across her front as she stared uneasily at the floor. As Megan looked to her, she remembered Sophia had had a black eye when she'd last seen her. It was still there, though the olive green had turned to a light yellow.

Sophia glanced up to Megan, then her gaze darted to Nicola, before returning to the floor.

'Sophia's been learning English in her free time,' Nicola said. 'She's improved so quickly. Hers is definitely much better than my Slovenian.' She laughed to herself, though nobody else joined in. 'It is Slovenian, isn't it?' she added, talking to Oleg. 'I didn't know if you speak Russian, or whatever?'

Oleg mumbled something that sounded like 'Slovenian', though he – understandably – didn't appear remotely amused.

Nicola hadn't seemed to notice the possible offence as she turned to Sophia. She spoke a little slower and louder than usual: one step from a Brit bellowing 'chips' at a Spanish waiter. 'My sister wants to ask you some questions,' she said laboriously.

Sophia's eyes switched to her father and then settled on Megan. Oleg was watching her, too, and so was Nicola. It suddenly dawned on Megan that this was her moment. She scratched her arm and coughed to clear her throat. From nowhere, this all felt like a terrible idea. All her dark thoughts and fantasies were wildly misplaced – and now she actually had to say some of it out loud.

'I, um, saw you in the stream the other day,' Megan managed. 'I sort of panicked when I saw you at the back of the café because, er...'

Megan wasn't sure where she was going. There hadn't even been a question there and Sophia glanced towards Oleg again. It would be bad enough even if the poor girl spoke perfect English.

'I suppose I'm just, uh, wondering if you're... OK?'

Sophia's nose twitched with what looked like confusion and it wasn't a surprise. It didn't matter how good a person was at a language, being asked if you were OK by a stranger was weird.

'Yes...?' she replied, although it sounded somewhat like a question – which was understandable given how confused she must be.

She wasn't making eye contact – but Oleg and Nicola were both looking expectantly towards Megan.

'Um... do you like working in the café?'

'Yes...?'

It was hard not to cringe. What else was she going to say? Her boss and her father were in the room. She was hardly going to say she hated it, even if her English had been perfect.

Megan's mind was racing as she tried to think of a question. 'How did you, um, end up in Hollicombe Bay?'

Sophia looked to her dad, eyebrows dipped with confusion. 'I don't, er—'

'We come for sunshine,' Oleg said. 'The beach. You need workers, yes?'

It was the obvious answer. The area *did* need seasonal workers – and despite the gloominess of the day, the weather was generally good during the summer. There would be worse places to live.

Megan couldn't stop asking obvious questions that had obvious answers, mainly because she didn't want to ask the one thing for which she was there. She didn't want the answer.

'How did you get the black eye?' Megan asked, while circling a finger around her own eye to make the point.

Sophia bobbed from one foot to the other and pointed across to the kitchenette. A cooker was built into the wall, next to a stainless-steel sink that was certainly stained. A single mug and plate sat on the draining board as a fridge likely older than Sophia buzzed with the ferocity of a pissed-off bee. Sophia pointed to her head and then the cupboards high on the wall that were more or less at the same height as her.

'You hit your head on a cabinet?' Megan asked.

That got a nod.

Megan desperately tried to think of something better than what she'd so far come out with – and then it came to her. She wondered why it had never crossed her mind before. It would explain everything.

'Do you have a sister?' she asked.

It was so obvious. Megan hadn't seen Sophia in the woods, she'd seen her sister.

Sophia didn't reply. She looked to Oleg with a frown on her face. 'Sister?' she repeated.

He said something back to her in what was, presumably, Slovenian – and they went back and forth for a few seconds. Sophia was nodding along, before turning back.

'No, no, no.'

Megan felt herself deflating. It would have explained almost everything.

If there was no sister, nobody else who looked like Sophia, then there was only one question remaining.

'Did I see you in the woods on Sunday?' Megan asked. 'By the stream?'

Sophia's features crinkled. 'Stream?'

'Like a river but smaller.' Megan realised she was making a swirly motion with her hands.

Oleg said something and Sophia shrugged at him.

'Stream? No stream.'

And that was that.

How else to explain things other than that Megan had seen something that wasn't there. Sophia *hadn't* been in the woods and she didn't have a sister.

Megan clutched her bag tighter to her side as if it were a comfort blanket. Except there was one thing that was definitely real. She unzipped the bag, reached inside, and pulled out the pink top.

That was all it took. When he saw what was happening, Oleg reached for it but he was too slow. Sophia had already bounded across the room and snatched it from Megan's grasp. 'Where?' she demanded. 'Where?!'

She'd exploded from a shy, quiet young woman, into a shouting, frantic wide-eyed ball of energy. She held the top to her face and smelled it, before holding it at arm's length. 'Where?'

Oleg started to talk, so Megan spoke over him. 'It's what the girl in the stream was wearing. What *you* were wearing?'

Nicola was frozen, staring in confusion at what had happened in what felt like a blink.

Oleg took a step towards his daughter and stretched to take the top. Sophia turned her back on him and snapped 'mine'. He continued trying to talk to her, voice getting louder, as she refused to hand over the clothing.

'Did you kick Trevor in the face?' Megan asked.

Sophia was still trying to avoid her dad, though she caught Megan's eye and there was something there between confusion and fear. 'Trevor?' she said.

Oleg had stopped a couple of paces away as he and Nicola both gaped at Megan. Everyone appeared confused.

'What do you mean?' Nicola asked. 'Like a real kick?'

Megan motioned a kick and then patted her face as everyone watched.

Oleg said something in his native language and then switched to English. 'This your British humour?' He was turning between Megan and Nicola.

Nicola had twisted to face her sister. 'I think so...?'

Megan was watching Sophia, desperate for the younger woman to make eye contact. Did she understand what she'd asked?

Oleg stepped in front of his daughter, and the message seemed clear enough. Nicola understood it, too.

'That's probably everything, isn't it?' Nicola said.

It was phrased as a question but didn't sound like one.

Nicola moved towards the door, leaving Megan little option but to follow.

'Thanks,' Megan called, as she backed out of the living room, searching for something better to add. It had been a strange turn and she wasn't quite sure what had happened. The last thing she saw before the door closed was Sophia clasping the pink top to her face.

THIRTY-EIGHT

SATURDAY

The walk up the hill from Sophia's flat had been largely uneventful. Nicola seemingly thought Megan had asked all her questions, which, in a way she had. She hadn't bothered to ask from where the top had come – not that Megan would have told her that it was from the back of Trevor's SUV. She'd also not brought up Megan's manic insistence of asking whether Sophia had kicked Trevor in the face. Megan doubted it was down to a lack of inquisitiveness and more to do with the fact she was past querying the things Megan said and did.

Did she really think Megan had gone through a proper breakdown?

But what about Sophia's reaction? Wouldn't Nicola have questions about that?

As Megan had lain on the bed in the attic through the evening, she'd found it hard to figure out what had happened. Sophia certainly recognised the top, though, unless she was hypersensitive to people touching her things, it was a baffling reaction.

Except there wasn't a lot more Megan could do. Sophia said she hadn't been in the stream and that she didn't have a sister.

There seemed little point in Megan continuing to insist she'd seen something that nobody else had.

The only thing left to ask Sophia was, if she hadn't been in the stream, how had her top ended up with Megan's handprint on it? It all felt so murky. Was there another explanation?

As she'd lain on the bed, listening to the sounds of the night through the open window, she'd decided she was going to return to Whitecliff. She'd been in her hometown for a week and it had taken that long to realise that it didn't feel like home any longer.

Except Saturday was the day of the summer festival and it seemed a waste not to experience something of a childhood flashback before returning to real life. That and Megan should probably say goodbye to Daniel. He'd been a beacon of sanity in a week that had been anything but.

The smell of coffee drifted through the house as Megan yawned herself awake. The sun blazed around the edges of the roller blind, signalling what was surely going to be a hot one.

When Megan got downstairs, there were croissants on a plate on the kitchen table.

Nicola was sitting with her laptop and peered over her glasses.

'Take one if you want,' she said. 'Leftovers from the café yesterday. There's jam in the fridge.'

Ben came in from the back and kicked off his shoes. He shot a smile at Megan and then sat at the table, where he took a croissant for himself and tore it in two.

The three of them made small talk as if the previous week hadn't happened. *Yes*, the weather did look nice. *Yes*, wasn't it lucky for the festival? *Yes*, it would be good to see the town all decked out.

'Better than last year when it chucked it down,' Ben said, as he dropped a croissant flake on his lap.

'Do you remember when Dad ran that ping-pong stall that year?' Nicola asked.

It was probably the first time Megan had thought about it in twenty-five years. When she'd been eleven or twelve, her father had set up a game stall that invited people to pay 50p which let them fire ping-pong balls into goals using a catapult. All the money had been donated to charity.

'He wouldn't let us win any of the prizes,' Megan replied. 'Said it would look like cheating.'

The thought had dropped into her head from nowhere. Absent for so many years and then shining bright.

'Do you remember when he used to take us into the woods with his catapult?'

Something else that now burned clear and vividly.

'He'd say we were hunting rabbits,' Megan said, 'but we'd never hit any.'

'Dad missed on purpose,' Nicola said. 'I figured it out years later. He could hit the knots on trees from miles away but he'd miss rabbits no matter how close.'

And of course it was true. Megan wondered how she'd never realised.

'Kinda weird how catapults were his thing,' Nicola said. 'I always wondered if he got it from his dad, something like that.'

Megan was now thinking the same. Some locals were into fishing, or pheasant shooting. Their father would take them into the woods and ping stones into trees from, as her sister had put it, 'miles away'. From nowhere, she had the craving to ask him.

A series of thuds came from the stairs and then Jessie breezed into the kitchen. She was showered, dressed and ready for the day. 'I'm gonna meet my friends for one' – Nicola began to interrupt, though her daughter spoke through her – 'but I'll be at the baking tent for three.' She reached for a croissant and offered it to Megan. 'Halves? I can't eat a whole one.'

'OK.'

Jessie tore the croissant in half and passed Megan the larger part. After the turbulence of the week, there was a bounce to her. It felt like eating in front of her mum was a direct response to any queries about problems with eating.

'Me and your dad are going to be at the café until about half-two,' Nicola told her. 'We'll meet you at the baking tent at *five-to*-three. Don't be late.'

Ben suddenly looked to his watch, as if he'd been electrocuted. 'I forgot Pam said she's going to be late. We're supposed to be opening up.'

Nicola picked up her phone and checked the screen. 'First I've heard of it.'

'We've got to go,' Ben said – and then the two of them were off. Laptop lid snapped shut, shoes retrieved, keys found, goodbyes said.

Jessie slipped into the seat where her mum had been sitting. She picked at the croissant, nibbling away flake by flake. 'I'm probably going back to bed for a bit,' she said. 'Only got up 'cos I smelled food.'

'How are things with your teacher?' Megan asked.

'I've switched classes for next term,' Jessie replied, though she said it so quickly that it sounded almost rehearsed. Certainly something she'd gone over in her head. 'I'm not going to see him anymore,' she added. 'So probably no need to tell Mum about any of it...?'

It was spoken as a question but it didn't feel like one. More of a firm request. Megan wasn't sure how to deal with it. The information felt like something Nicola probably *should* know – and yet Jessie was close to being an adult in her own right. That and the concept of adulthood in respect to age always seemed so strange anyway. A person could be seventeen and 364 days old and treated one way but, a day later, and there were different expectations.

'If you don't want me to say anything, I won't,' Megan said. 'But if you want to know what I think, you should probably tell her. Maybe not now but in a while.'

Jessie nodded along as she continued to pick at the croissant. 'Thanks,' she replied – although Megan knew there definitely wouldn't be a daughter-mother conversation about such things. She had another bite and then stood. 'I'm going back to bed,' she said.

Megan was left at the table half-eating her own part of the croissant. It had gone soft and tasted a bit too much like microwaved tissue paper for her liking. She considered texting Paul to let him know she'd be back at the house within a day or two – but she didn't. Then she thought about texting Daniel to say she was leaving at some point too – but she didn't do that either. He'd gone out of his way to get Trevor away from his farm in order for Megan to embarrass herself. At least it was only him who knew. A day on, and she couldn't quite believe why she'd done it, or what she'd been thinking. She'd throw the tooth away and try to forget she'd ever found it.

She should never have come back.

Not wanting to waste food, Megan forced down the rest of the croissant, downed a cup of coffee and then got dressed.

Outside, and the day of the summer festival was as Megan remembered from her youth. Not just the time her dad ran that stall with the catapult, she couldn't remember any occurrences when it had rained. Nicola bringing it up that morning had triggered new-old memories. There was the time the two sisters had been on camel rides along the seafront. They'd bumped up and down on the saddle, while giggling as if on a rollercoaster. She wondered where the camel had come from. Did the owner tour the creature around various fetes and festivals across the year, as if it were a musician doing Glastonbury, V, and Leeds?

The hill down to the centre was lined with various bric-a-brac stalls as residents had dragged any old rubbish onto the kerbside in an attempt to make a few quid before it ended up in a skip. Some kids were selling cans of Coke for a quid from a cool box and Megan admired the sheer cheek of it.

There were roadblocks towards the bottom, and a man was out of his car arguing with a police officer about 'needing' to go 'that way' as he pointed towards the seafront. The officer was patiently trying to explain that signs had been up for weeks and the festival happened every year – but the man was still raging as Megan continued onto the main street.

There were stalls selling candy floss, sweets and baked goods, plus at least four ice cream vans. The bacon butty truck was doing a roaring trade – as was the one serving a full English in a bap.

'Hungry?' someone asked.

Megan turned to see Daniel standing next to the bench on which they'd sat while watching the kayaker head up the boating ramp. Of course she'd run into him.

'I can feel my arteries clogging just looking at the sign,' Megan said.

'Smells good, though, doesn't it?'

That was the truth.

'How are you?' Daniel asked – and it was such a loaded question. She'd not been in contact with him since the day before when her silly little plan had come to nothing.

'I met Sophia,' Megan said.

He didn't appear surprised. 'How did it go?'

A shrug. 'She's fine. Normal. The big guy – Oleg – is her dad. They live above the chip shop, or maybe it's just her? I didn't ask.'

Daniel was nodding along. A simple explanation of sorts. Still hard to explain Trevor's tooth and Sophia's reaction to seeing the pink top – but perhaps some things weren't supposed to be answered. Megan was going to drive herself mad if she kept digging. She didn't particularly approve of her sister exploiting Sophia's labour, but it was hard to say as much. She'd burned too many bridges as it was.

'I think I'm going back to Whitecliff,' Megan said. 'I was going to text you but...'

I wanted to sneak off, she didn't add. He understood.

'Where are you going to stay?'

'In my old house. My husband's moved out and said he'll stay away.'

Daniel offered his hand and Megan wasn't sure what he wanted. After a second of awkwardness, he reached further and took hers in his. 'It's been nice getting to know you,' he said, as he squished her fingers a little harder. 'I want you to be happy.'

'Nicola said the same.'

That got a soft smile. 'Is it a problem that people want you to be happy?'

'I guess not.'

They held hands for a few seconds more and it was what she wanted.

Enough.

Then he let her go.

'I need to get to the arcade. It's the busiest day of the year. Am I going to see you again before you go?'

Megan smiled at him and that was the answer.

He nodded and then turned in the other direction. 'Look after yourself,' he said.

She watched him go and, maybe, there was a glimmer of an alternate life. If it hadn't been for the fire, for what had happened to her father's friend, for those things and everything else, maybe there was a version of her life in which she'd remained in Hollicombe Bay and married Daniel. Nicola would still have married Ben – and they'd have cosy sister nights in once a week. No Paul, no Lucy.

Megan dwelled for a moment too long, allowing the melancholy to consume her. Real life was calling – and it wasn't far away.

The festival was a welcome distraction. Megan walked

along the seafront and then back along the parallel street. She
gave in and had a fried egg sandwich that was as wonderful as it
was disgusting. A small football goal had been set up a little off
the beach for a penalty competition – and Megan watched as a
boy booted the ball hard into his father's face. There was blood
and stifled laughter. The only person not finding it funny was
the guy with the busted nose.

A different dad was frantically trying to win a cuddly toy at
a coconut shy as his wife told him he would put his back out
again if he kept trying so hard. A mum was spiking playing
cards with darts in a different game. The arcade chuntered with
activity, and the line for the Portaloos lengthened as those
breakfasts in a bap had their revenge.

Everywhere Megan walked, there were families, couples,
friends and singletons like her enjoying themselves. She was
glad she stayed. Not everything about her return home had
been awful.

It was a little after one that Megan spotted Jessie and a
group of young women roughly her age hanging around on the
green, close to where she and Nicola had sat the day before.
They were multitasking on their phones while seemingly
holding a nine-way conversation at the same time.

Megan completed her third loop of town and considered
returning to the house. The alternative was to head across to the
baking tent to meet Nicola's father-in-law and see what all the
fuss was about.

She was near to one of the ice cream vans when she spotted
someone she recognised. A man, standing with people who
were, presumably, his wife and daughter. The girl was maybe
seven or eight and, though she knew his face, it took Megan a
few seconds to realise who he was.

It was Jessie's drama teacher.

THIRTY-NINE

Megan watched the family of three for a while and something ached within her. His wife laughed at something he'd said and then crouched to wipe a mark from their daughter's face. The girl pulled away and crinkled her nose as the parents laughed.

It was hard to know why he cheated, especially with a teenager – except, of course, it was never really about that. It wasn't about how good somebody's life might be, or not. It could be about power, or impulse control, or – most likely – simply horniness.

The two parents said something to each other and then mother and daughter crossed the road and headed into a cluttered vintage clothes stall. Lucas took a few steps backwards and sat on the wall, before taking out his phone and starting to scroll.

Megan didn't particularly think, she crossed the road and plonked herself at his side. He glanced sideways to her, smiling in a curious *Who's this nutter?*-kind of way. She could have sat anywhere.

'Your phone works, then?' Megan said.

He glanced down to the device and then back to her. 'Huh?'

'Lucas, isn't it?'

His eyes narrowed. 'Do I know you, or...?'

'You don't *really* know me – but I suppose I'm surprised your phone's working so well.'

Lucas locked the screen and started to stand.

'Jessie Harris is my niece,' Megan said.

He froze. 'Oh.'

'Your phone didn't seem to be working when she was trying to tell you she was pregnant.'

'*Shush!*' He lowered himself back onto the wall, eyes fixed on the stall into which his wife and daughter had disappeared. 'Can you keep your voice down?'

'Can you keep your dick in your pants?'

He swore under his breath, teeth clenched.

'How's the wife?' Megan asked, nodding towards the stall. 'And your daughter?'

Lucas sunk onto the wall, almost as if he was trying to swallow himself. 'What do you want?' He lowered his voice to a whisper. 'Jess said it was a misunderstanding, something to do with dates. She said she's not pregnant.'

The last word came out so reluctantly, it was as if he'd never heard or spoken it before.

'You're having an affair with a seventeen-year-old *student* and that's the best you can do? *A misunderstanding?*'

Megan had kept her simmering fury in check when she'd been around Jessie, but it was impossible to keep down now Lucas was in front of her.

How *dare* he.

Lucas craned his neck, trying to peer into the clothes stall. There was a bustling mass of people coming and going, but no sign of his wife or daughter.

'Look, it was an accident,' he said.

'You slipped and fell *into* her?'

'Not like that.' He shook his head. 'You don't have to be crude.'

'Are you joking?'

He sucked in his cheeks and took a breath, then tried again. 'It was a misjudgement. I'd be the first to admit it.'

'Don't start with that,' Megan replied, just about holding onto her fury. 'I don't know what happened but it doesn't really matter. Even if you think she led you on, or flirted, whatever – which I doubt anyway – she's seventeen and you're twenty years older. You're her *teacher*.'

Lucas was steadfastly making sure not to look in Megan's direction. His gaze had barely left the stall. He gulped, probably wondering how she knew his age.

'Does anyone else know?' he asked.

'Like who?'

'I dunno, her parents?'

Megan laughed at that. 'You wondering if she's got some brick-shithouse dad?'

Another gulp, because that was obviously what he was thinking. He was one of those hill-walking types. All skinny and lean, who'd be blown over in a strong breeze.

'I know your name,' Megan said. 'Your wife's over there. I know where you live and where you teach. I know the name of your boss and their boss. I know the girl on the local paper and I know your local MP. And if I hear even a *whiff* of you looking at another girl for a second too long – one second – I'll send all the evidence to everyone I just mentioned.'

It was largely bravado but Megan knew she had him.

Lucas rubbed his eyes and then his chin. 'What evidence?' he asked.

'Do you really want to find out?'

He didn't reply to that. He might wonder whether she was bluffing but he'd be a fool to risk it.

'You can't,' he said, though he sounded defeated. 'Faith is only seven. Her mum will leave me. You'll ruin her life.'

Megan's stomach twisted. She knew what he was doing and, as she looked back to the stall, she saw Lucas's wife pick something purple from one of the rails. She held it up, showing it to Faith and presumably asking what she thought.

He was right, of course. It probably would ruin Faith's life, at least in the short term. Megan knew what it was like to be centre of attention after something awful happened.

But it wouldn't be her ruining Faith's life. It would be her father.

'Nothing will happen if you keep your hands to yourself,' she said, trying to keep her tone level.

'Fine. It's not like—'

'Know when to stop talking.'

He did – but not for long. 'Is it secure?' he added, lips barely moving.

'Is *what* secure?'

'Your evidence. The texts, or whatever.'

Megan was on slightly shaky ground, considering she had no evidence. 'What do you mean?' she asked.

He huffed in annoyance. 'Say I believe you're not going to share what you have, what if someone else has access? There are always extra copies in the cloud. So I'm asking if you have hard copies, and if they're in a safe somewhere? If it's screenshots, or whatever, are they in a place only you can get them?'

Megan tried to think of the best way to bluff it and in the end went with a straightforward: 'Nobody else has access. I think you—'

Lucas didn't wait for the rest of the sentence. His wife and daughter were heading out of the stall and he sprang up from the wall as if he'd been stung. He practically galloped across the street and met them with an overenthusiastic enquiry about what they'd bought. As they began walking along the street, he risked a glance back towards Megan and gave the merest of nods. They had an understanding.

'In a safe somewhere,' he'd said. A safe...

Nicola had asked whether Megan had brought her passport to Hollicombe Bay. Megan hadn't but Nicola said hers, Ben's and Jessie's were all kept in a safe, along with their birth certificates.

But Megan had been in her safe – and none of those things were there.

It could have been a turn of phrase, but it didn't feel like it. If those things truly *were* in a safe, then that meant her sister had more than one.

In which case, what else could Nicola be hiding?

FORTY

It was a minute to three and The Great Hollicombe Bay Bake Off would be beginning soon, subject to copyright issues. Megan guessed it would probably take an hour, something like that, until it was either finished, the tent was on fire, or people got bored.

Megan hurried up the hill, past the now abandoned bric-a-brac stalls, some of which now had crude cardboard 'free' signs leaning against them. She reached Nicola's empty house at nine minutes past and burst through the front door, a sweating, swearing mess.

No time for that.

She checked the downstairs safe, entered those same four numbers again and pulled out the contents to double-check she definitely *hadn't* missed the passports and birth certificates, which she hadn't.

Suddenly, the day before felt off. It was hard to say precisely why, or how. Perhaps it was the way they'd gone directly to Sophia's flat – and that she had just happened to be in along with her dad. That the place was so empty of furniture and anything else. No phone chargers, no random cables. Just one plate and mug on the draining board. And this young woman had barely blinked when she was dragged in front of a stranger who wanted to ask her questions. And that reaction when Megan had taken out the pink top.

Had that conversation been set up?

Megan knew she'd seen Sophia in the stream, she *knew* it. It wasn't her imagination and she hadn't had a breakdown. She gave her chest compressions. She left those marks on her top. It had happened.

Megan had already searched the downstairs when hunting for the safe the first time. She checked behind a couple more cabinets as if the house was part of a bad spy movie.

Nothing. Obviously.

Could there be a second safe at the café? It felt unlikely – especially if passports were within.

Upstairs and it didn't simply feel like a betrayal, it *was* one. Megan went into her sister's room, to be surprised by the mess. There were socks and underwear across the floor, plus a pile of unwashed clothes against the radiator.

No time for regret, or thinking herself out of it. The clock was ticking.

Megan checked the cluttered wardrobes, then the drawers, and then under the bed. Nothing.

There was nothing to be found along the hall – and Megan didn't think it would be in Jessie's room, even if she wanted to look, which she didn't. The bathroom felt even more unlikely, so she returned downstairs and went into the garage. The car took up much of the space and there were tools and a workbench in the back corner, next to a boiler. There wasn't much room for anything and, even if there was, nowhere to hide it.

Back into the house and Megan did another flit through the living room. She checked under the furniture and behind everything.

There was no safe. There was nothing particularly out of

place. It was also twenty-five past and Megan didn't know how long she had until someone got home.

It was only the attic she hadn't checked.

And then Megan knew.

Everything had seemed out of place from the first night she slept there.

Megan tore up the stairs as if half her age. She burst into the attic and headed for the stupid chaise longue that was too big and too in the way. There was no reason for it to be pressed up against the bed – but it was like that for a reason. Her shoulders screamed as Megan dragged it across the floor to reveal that the smooth off-pink carpet wasn't as complete as it seemed. A square had been cut in the space underneath and, though a piece of matching carpet had been put in place, it stood out like a vegan at a barbecue.

The carpet square came up along with the floorboard it had been stapled to – and, there, sitting barely a pace from where Megan had been sleeping for a week, was a safe.

It was the same size as the one downstairs – and Megan again typed 7-7-2-7 into the pushpad on the front. There was the now familiar *click-clunk* as the lock disengaged. Megan was on her knees but paused for a moment, rocking on her heels, wondering if she really wanted to know. This was her *sister's* secret.

'It's just passports,' Megan said out loud, even though she hadn't looked.

Megan reached into the safe, and it was quickly apparent there *were* passports inside.

Not three.

At least twenty.

Megan took them out, one, two, four at a time until there was a stack on the carpet. Some were pristine, others looked as if they'd rattled around the bottom of a bag or two. She couldn't quite believe what she was holding. There were three British ones in the pile – Nicola's, Ben's and Jessie's. Of the others, most had crimson covers, with gold type on the front. 'Polska', 'România' and 'Slovenija' were some of the countries named.

As she opened the first, Megan thought of the spy films she'd seen, where the lead character's face would be in a foreign passport with a different name. She half expected to see her sister or Ben's face but it wasn't that.

The first passport had 'Polska' on the front, and the photo inside was of Jessie's friend. Helena Zielinski was nineteen years old and her face stared emotionlessly from the page. The next passport belonged to someone from Romania and it took Megan a few seconds to realise she knew him too. He was the person who'd exited the café's kitchen a little after Sophia. There were more faces and names Megan didn't know and almost all the passports belonged to young men between the ages of nineteen and twenty-four.

The first Slovenian passport belonged to Sophia – except that wasn't what she was called. Megan had only heard people say it, never written down. The young woman's *actual* name was Zofia Kovač. She was twenty, but seemed like a child in her photograph. There were freckles and longer, lighter, hair – with the youthful fresh face of a person who had their entire life ahead of them.

Megan checked the next passport and there was a twinkling fraction in which it felt as if someone had slapped her in the chest. She had to remind herself to breathe and it all came out as a frantic gasp.

Zofia's face was staring out from a second passport, except that wasn't her name. Valeska Kovač had the same face as Zofia and, when Megan went back to check the previous passport, she also had the same date of birth.

It wasn't Zofia, of course – and she didn't *only* have a sister. She had a *twin*.

FORTY-ONE

It was no wonder Zofia had been so shocked at seeing the pink top. It wasn't hers, it was her twin's. It wasn't Zofia in the stream, it was Valeska.

It was Valeska whom Megan had tried to save, probably Valeska who'd kicked out Trevor's front tooth.

Megan wondered whether Zofia knew her sister was almost certainly dead – although her reaction probably gave it away. Would she really have been answering Megan's silly questions in the flat barely days after her twin's death? Would she continue working in a kitchen as if nothing had happened?

The attic was hot but Megan shivered at the likely answer.

Whatever was going on around town, Nicola had to be in on it. *She* was the one storing other people's passports in a hidden safe. *She'd* taken Megan to Zofia's flat as a way of ending a mystery that Megan wasn't letting go.

Megan looked deeper into the safe. Nicola, Ben and Jessie's birth certificates were flat across the bottom, there was a bundle of cash that Megan didn't have time to count, and a series of keys with coloured tags and small printed labels. Megan sorted through ones marked 'café', 'sweets', 'chips', 'pub' and 'base' – whatever that meant. There were around twenty in total.

And then something else occurred to her. There were passports for close to two dozen young people in front of her and, as far as she could tell, she hadn't seen one of them walking around the summer festival.

Wasn't that strange?

Megan had seen Jessie with her friends, not to mention dozens, maybe hundreds of other teenagers hanging around.

A horrible, creeping realisation was beginning to dawn.

It was 3:37 and Nic's café was due to close at half-past four. Megan took the key marked 'café', returned everything else to the safe, replaced the carpet square, and dragged the chaise longue back into place.

Using Nicola's bike, Megan managed to get to the café in a little over ten minutes. She'd have been proud of the record at any other time – and her legs certainly weren't happy about things – but Megan expected to have only a short window to do what she wanted.

The festival's daytime activities were winding down and residents were making their way back up the hill, while visitors headed for their cars. Megan climbed off the bike in the courtyard at the back of the café. There was no SUV parked outside, which Megan guessed meant Oleg hadn't yet arrived.

And it *was* a guess.

Megan had spent much of her time in Hollicombe Bay confused, or doubting herself but, for the first time since arriving back, there was a tingle of fear.

She retrieved the stolen key marked 'café' from her bag and tried it on the door at the back of the café. It slipped so cleanly into the lock that it almost turned itself.

The heat hit Megan as soon as she stepped into the kitchen. After a week in the oven of an attic, she was partly used to it – though it was still a shock as her face flushed. She closed the door into the frame behind her but didn't shut it all the way. On the other side of the kitchen a pair of figures were shuttling from side to side with their backs to her. Megan craned to look into the corners, where there was a pair of freezers on one side and a row of tall cupboards in the other.

No Oleg.

One of the figures turned and headed across to what turned out to be a store cupboard – and Megan recognised him as the person she'd seen in the Romanian passport. She couldn't remember his name but she knew he was twenty-two.

And then they saw each other.

Zofia had been standing close to a deep-fat fryer when she turned and spotted Megan.

'Hi,' Megan said.

FORTY-TWO

Zofia looked from side to side and reeled back towards the counter.

'You're safe,' Megan said, holding up both her hands to show she wasn't carrying anything except the key.

The young Romanian man had noticed Megan and was edging towards Zofia. He said something to her in a language Megan didn't understand and Zofia nodded. Both of them had an air of rising panic. Zofia was within reaching distance of the door that Megan knew led into the café. It was the one through which Pam had stormed to fix the hatch.

'I think I saw your sister,' Megan said. 'Valeska...?'

Zofia might not have understood everything – but her eyes widened at the name of her twin. She pointed towards a bottle of bleach that was sitting at the end of a counter and it took Megan a few seconds to realise it wasn't the bleach specifically, it was because the bottle was pink.

'Yes,' Megan said, while nodding. 'Pink. Her pink top.'

Zofia said something to the man, who replied to her, and then switched to English to talk to Megan.

'You know Valeska?' he asked.

Megan shook her head. 'I don't *know* her. I *saw* her last weekend.'

He translated that back for Zofia and then: 'They said she escape?'

It sounded like a question and Megan was so close to revealing the truth. She glanced to Zofia's expectant features and, suddenly, she knew.

They weren't being paid cash under the table. They weren't being paid less than minimum wage.

Nicola had their passports because they were being *forced* to work. Daniel had practically told her that the other owners from the business association couldn't understand why seasonal workers weren't showing up to do the menial jobs.

And, here, now, they had their workers.

No, not workers. Workers didn't talk about 'escape'.

Slaves.

Megan shivered at the thought. No wonder none of the faces she'd seen in the passports were at the summer festival, enjoying the weather and the day. They were all locked up in kitchens, offices, or wherever else. Oleg, Trevor, or someone else would drive around at closing time and pile them all back in the SUV to take them... where? That flat above the chip shop?

There was something else Megan realised. She'd never actually told Zofia that she'd seen her *dead* in the stream, simply that she'd seen her in the water. Oleg had interrupted the first time they'd met at the back of the café. Then, in the flat, Oleg had done the translating. Zofia hadn't denied having a sister, she'd denied whatever Oleg had said to her.

She thought her twin had got away from the hell they were in.

'You saw her running?' the man asked – and, as Megan desperately tried to avoid Zofia's stare, she knew she couldn't be the one to tell her the truth. Not now. Not in this kitchen, where there was nowhere to go. It would come another day, when she was safe. For now, all Zofia had was the belief that her sister was out there.

'Yes, running,' Megan replied.

The man said something to Zofia and she clutched her chest, her *heart*, as she broke into a smile. 'Worry,' she said to Megan, before saying something else to the man.

'She asked something about a pink shirt,' he translated.

Before anyone could say anything more, the three of them jumped together as the bell from the hatch dinged. Megan had sounded it herself from the other side, though it had never seemed as loud.

The man took a few steps to the side and picked up the scrap of an order that had been pushed through, before adding it to a corkboard.

They just don't like being bothered while they're working.

That's what Pam had said, so she knew what was going on as well. Nicola had repeated it almost word for word. Megan wondered how many were in on it. Daniel had warned her about the divisions of the local owners – and it now seemed obvious that's why Ben had warned her away from him.

'What's your name?' Megan asked.

'Elias.'

'I'm Megan,' she replied. And then: 'I found Valeska's top. She must have dropped it.'

Elias relayed that back to Zofia who nodded along. There was no follow-up. She believed her sister was safe.

The three of them stood in an awkward triangle until Megan nodded towards the fire door, which was still open.

'Do you want to... go?'

She looked from Zofia to Elias and was wishing she'd brought their passports. They exchanged a look and something was uttered that Megan didn't understand. There were hand movements that didn't seem particularly friendly and then a sharp 'no' from Zofia.

Elias turned to Megan. 'No,' he said.

Megan struggled to know how to reply. In her naivety, she had been certain they'd say 'yes', not that she had a plan. What would they do? A double backsie on her bike as Megan pedalled for safety? Wherever that might be.

The idea of calling the police flittered into Megan's mind, except they'd been *so* dismissive of Megan the previous weekend that small conspiratorial whispers told her they were involved, too. Even then, what would happen? Would these poor young people end up back in the clutches of Oleg, Trevor, and whoever else?

'Where are you staying?' Megan asked. She'd come back for them another time – and she'd bring their passports. 'Above the chip shop?'

That got a shake of head from the man, who didn't bother to translate.

'The farm?' Megan asked.

Another shake of the head. He was swirling his hand in front of his face, searching for the word. 'Base,' Elias said.

'Where's the base?' Megan asked.

And then it came. Somehow entirely predictable, even though Megan had missed it: 'Arcade.'

FORTY-THREE

Megan reached for the nearest counter, as she felt her knees give a gentle tremble. 'Arcade...?' she managed, although Elias didn't respond. He was pointing to the latest food order and talking to Zofia.

Except it was obvious. Daniel was a business owner like the rest of them. They were *all* in on it, including him. He'd even told her about the 'many storerooms at the back' of the arcade.

When Megan had confided in Daniel and he'd got Trevor away from the farm, it was in the afternoon. If there was anything in the space under the barn, Trevor would have had all morning to clear it out. They had probably sat in the office of the arcade having a good laugh about it. About her.

Not only that, Megan had run into Daniel late at night and he'd joked about them being night owls. While she had simply been out for a walk, he was probably doing the same thing as Trevor, and ferrying around those poor people.

'Do you all *live* at the arcade?' Megan asked.

Elias was emptying a basket of fries onto a tray lined with paper towels. 'Yes,' he said, when he turned.

'And Oleg lives with you?'

He frowned, probably at the mention of Oleg's name, though he understood. 'He has flat.'

Of course he did. The flat above the chip shop, where they'd taken Megan the day before. It didn't seem like the sort of place a woman in her late-teens or early twenties might live – but Megan could picture Oleg there. She doubted Zofia was his daughter, although it didn't seem worth pushing in the moment. His passport hadn't been with the others.

'I'll get the police,' Megan said. They couldn't pretend to ignore close to two dozen people being holed up in the storage rooms at the back of the arcade. They couldn't fail to believe her now.

'No,' Elias called. 'No police. No.'

Zofia must've understood the word 'police', because she was shaking her head. 'No, no, no,' she said, until Elias placed a hand on her shoulder and muttered something.

'No police,' Elias repeated.

Megan held up her hands again, trying to tell them she didn't mean any harm. She didn't understand. 'OK, no police.'

Elias was swirling his hand once more, searching for the words. His English was a lot better than he seemed to think, although, unlike his natural voice, it came with the gentlest hint of an American accent. 'They threaten family,' he said. 'At home. Threaten them there. Say we run, they kill.'

Megan glanced to Zofia and wondered what she was thinking. She thought her sister had escaped, though she must be worried whether that had an impact on what was going on back home.

It had to be Oleg. He was the link from here to wherever 'there' happened to be.

'No police,' Elias repeated.

'No police,' Megan confirmed.

'You go now,' Elias said, pointing towards the fire exit. 'You go.'

Megan took a step towards the door. 'Don't tell anyone I was here,' she said, while waiting in front of the exit. 'Do you understand?' she asked.

Elias nodded.

'Tell Zofia.'

Another nod. 'You go.'

Megan did. The light of the afternoon blinded her as she slipped off the step into the courtyard. The fire door banged closed behind her as she reached for the bike.

Their families were under threat. No wonder they didn't want to be rescued.

She wondered how far and how deep it all went. Her sister didn't only know, as if that wasn't bad enough, she was in on it. She was keeping their passports in her house. Her *actual* sister.

It was the previous day they'd sat together and Nicola had said that if they lost the café, the house would be gone as well. They owed so much money. Megan had thought the forced defiance was Nicola trying to convince herself that stealing money from their father was OK. And perhaps it was that – but it was trying to justify *this* as well.

Then there was Daniel and how naïve she had been. She'd been blinded by a teenage crush. Ben and Nicola had warned her away, maybe because they feared her discovering their own secrets – but perhaps because he was at the centre of everything. The workers, the *slaves,* were living in the back of his arcade.

Megan didn't know what to do. She kept circling back to telling the police – but what if something happened to the families of Elias and Zofia and the others?

She wheeled the bike onto the high street, where stalls were being taken down. The beer gardens were rammed and, with traffic still barred, people were sitting on the kerbs with drinks and takeaways. It was going to be a long beery night. One of not very many in the town – and Megan wondered how many of the faces she'd seen in the passports would be locked in kitchens making food, or cleaning up. Hidden away, where no one would discover them.

They were stuck, and so was she. She couldn't drive and, even if she could, where would she find something that could hold twenty people? And where would she take them?

She didn't know.

And then she did.

FORTY-FOUR

When Megan arrived back at her sister's house a few hours later, everyone was already home. They spent some time sitting in the living room, pretending everything was fine. Nicola's father-in-law had pulled off a disaster at the baking competition. His attempt at making some sort of pear cake had turned into what Jessie described as 'soup'. He had blamed it on the heat, raged at the organiser for having favourites, and then kicked a fridge. He'd finished last and probably wished none of his family had been there, let alone all of them. Happy birthday, and all that.

They ordered a takeaway and, for the first time in the week Megan had been staying there, the four of them ate together. It was, admittedly, from their laps while scattered around the living room but everyone seemed to enjoy it – including Megan in some ways. She told them she was returning to Whitecliff the following day and the family meal felt like an end, which it was.

Jessie drifted up to her room not long after the food was gone. Her mum was seemingly convinced the eating disorder truly was over. Megan listened to her footsteps on the stairs, then her door opening and closing. One way or the other, it would be a new world for Jessie tomorrow and a large part of Megan wanted to warn her – even if she knew she couldn't. None of this was her fault.

Then it was three of them and Megan allowed herself to be drawn into conversations about everything and nothing. Yes, Saturday-night TV was awful nowadays. Yes, they were too old to be out on the town at this time of night. No, she had never got into red wine. No, she'd never played Settlers of Catan and didn't want to start now. Yes, heading back to Whitecliff probably would be good for her.

It was the most amount of continuous time Megan had spent with her sister in years and, in short bursts – when she allowed herself to live in those moments – it was back to that glimpse of an alternate life. A life in which they'd stayed in the same town, enjoyed the same things, lived in each other's kitchens and living rooms. Maybe even had children the same age, who'd play together.

Then Megan would remember the other stuff – and it wasn't that at all.

Ben was the first to stretch and yawn. He picked up his and Nicola's empty wine glasses, plus the drained bottle, and dispatched everything into the kitchen before saying he was heading to bed. Nicola said she'd join him and they both looked to Megan expectantly. She said she'd head upstairs, too, so the lights were switched off, the dishwasher was put to work, and to bed they went.

Megan lay, listening to the night through the open attic window. It was how it had all started and there were so many what ifs. What if Megan hadn't decided to leave Whitecliff? Or if she hadn't asked her sister if she could stay over? Or if she'd gone out that Sunday afternoon? Or if the attic hadn't been so hot and the window was shut? Or if she'd ignored the scream and put it down to someone's telly being too loud?

And so on.

Megan didn't know whether she'd slept, or if she'd been awake the whole time. Her phone beeped quietly to tell her it was 1 a.m. – and then she climbed off the bed and scooched around the chaise longue. It was perhaps hard to know why Nicola and Ben had left so many valuable things in a safe barely a reach away from where she'd been sleeping. Except, why would Megan move furniture? Why would she notice the cut-out square of carpet? Why find the safe? Why guess the code? Why, why, why?

Everyone had underestimated her.

She crept down from the attic and through the house, grabbing her shoes from the hall and quietly leaving the house. The walk down the hill towards town was in near silence, save for the rhythmic wash of the ocean.

Megan avoided the seafront, instead keeping to the darkened back alleys and delivery lanes as she weaved around overflowing bins and discarded festival signs. She slowed as she moved into the centre of town, listening for voices or vehicles. It was late and had been the longest of days. Aside from a couple of stragglers on their way back to the various campsites, the town was quiet.

A pink rubber circle was clipped to the rounded end of the key marked 'base' that Megan had taken from the attic safe. She wasn't entirely sure why her sister had keys to many of the businesses in town, though she had her suspicions. Everyone who was in on whatever was going on had their own collective responsibilities, meaning they were in it together. If someone's conscience came calling a bit too strongly, they wouldn't be able to take anyone else down without destroying their own life and business. Trevor, Nicola, Ben, Daniel and anyone else needed each other.

Megan glanced up to the camera over the door at the back of the arcade. She knew it broadcast back to the office, though had no idea whether it went anywhere else. Given the time, it was a calculated gamble that nobody was watching a feed at that moment.

The key slid into the lock for the back of the arcade and the door popped open with a clunk. The inside was gloomy, though not entirely dark and, as Megan stepped inside, she spied the rows of mattresses across the floor. She looked around, taking in the rest of what looked like a scene from a refugee camp. Clothes were in piles next to the mattresses, or balled into plastic bags. There was a row of canvas floor-to-almost-ceiling dividers on one side, with jerry-rigged festival-style showers hanging above.

Daniel had told her there were storerooms at the back – and the walls were lined with rows of battered machines, plus towers of file boxes.

Then there were the people. Some were sleeping but most weren't. Megan recognised faces from the passports as three gathered around a table with a dim lamp and a deck of cards. Others were lying on mattresses, or sitting and chatting in small groups.

Helena was there, lying on her bed, scruffy paperback in one hand. Megan had never met her, though she'd seen her through that window doing the night shift in the sweet shop kitchen. She wondered why she'd been allowed out for a while at least, to become friends of a sort with Jessie. Perhaps it was soon after being brought to the area, when she would have been full of hope and excitement? Then someone decided to put her to work and that's why, in Jessie's eyes, the other girl had disappeared.

Elias had been at the table playing cards but he slid out from his stool and stood, staring in Megan's direction.

Then there was Zofia, who had wet, newly showered, hair and had been sitting on a mattress with another girl about her age. Valeska's pink top was folded tidily next to her pillow and

Megan had to remind herself that Zofia currently believed her twin had escaped.

One person staring became two, became ten. More. People were talking over each other, all in languages Megan didn't understand. She peered through the throng towards Elias.

'Will you trust me?'

He had been walking towards her and his brow wrinkled. She unhooked the bag from her shoulder and dug inside, before pulling out a handful of passports, which she offered to him. He was in front of her now, muttering under his breath as he took them. The chatter had gone silent as he thumbed through the pile until reaching his own.

Megan removed the rest from her bag and offered them too. 'I can get you all out,' she told him. 'But we need to go now and everyone has to be quiet.'

Elias flipped to the next passport and checked the profile page. Then another. He called to the man nearest him and passed him the passport. They spoke back and forth, using their hands as much as their words, and then Elias called across to Zofia as he held up hers.

'We have to go now,' Megan told him as she failed to hide the desperation. The confidence she'd felt through the evening while acting as if everything was fine had deserted her. As she offered the final stack of passports, her hand was shaking. 'If we're quick, we can get you somewhere safe before anyone notices you've gone. Then we can get your families safe, too.'

Megan wasn't certain about that part. It was a big promise that she wasn't sure anyone could guarantee, least of all her. But she was confident about the first part. Or that's what she told herself.

Elias had passed the first pile of passports to the man at his side and had reached for the next. Megan's bag was open and she juddered as the phone inside started to buzz. Without taking it out, she could see who'd messaged her.

Daniel.

FORTY-FIVE

Megan took out her phone and read the message.

Where are you?

She typed back a quick:

Past the greenhouse, near the woods

and then put the phone back into the bag.

Daniel was currently getting a taste of his own medicine at Trevor's farm. Megan had messaged him to say she'd found out something *really* important about the farm and asked him to meet her there. She pictured him skulking around, looking for her, while Trevor watched from the farmhouse, unseen.

What it did mean was that neither of them could be watching the camera feed from outside the arcade door.

'We've got to go,' she told Elias, with a firmness that surprised even her.

Elias had seemingly made his decision and began talking quickly to the others. Some were gathering items from the mattresses, or retrieving their passports. Others were chattering excitedly – and a couple more were waking up, wondering what was going on.

Within a minute at most, Elias appeared to have rallied everyone. They were putting on shoes and clothes as he turned back to Megan. 'Where?'

Megan's phone buzzed again but she ignored it as she hurried to the door. She expected Elias to be directly behind but he waited, urging others to follow her as she led them into the alley. It was what Megan had planned earlier in the evening, before returning to the house but a surreal sense of confidence slipped through her. This was actually happening. There was no going back.

She led the swelling group along the alley and around the front of the shops, before crossing the road towards the boat launch dock. It hadn't been that long since she and Daniel had sat on the bench watching that kayaker. Daniel had lied to her about everything and she'd trusted him. Now, as her phone buzzed again, he was the one who'd been naïve.

It had taken two or three minutes for Megan to get from the back of the arcade to the boat launch. The crowd of tired young people massed around her when she stopped. A few seconds on and Elias drifted through the numbers until he was in front of her. Zofia was at his side.

A growling rumble was chuntering in the dark and then a bright white seared through the night, from the end of the dock.

Megan pointed towards the boat as she spoke to Elias. 'That's Cliff,' she said. 'He's got enough room for all of you and he's going to take you somewhere safe.'

Elias reeled a little as he, understandably, hadn't expected a boat. He exchanged a look with Zofia, said something to the man closest to him, and then looked back to Megan.

'Boat?'

'There'll be people on the other side,' Megan said. 'You'll never have to come back.'

'How long?'

'About half an hour. Thirty minutes...?'

Megan wasn't certain but she needed to sound sure and confident. This was the important part.

A second passed. Two. And then Elias nodded. He started waving an arm, beckoning his friends towards the boat.

Cliff was a silhouette against the light and he was helping people up, calling them 'love', 'dear', 'mate', 'pal', 'big lad', and 'fella'. The affability sounded like Megan's father before the fire.

Some seemed happy to head for the boat, others dragged their feet, or spoke harshly to Elias, who simply shrugged. Megan didn't understand the words but she got his response. Whatever was on the other side couldn't be worse than what they'd gone through.

Megan's phone was still buzzing with incoming messages. And then it was just her, Elias and Zofia – who was still clasping the pink top. There would be a conversation about that item of clothing, but not tonight.

'Thank you,' Zofia said.

'You're welcome,' Megan replied. 'But you have to go.'

The seafront was quiet but there were lights, probably from a car, far up on the hill. Maybe nothing but that wasn't the point.

'Where are we going?' Elias asked.

'Whitecliff,' Megan told him, pointing towards the furthest side of the bay, past the lighthouse. 'Along the coast. It's where I live. People will be there.'

He nodded, although she wasn't sure he'd understood.

'Go,' Megan hissed – and then he did. He was the last person on the boat as Cliff heaved him up and said something that sounded a lot like 'welcome aboard'.

The engine grumbled louder, which at least muffled the

sound coming from Megan's phone. She watched as the boat rocked slowly forwards, then backwards, and then surged ahead with a booming snarl. It was almost as if it had backfired, except it was shrinking as it started its journey across the rippling inky black of infinity.

Megan continued to watch as the chundering of the engine dipped and disappeared. Time passed and she couldn't bring herself to look away as the lights slowly withered to dots. When the boat passed the curve of the cove and drifted past the lighthouse, Megan allowed herself to breathe properly. Her phone had long since stopped vibrating and she knew a reckoning was coming.

At least they were safe.

She sensed him, maybe. Or perhaps it was an accident of timing, a striking moment of synergy, Megan turned towards the high street and Daniel was on the other side of the road, at the exit from the alley. He stepped off the kerb, walking towards her breathlessly, one hand on his chest. It sounded like he'd been running, probably because he had.

He looked between her and the horizon as it dawned. That beautiful face of his was gone, twisted into something horrified.

No.

Not horrified. *Frightened.*

Megan wondered if it had happened in the moment, or if she'd been blinded by her teenage memories since the first evening she saw him.

He eyed Megan and then glimpsed past her into the night. He might not know *exactly* what had happened, but he must have some idea.

'You know you've just killed all their families, don't you?' he said calmly.

FORTY-SIX

Megan pulled out her own phone and looked at the screen. There were fourteen unread messages and three missed calls. It must've taken Daniel a while to realise she hadn't been at Trevor's farm.

'Calling someone won't help,' he said, misunderstanding why she'd taken out her phone. There was a sneer to his voice that she hadn't heard before. 'It's too late,' he added. 'I just need to send a text, one text, and it's over. You can't believe how stupid a thing you've done. All their families are going to die and it's going to be horrible.'

Megan returned her phone to her bag and zipped it. 'Do it,' she said, finally looking him in the eye. They were under a street light, painted in the orangey glow.

Daniel had been about to say something else but stopped mid-word. 'Fine. This is on you.'

He took out his phone and started tapping at the screen before the confusion dawned. He patted the device a few more times, turned it over and looked at the back for some reason and then lowered it.

'What have you done?'

Megan almost laughed. Everyone in town loved to complain that there was only one phone mast. Including her sister. She nodded up to the hill – and the flickering, swelling fire that was beginning to take hold. The timing had been impeccable.

'The police are waiting at the other end for the boat,' she said. 'There's a journalist there, too. Some guy from Whitecliff who already has the details about everything that happened here. I emailed him everything, including your names.'

Daniel looked to his phone again, as if the answers might be there, before he paused to stare up at the fire. He must have been wondering how she'd had time to start that while also being on the seafront at the same time. It was a fair question – but he never asked it, because the SUV with the dented bumper screeched along the high street, before parking crookedly on the far side of the street.

Megan had expected Trevor to show up at some point, probably Oleg, too – but they had the full house, because Nicola and Ben clambered from the back seat. Nicola was still in her fleecy, cosy-looking pyjamas, walking boots on her feet. Ben had seemingly taken longer to get ready because he looked like he was ready for a country ramble before a Sunday roast. He was even wearing a padded gilet that couldn't have said 'prick' more than if it had been stencilled across the front.

The four of them crossed towards the boat dock, where Megan was still standing. She hadn't been sure things would end here, though it had always been likely to be somewhere in town.

Nicola looked to Daniel first. She was holding her phone. 'We got your text but there's no reception. We came right here.'

Daniel wasn't looking to her, not properly, and she followed his gaze up the hill towards the burning mast.

'What happened?' Nicola said.

'Ask your sister.'

And then all eyes were on Megan. She had never wanted to

be centre of attention, especially after the school fire. She'd craved obscurity, to start a family, and live a normal life.

She yawned. It was late, after all. 'Not as much of a night owl as I thought,' she said, talking to Daniel.

Nicola wasn't ready to be ignored. There was a snap to her voice as she pointed up the hill. 'Did you do that?'

'Not me personally.'

Megan risked a glance to Oleg, who didn't need to do an impression of some giant, pissed-off henchman. He was naturally fitting the role.

'Why?' Megan asked, focusing on her sister. 'Why did it come to this?'

The two sisters stared at one another, although Nicola's eyebrow was flickering.

It was Daniel who answered. 'I told you,' he said, and his voice was calm. 'The town's dying.'

Megan looked to him and he was holding his hands open and wide, showing off the scars.

'We almost *died* in this town,' he added. 'Someone had to rebuild it. Someone had to do something. I was tired of listening to all the clowns at the business association meetings with their dumb ideas. Take out all the wages we throw away to people who don't appreciate it, and everything's fine.'

'You can't just take away wages,' Megan said. 'If you can't afford to pay people, you don't have a business.'

'Oh but we do,' Daniel said.

'You *did*,' Megan corrected him, although it didn't feel particularly good to say so. Nicola had said that losing the business meant losing the house – but even that was small if Daniel was right. Losing the businesses – multiple – meant losing the town. He'd told her something similar at least twice and she'd still somehow thought he was a good guy.

'Why do you think we told you to stay away from him,' Nicola said, and Daniel laughed at her. At Megan too, probably.

'It wasn't *our* idea,' Ben said, as he literally pointed a finger at Daniel. 'We kept telling *him* it was a bad idea.'

'You went along with it like everyone else,' Daniel scoffed.

'We *had* to,' Nicola replied.

'You didn't *have* to do anything.'

Ben was pointing to Trevor now and his voice had gone up by at least an octave. 'He's the one who brings them into town,' he said, before switching to jab a finger at Oleg, 'and he gets them into the country.'

'Domestic servitude,' Megan said carefully. She'd looked it up. 'Slavery.'

'It's not slavery,' Ben said. 'They get paid in things like accommodation and food.'

'Is that their choice?' Megan asked, which went without a response. 'You had their passports,' she added, talking to her sister. 'You had the keys. You could've ended it.'

Ben sighed and looked to Nicola. 'I told you we should've moved that stuff.'

If Megan had any doubts, which she didn't, it was gone with that. There was no contrition for what they'd done, only that they'd been caught.

Daniel was glaring at Megan and, though she could feel its weight, she tried to ignore him.

It was Trevor who spoke next. He'd been largely silent since arriving, aside from a series of grunts.

'Why do you care?' he asked – and it sounded that he was actually interested.

'Because they're people,' Megan replied.

'But you don't know them.'

Megan wasn't sure how to reply. She still had his tooth and figured it would be evidence at some point. Maybe.

'Anyone wanna give me a lift home to Whitecliff?' she asked.

It was largely a joke, a bad one, and nobody reacted.

'I don't know why you're looking so smug,' Daniel said. 'The police aren't *here*.'

Megan finally shifted her gaze back to him as he pointed along the empty road.

'Where are they?' he added. 'Where's anyone? You might've got *them* to safety but *you're* still here.'

There was a glimmer of something between him and Oleg, a momentary arc of the finger, and that was enough for the brute to take a step towards Megan.

FORTY-SEVEN

'You can't,' Nicola said, which stopped Oleg a couple of metres away from Megan. He was so big, he was blocking most of the orange of the street light, which left him haloed by the glow. 'She's pregnant,' Nicola added.

Megan realised she'd been holding her breath. She wasn't sure what would happen to her after she got everyone to safety. A part of her wasn't bothered. What did she have left? A cheating husband. The best friend who'd betrayed her. A sister who'd done *this*. A hometown that hadn't been home for a long time. And an adopted town that didn't feel much like home either.

That didn't stop her from wilting under Oleg's hulking frame.

Except he *had* stopped. He moved to the side and Nicola was standing a fraction behind him. Her face before had been mainly confusion but now it was untampered fury.

'We took you in!' she raged, jabbing a finger towards Megan. 'You've cost us everything. We'll lose the house and the café. You've destroyed Jessie's life. How can you live with yourself?'

And maybe it was true, especially the bit about Jessie. Their family had a history of destroying the lives of its teenage girls.

'She'll always have an aunt,' Megan managed. There was a lump in her throat.

'You wreck everything and then you run away,' Nicola spat and Megan didn't deny it. Nicola pointed to the imagined foetus in Megan's belly. 'You'll wreck that baby, too.'

Oleg took a half-step ahead but Nicola slapped an arm across him. He reacted like a toddler who'd just had his favourite toy snatched, by batting her away.

'She's pregnant,' Nicola repeated.

'So?'

'So, you can't—'

Nicola didn't finish the sentence because the beast of a man shoved her to the ground. There was a crunch as she slipped from the kerb and her leg folded underneath her. Not that Megan could see much because, this time, Oleg was truly upon her. She tried to step away but he was too big, too fast – and his fingers were reaching for her throat.

FORTY-EIGHT

Oleg's face detonated in an explosion of red. He whirled backwards, away from Megan and toppled over the top of Ben, who had been trying to help Nicola up from the ground. Limbs warped into each other as Ben yelped and Oleg clutched his head while screaming. Ben managed to disentangle himself, though his forehead was drenched with blood from Oleg's spurting wound.

'What—?' Ben managed, though he didn't get any further. With Oleg now free, a second rock thrashed into his head, this one hitting him in the eye. He cannoned backwards, slamming into the tarmac, arms limp.

Ben screeched this time, covering his head as he ducked instinctively for cover. At some point, Trevor had retreated towards the SUV but Daniel was a stunned statue as his head flipped from side to side.

'What's happening?' Ben shouted – but his wife knew.

After crumpling to the floor, she'd managed to pick herself up, though she crouched and snatched the rock that was almost the size of a fist.

And then, twenty years too late, he was there. Megan wasn't

quite sure from which direction her father had appeared – but he was as good with a catapult as he'd ever been. Thankfully, fishing had never been his thing.

He held the improvised weapon in one hand, and fished a rock from his cargo pant pocket, holding it up as he neared Megan's side. 'You want one, too?' he said gruffly, talking to Daniel.

Probably wisely, Daniel held up his hands in surrender.

'You all right, love?' her father asked.

'Not really,' Megan replied – and she wasn't. But maybe she would be.

There were spinning blue lights in the distance now, snaking their way down the hill, as the phone mast fire raged on the hill behind.

'I guess the landlines still work,' Megan said.

FORTY-NINE

THREE DAYS LATER

Judy at the bed and breakfast might have had dodgy beds that were too soft – but she could certainly make breakfasts. And, sure, her dining room had a shrine to Princess Diana but there was something about the way she cooked eggs that made all that forgivable.

She'd been feeding the rescued workers after taking in as many as she could fit. The other local hotels had also been helping, ensuring everyone had a safe place to stay. The Whitecliff community had come together to welcome the newcomers in a way that hadn't happened along the coast.

Some were already on their way back to their home countries, while others wanted to stay. Megan had helped rescue twenty-three in total and everyone had their own story. Some wanted to tell it, others not so much. The police had accepted Trevor's tooth and listened to Megan's story of where it came from, plus everything else. So had a misfit pair of reporters that included a woman Megan vaguely recognised and some shambling old geezer twice her age. He somehow knew both Cliff and Megan's dad.

But there was one story that was for Zofia and Megan.

They'd pieced it together from their respective shared knowledge, with thanks to Elias as their go-between, plus odds and ends the police had passed on.

Zofia and Valeska had been in the back of the SUV on their way back from work the day that Megan had heard a scream. Oleg had been driving, with Trevor in the passenger seat. Usually there were child locks but, somehow, some way, the back doors weren't secure. Valeska had thrown herself out of the vehicle when it stopped at traffic lights. She was part-way up the street before Trevor had set off after her.

That was the last time Zofia had seen her twin. Later, Trevor told Zofia that Valeska had got away. He'd added that as long as she stayed put, and did what she was told, then nobody back home would be harmed. Zofia had settled for that, mainly because she believed her sister was safe. She'd dreamed of her running somewhere safe and living a good life. Maybe they'd meet again some day.

Zofia had met Megan in that flat because Trevor had told her she had to. That her family back home would be harmed if she didn't. And then she'd seen the top her sister had been wearing when she'd run and... the poor girl didn't know what to make of it.

Which left her, Megan and Elias sitting in Megan's back garden on the furniture set she and Paul had bought so they could 'entertain'. Such a notion was a long way off for Megan. This was the one thing she had to do herself.

'Valeska was dead,' she told Elias, who nodded solemnly. He already knew and so did Zofia. The police had told them – but they didn't know everything Megan did. 'I found her in the stream in the woods. I didn't have my phone and by the time I'd called the police and got back, she was gone. I'm really sorry I told you I'd seen her running. I wanted you to be safe before I said anything.'

Elias converted that into something Zofia could understand.

The younger woman was staring at the floor, her legs curled underneath her. There had already been pained, streaky rings around her eyes when she arrived.

'I told the police but they didn't believe me,' Megan said. 'They do now. I'm so sorry.'

She reached for Zofia's hand and gently squeezed her fingers. The younger woman let her as Elias translated. She said something back to him and then he spoke to Megan.

'She asks if Valeska seemed peaceful when you saw her?'

And she had, she *really* had. Megan said that it looked as if she'd been sleeping. That there were no marks on her face. Elias told that to Zofia, who nodded acceptingly.

Nobody yet knew precisely how Valeska had died. Trevor had to know, though he wasn't talking. He must also have been somewhere near that stream, bleeding from the mouth, when Megan arrived. He'd have been panicking that she'd raise an alarm, or – maybe – plotting to get rid of Megan as well.

Once Megan had disappeared off to call the police, he'd moved the body – probably to somewhere not that far away until he could go back for it.

Valeska had been found buried in the patch of disturbed dirt close to Trevor's greenhouse that Megan had walked across the previous week. She'd barely even given it a look.

'I found Trevor's tooth by the stream,' Megan said, talking to Zofia. 'Your sister fought. The police have it now. He won't get away with anything.' A pause. 'I know it won't bring her back...'

Elias took Zofia's other hand and squeezed too. He translated that and she rested her head on his shoulder.

Megan didn't know what else to say, other than sorry. There didn't seem much point in telling her that the police reckoned the bunker under the farm was used to temporarily host new people when Oleg smuggled them into the country. She probably already knew that.

'You can stay here if you want,' Megan said. 'Both of you. Or either of you.'

Elias frowned, not quite understanding as Megan pointed towards the house behind them. 'This is mine,' she said. 'And the only people living here are me and my niece. There's plenty of room. Stay as long as you like.'

Megan had always envisioned a house full of young people, though not like this. Not anything like this.

Elias said something to Zofia, who said something back. 'She says yes,' he answered.

FIFTY

Whitecliff Pier appeared to have its own microclimate. The prom had been so warm that Megan had worried about sunburn. A couple of minutes' walk away, sitting on a bench above the mud flats, a hurricane was seemingly in full flow.

Megan hugged her arms across her front as she sat watching a boat out towards the horizon.

'I've not been here in years,' her father said.

There was booze on his breath and cancer in his cells. None of that had changed and it wasn't going to. But his mate, Cliff, was the local hero who'd rescued twenty-three trafficked victims to safety.

Not everyone thought he was a hero, of course. The war of words was in full swing back in Hollicombe Bay over who knew what and when. Those blind eyes that had been turned were coming back to haunt. It was too early to know who'd get away with what.

'I didn't want to ask you to burn the mast,' Megan said. 'I couldn't think of another way.'

Megan had visited her father's caravan before heading back to Nicola's house on the night of the festival. She didn't know how sober he'd be, let alone how capable, but there had been no one else. Shutting down that mast was the only thing she could think of that would stop Daniel, Oleg, Trevor, or anyone else from easily and immediately contacting the outside world and bringing harm upon the families of the victims. Of course any of them could've gone home and hopped on the Wi-Fi to make a data call, or send an email – but nobody was thinking with such clarity, and it had at least bought some time.

Megan's father didn't reply. He was watching the boat, too.

'I know, Dad,' she said.

'Know what?' he croaked.

It had seemed perfectly normal at the time to occasionally see her father in the school corridors, even though he didn't work there. There'd be security gates and codes now. Sign-in sheets at the very least. Different times and all that.

'The caretaker didn't actually smoke,' Megan said. 'You used to get through a couple of packs a week but you never had another one after that day.'

She wondered if Nicola had ever figured it out. If she had, they'd never spoken of it. The clarity had come over time and with age. Their dad would even joke with them at times about how he was going to pop into the school to have a whisky and cigarette with his mate – and maybe he'd see them around. More different times.

And yet the caretaker had no children. He'd taken the blame and left whatever savings he had so that Nicola and Megan's father could care for his. This man, who Megan had never really known, and whom everyone believed to be a villain, gave up everything for two young girls who weren't his.

Megan had guessed the origins of her father's descent a while back. A decade and more. He wasn't simply grieving for his friend, he was grieving for the sacrifice and struggling with the encompassing guilt. And every time he drank, every time he spent that money, the guilt grew. His friend had allowed himself to be the scapegoat and Megan's father threw it away. He knew it. It was why he was so broken. He hadn't only let down his daughters, he'd let down the man who took the blame.

Yet Megan had still asked him to start another fire, this one on purpose. And he'd done it. Then he'd somehow got back down to town with his catapult in hand. The one thing he was actually good at.

'For you,' he said quietly – and it was almost lost to the raging wind, though Megan still caught it.

'Nic will never forgive me,' Megan said.

She'd heard that morning that Ben had taken the blame for everything and was claiming Nicola didn't know. Perhaps she'd get away with it, perhaps not. The sisters had not spoken since the night near the boat dock. For all Megan knew, Nicola still believed she was pregnant.

Pam was apparently claiming she knew nothing about what had been happening in the kitchen either. Megan had the sense that a lot of people in town were making similar calculations about what to admit and what to deny. For now, Jessie had moved in with Megan. It was a lot for a young person to realise their parents were fallible. Megan had learned that a long time before.

Her father didn't reply, though Megan reached and took his hand. She'd seemingly held onto a lot of people's recently. His was gravelled and freezing. She felt the joints creak as he interlocked his fingers into hers.

Maybe it wasn't for her to say because she wasn't the only one trapped in that classroom – and because too many hadn't walked away. But she couldn't speak for them, though she could speak for herself. So she said it anyway because, now, after everything, she meant it.

'I forgive you,' Megan said.

PUBLISHING TEAM

Turning a manuscript into a book requires the efforts of many people. The publishing team at Bookouture would like to acknowledge everyone who contributed to this publication.

Audio
Alba Proko
Sinead O'Connor
Melissa Tran

Commercial
Lauren Morrissette
Hannah Richmond
Imogen Allport

Cover Design
The Brewster Project

Data and analysis
Mark Alder
Mohamed Bussuri

Editorial
Ellen Gleeson
Nadia Michael

Printed in Great Britain
by Amazon